For Joseph, S

CW00863879

Dear Kelbo,

Thank you for your
continued interest in
my novel,

I hope you enjoy

Benjamin Leon Dodds

@WinsWinters
www.WinnerWinnerNovel.com
Cover Art by Levi Chang

Aknowledgements

First and foremost this novel would never have been written without the love, support and patience of my wife, as well as the inspiration of my children and their occasional tantrums.

Additionally; I could not have built Winner Winner without the astonishing insights and ideas of the following authors' work:

Daniel Kihneman – Thinking, Fast And Slow

Carol Dweck - Mindset

Daniel C. Dennett – Conciousness Explained

Richard E. Cytowic – Synesthesia

Matthew Syed – Bounce / You Are Awesome

David Shenk – The Immortal Game: A History Of Chess

Gary Klein – Seeing What Others Don't

Perhaps the most important of all my muses were provided by the albums Dreamrider and Redline by the musical artist Lazerhawk; without which I would not have been able to visualise Winner Winner. These two albums played over every keystroke made in writing this novel and were instrumental to shaping the feel and tone of Winston Winters' story.

Winner Winner

A novel by Benjamin Leon Dadds

4

5

1: School Daze

Winston "Wins" Winters had visited Aldershot Academy before the summer for an 'orientation day' with some of the other kids from Mont Primary. Strangely enough, the day had done little to orient him, quite the opposite in fact. Wins was used to the small primary school where he'd been comfortably swimming for years amongst kids who never bothered him one way or another. If Mont Primary had been an aquarium, Aldershot Academy seemed like the deep blue sea. Prison-like from the outside; tall walls topped with even taller fences all around, encrusted with old Victorian brick and tile. Wins soon found out how many kids such a behemoth could hold in its belly.

Arriving on his first day Wins was overwhelmed before he had even entered the gates. So many children... so many *bigger* children, were all rushing and shoving and running and shouting on their path through the main gates into the playground. Wins wondered how they could all know where they were going, and why they didn't seem nervous like him. He tried his best to gather up all his worries and push them down inside so he could put on a brave face as he made his way to the playground.

Following the flow of footfall and bustle he arrived in the biggest playground he had ever seen. At least, that's what it was called; 'The Playground'. Not that there was actually anything there to play with. No climbing frames, no swings, nothing. Just a huge expanse of rough concrete filled with intimidating identically dressed titans. Desperately looking for his best friend Rish, Wins was bumped by a bigger boy. "Watch out small fry!" the bigger boy growled, pushing past him.

Wins felt utterly lost.

A whistle blew and everyone began walking into the building. Getting closer Wins could hear a teacher conveying something to the influx of pupils "Everyone to the hall, first-day assembly, everyone to the hall." In the rush of the crush, he noticed a few familiar faces from summer camp and remembered that he wasn't the only year 7 kid in the school, a thought that soothed him slightly. Rounding corner after corner Wins' view opened up upon a grand ornate wooden archway into which hundreds of children were pouring. A different teacher was directing droves of children to their assigned seating. "Year 8's, that's *new* year 8's *Kevin*, to your right... *that* side of the room please Kevin." "New year 7s, to your left, NEW YEAR 7s, SIT ON THE LEFT SIDE OF THE HALL, PLEASE!"

Wins found a seat and sat down between a pair of kids he'd never met before. They looked just as frazzled as he felt. Wins couldn't believe how many kids were in the assembly hall and couldn't recall ever seeing so many children in one place. Then he saw the balconies. Twice as many kids sat above him, twice as many *bigger* kids. "How many kids come here?!" he said under his breath. Out of nowhere he felt a sharp shove to his shoulder and snapped round not knowing what to expect.
"Dude!" Rish greeted him warmly. "I can't get over the size of this place. I feel like I'm gonna get lost just trying to find the toilets." "I know right," Wins enthusiastically replied, glad to find a friend amid the ocean of others. "I hope we're in the same class Rish, I'll be gutted if they split us up." Before Rish could reply, the headmistress, a looming stern looking lady, shattered the hubbub. "Good morning Aldershot Academy and welcome to a new school year."

"Good morning Miss Maude," the older years answered instinctively.

Miss Maude continued, "Now, before we start the proceedings I would like you all to join me in welcoming our new pupils to Aldershot Academy on their first day of secondary school." Without warning, and quite unceremoniously, hundreds of kids on the upper balconies started chanting "SHRIMPS! SHRIMPS! SHRIMPS! SHRIMPS!" in crashing waves like a baying mob of football hooligans, the volume of which was challenged only by guffaws of laughter from the kids who were not chanting. "Settle down! Settle down! That's enough!" commanded Miss Maude. "Are we finished?" she asked rhetorically, her silencing glare sweeping the hall like a lighthouse's beacon.

"Right, the first order of the day is to assign the form-classes for our new students."

Wins looked around at the expanse of kids in the huge hall. All at once, a recollection came to the front of his mind; the time he found himself struggling to keep his head above water at the seaside and his dad had to rescue him from the waves.

"When your name is called, please go to the archway at the back of the hall where your new form tutor will meet you and take you to registration. There you'll be given your time table and meet your new classmates."

The school was situated on one of the most bizarrely named streets Wins had ever seen. 'Valkyrie Road'. He had no idea who, what or where a Valkyrie was but he was starting to think he didn't want to find out. Each of the classes at school was identified by its year group and one of the letters from its street address on Valkyrie road. Thus one of the year 9 form classes might be 9K, whilst one of the year 11 form classes could be 11V, and so on.

Wins and Rish listened for their names as kid after kid upped and left the hall with their new form-classes. Rish was called, prompting a good-luck pat on Wins' shoulder as he made his way out. Name after name was called and just as Wins started to think he'd been forgotten "Winston Winters" crackled over the PA system, with a sense of relief he went to join Rish at the back of the Hall. Recognising some other boys and girls from his previous school waiting alongside the kids he didn't know, Wins realised that they must have kept primary school groups together. A kind-eyed teacher greeted them "Good morning 7Y, I will be your form-tutor, Miss Hussain. Come with me and I will take us all to our form-room". The newly formed class followed her along.

Glad to have been kept together, Wins and Rish quickly found a desk near the window, a prime spot for keeping an eye on outside events, whilst the other children scurried to find their seats. From its position on the top floor, their form room's large window's vista covered most of the playground, the sports hall and playing fields.

"Good morning 7Y," Miss Hussain began "I realise some of you may feel a bit out of sorts this morning. I want everyone to know that if you have any concerns or problems please come and see me and I will do my best to help." Regarding her new pupils she went on, "In a moment I'll hand out your class time tables and maps of the school- we don't want anyone getting lost on their first day."

Over the next twenty minutes Miss Hussain explained their weekly schedule, talked them through a map of the school and showed them where the various classrooms for their subjects were located. Somewhere nearby a bell rang and the whole class was left to make their own way to their first lesson; Science.

Unlike his sister, Zoop, Wins had never been much of a scientist. Whilst he enjoyed science fiction films and superhero comics, all the actual technobabble and textbooks that seemed to accompany the actual doing of science, not to mention the endless tables of measurements and drawing out of graphs, bored him. He never really saw the appeal next to exciting subjects like History (all tales of battles, ancient secrets and far off exotic places), Drama (which was basically being positively encouraged to pretend), and most of all- P.E. Despite the events of *'That Day'*, Wins remained excited about P.E. at his new school, he had heard they had loads of gear and facilities for all kinds of assorted activities, like a swimming pool, cycling, and even a climbing wall. But for now, Wins sat down and awaited his Science teacher's lesson.

Rish rushed in five minutes late. "Sorry Miss," he spluttered "I got lost trying to find the toilets." A rumble of sniggers circulated the room. "Well, you're just in time" Miss Walters prompted Rish to find a chair, which he did right next to Wins.

"What is science?" Miss Walters asked. The class answered with silence. Unperturbed she persevered, "OK guys, it's like this. This is science class and the first rule of science class is always, *always* ask questions. Asking questions is the second step to learning. If you don't ask a question, to your teacher, your classmate or even *yourself…* how can you possibly find any answers?"

So, I'll ask you again, "What is Science?" Rish put up his hand. Acknowledging him Miss Walters spoke, "Yes ermm, Rish right?" "What's the first step Miss? You said asking questions was the second step of learning, what's the first step?" With a smile growing over her face Miss Walters answered Rish, "I'm glad you asked me that Rish. The first step to learning is knowing that you *don't* know something. People think scientists are smart" behind her hand she loudly whispered, "which most of us are." She winked. "But being smart doesn't mean that you know everything, or even that you have all the answers. Being smart means you know how to *work things out*. So the first thing you need to be able to do is to realise that there is something you don't already know. Once you realise that you don't know something it means you can start asking questions about it. Easy right?"

Addressing the entire class she asked once more, "So, what is science?" A girl with long plaited hair asked: "Trying to work things out, Miss?" "Yes Cassie," Miss Walters eagerly encouraged. "Science is the study of nature. Not just living things like plants and animals… and us… which is biology, but everything in the universe. That means anyone who tries to work out how and why things happen the way they do *and* can prove it with repeatable experiments is a scientist. And this term, we are going start trying to be some of those people."

Wins' mood had shifted from bored to intrigued. It occurred to him that perhaps there was something interesting to be found here after all.

Miss Walters placed three buckets on the front desk and looked at the class without a word. After a curious minute Wins asked,

"What's in the buckets Miss?" Miss Walters cracked a grin. "A question! Thank you, Winston." "Wins." Wins interrupted. "Pardon?" said Miss Walters, taken aback. "Its Wins, Miss. No one calls me Winston." Miss Walters scribbled something on her desk and continued, "As I was saying a question, and a good one at that." Putting her hand in each bucket and dramatically drawing out its offerings she named their contents aloud in turn "We have, sand….. salt …. and water. Now, let me ask you all a question. Where did all this come from?" "What do you mean Miss?" Wins blurted out, now fully engaged with the theatrics but suspecting some kind of trick question was around the corner. "How did all this sand, salt and water come to be in these buckets on this desk?" Miss Walters asked. "You bought it in a shop Miss?" someone suggested. "Well yes, but before that, how did it come to be in the shop?" she prompted. "Miss? From the beach Miss?" another pupil asked "Good," Miss Walters pulled on the conversation "…and how did it all end up at the beach?"

A hushed wave of whispers and curiosity flowed through the class as everyone pondered the mystery. Wins spoke up, "Well, the water comes from the rain right Miss, but my Dad said the rain comes from the seas and lakes so, where does that come from?" "Ah-ha!" Miss Walters sparked "We are now digging down to the real question. Does anyone know where all the water and salt and sand on our *planet* came from?" Wins looked at Rish, Rish looked at Wins and they both looked around the room and saw everyone else looking at each other in absolute bafflement. Allowing their bafflement to brew into wonderment, Miss Walters built on their growing attention "Do you remember the first step for learning?" Rish jumped up out of his seat. "Knowing that you don't know something Miss!" he sang.

"That's right" Miss Walters chimed back "So what have we just found out 7Y?" Cassie chipped in, "We don't know Miss, we don't know where it comes from!" Exuding glee Miss Walters drew them in for the big reveal "WONDERFUL! So what do we need to do?" "Ask where it came from Miss!" the class sang in unison.

"Right!" Miss Walters walked around her desk. "All this sand, salt and water started out a long time ago squeezed down in the tiniest point imaginable, along with everything else in the entire universe." She paused. "That's everything in this room, everything in this building, everything in this city, this country and the whole world." She didn't stop "The sun, our moon, all the planets everything in our solar system, our galaxy and all the billions of other galaxies- all squished down into a single point…. then… BANG!" She clapped her hands together. "In an instant it all exploded, expanding out, blinding-bright, blazing-hot and unfathomably fast. All this stuff, let's call it 'matter' was almost entirely in the form of the simplest chemical element there is… hydrogen." She pointed at a large poster on the wall covered in little squares; it looked like a Lego castle with a moat underneath.

"Right there," she pointed, "At the top left corner, can you see it, that little box with the 'H' in it; that represents 'hydrogen'. All these boxes represent the different chemical elements that make up our world, our universe. Hydrogen is the simplest element because it is made of only two pieces; a heavy positively charged 'proton' in the middle, and a tiny negatively charged 'electron' flowing like a wave around its outside."

"Is that like electricity Miss?" Rish wondered. "I like your thinking Rish." Miss Walters explained, "Electricity is the movement of electrons, however, that doesn't really happen in hydrogen, on Earth at least, but that's a story for another day."

Miss Walters returned to her tale. "Now remember, back then, billions of years ago, all the matter in the entire universe was made of hydrogen with a tiny bit of helium in the mix" She pointed at the other side of the poster to a little square with 'He' written in the middle. "Like you put in balloons Miss?" a spectacled boy at the back of the class asked. "Exactly!" said Miss Walters, throwing enthusiastic thumbs-up his way. "All this hydrogen and the little bits of helium were floating about in space for millions of years until great swathes of it started to become drawn together by the power of its own gravity. You see, the more stuff you have in one place the heavier it is, right, but the heavier it is the more gravitational force it exerts… that is to say… sends out, to pull on other matter nearby. So the more hydrogen and helium that got pulled together, the more it pulled even more matter in on itself. Faster and faster, harder and harder, these clouds of gas grew bigger and bigger and heavier and heavier until CRUNCH! They squeezed the hydrogen so tightly it got squished into helium and in doing so these clouds re-made themselves, changed themselves into something new… they were suddenly born a-new as shining stars."

Miss Walters shone her laser pointer from the 'H' square on the poster to the 'He' square on the other side. "This process, squished hydrogen into helium, releases tremendous amounts of energy, in fact, this is what's happening in our star right now."

"Our star Miss?" the spectacled boy asked. "That's right Asher.

Our sun is a star much like billions of others in the universe, but smaller."

"Smaller Miss?" another girl asked. "I thought our sun was enormous, I saw it on a poster". "It is enormous Rikita" Miss Walters responded "But by no means the biggest. After some of these hydrogen-helium stars used up all their hydrogen they had pulled in so much of it that they were gigantic giants. They were so large and heavy that they could crunch down all the helium to make even heavier elements... all the way up to iron" Miss Walters shone her laser pointer along the first few rows of little squares on the poster stopping at one in the middle labelled 'Fe'.

Returning to her original train of thought Miss Walters continued, "After the stars had used up all their lighter elements to make iron, they just couldn't carry on, they stopped producing all that energy, all that star-light and they exploded in supernovae, blasting their contents out into the universe. All those elements being spewed out from the middle of these enormous exploding stars were smashed with an intense tsunami of another type of tiny particle, the third piece that makes up all the elements; neutrons. They crashed straight into the other elements and made new, heavier elements- right up to uranium, the heaviest naturally occurring element."

Again she whipped her laser pointer over the rest of the poster settling on a square near the bottom marked 'U'.

Summing up Miss Walters asked, "Well, what does this all mean?" "It all came from exploding stars Miss?" Wins answered, "All the stuff, all the matter I mean, the water and sand and salt".

"That's right Wins," Miss Walters continued. "But not just that, everything, everything you are made of, the carbon, the phosphorus, the iron in your blood the oxygen we breathe, the gold in our jewellery and computers, everything, *everything* came out of an exploding star. In the end... we are all made of star-dust!"

The whole class gasped in awe just as the bell rang. "OK 7Y," Miss Walters concluded, "I want you to keep a look out for problems you can solve like scientists, have fun and don't stop asking questions!"

2: That Day

Whilst on the surface Wins was mostly thought of as a 'good kid,' he did have a rotten streak underneath. Wins didn't so much hate to lose as much as he hated *not* to win. Indeed, in recent weeks he had become insufferable. He would turn as rapidly incandescent with rage and frustration when a game ended in a draw as when it ended with his loss.

And so it was that Wins' family witnessed another of his increasingly frequent tantrums, the worst since *'That Day'*. Wins, Zoop and BB had been playing a new board game that BB had just received for his 2nd birthday. Each player was tasked with taking their pirate booty of gold and diamonds around the game's board, through secret tunnels and over cliff-side paths, to their pirate ship; all the while... a large plastic dragon looked ominously on.

When Wins rolled the dragon icon on the treasure-chest dice, he'd ecstatically enjoyed activating the swinging swaying dragon in hopes of knocking Zoop and/or BB off the board, sending them back to the start of the game, but as yet Wins hadn't succeeded in his hopes of ruining their chances.

Wins was closing towards the pirate ship, only one roll of the dice away, when BB rolled the dragon icon. Grinning from ear to ear BB had screamed with excitement as he hit the dragon's activation button causing it to swing, sway and swipe Wins' piece, treasure and all, clean off the board. Wins exploded, "ITS NOT FAIR!" and flipped the entire board over, causing Zoop and BB's pieces to fly across the lounge and under the sofa. Unsurprisingly BB had erupted into the righteous, indignant tears of fury only two-year-old children can muster, prompting Zoop to turn towards Wins and twist the knife of his frustration. "Well done **Wins**, why don't you smash up all his other birthday presents too?!"

"It's not fair! IT'S NOT FAIR!" Wins was repeating as his Mum and Dad came rushing in, not to find out what had happened, as they were fully expectant of these upsets by now, but to try and calm everyone down. "What's going on?" asked Ed as he looked about the room realising his question answered itself. Seeing the prospect of parental attention approaching, BB began crying even harder and pointed at his new game strewn across the carpet. "Wins, what did you do!?" Ed asked pointedly, "ITS NOT FAIR!" Wins bellowed again, "I never get to win! And BB only won because of the stupid dice!"

Unfazed by Wins' tantrum Zoop interrupted, "BB didn't even win **Wins**. You ruined the game before anyone else had a chance to try." "I don't care!" Wins snapped, visibly trembling with the upset. His Mum, ever the peacemaker, was trying to calm him down. With a comforting hand on his shoulder she offered, "Wins, you can't win every time you play a game."

"Yes I can! I should be able to win *every time.*" he spat.

"Think about it Wins, imagine what life would be like if you won all the time," Anne said futilely trying to reason with him. "What would be the point of playing at all? Everything would be so boring!" Not missing a beat Wins replied, "No it wouldn't, life would be *wonderful*. Life would be *perfect*. Nothing would make me happier than *always* being the winner!"

Ed, ever the well-meaning but catastrophically clumsy conversationalist butted in, "Wins, say sorry to BB, clear up the game and go to your room to think about how mean you were to your baby brother". "No!" Wins snapped again, storming off, slamming the door, stomping up the stairs to his bedroom and throwing himself into his hammock.

Picking up BB and giving him a cuddle, Anne asked her husband "What are we going to do Ed? He only started at Aldershot this morning; he's never going to learn anything with that attitude. He's starting to remind me of Uncle Quentin!" Ed shuddered, knowing better than to get drawn into a conversation concerning his least favourite in-law he said: "I'll go and talk to him." "You'd be better off going and listening to him Dad," Zoop suggested. "OK, you're the expert," Ed agreed, setting off to see Wins.

"I'm back in the lab tomorrow," Anne said, seeing the situation was moving on. "I better get everything ready; we are running the first set of trials this week." "Sure Anne, good luck." Ed said, relieved that the tumult of the evening's events was coming to a close. BB, calmed in his mother's arms, snuggled in and whispered "Book?" in his Mum's ear. "Oh I do love you, you little monster," she giggled, tickling him as they went to the playroom.

"Knock Knock." Ed rapped on Wins' bedroom door. "Go away, Dad." a grumpy voice replied. "May I come in Wins, I just want to know what's going on. I just want to help." "Go *away* Dad." a more subdued voice murmured from behind the closed door. "I don't want to talk about it, I just want to be left alone."

"Ok Mister," Ed reassured him, "But if you ever want to talk you know I'm always ready to listen." Silence followed, so Ed went back downstairs to finish the washing up.

Curled up in his hammock, Wins was deep in a cycle of maladjusted memories. His mind was stuck upon the day it had all gone wrong, the day his enthusiastic hopes and perceived prospects of popularity had been trampled, the day that had become known to him alone as *'That Day'*.

Summer camp had been a boon for Wins. Four of the six weeks of the school holidays spent with his friends getting muddy, climbing obstacle courses, constructing outlandish art projects and most importantly playing games; board games, computer games, sports games and more. When Wins was playing a game there was nothing else, there were times when he was so absorbed that if someone had asked him his name he would have to stop and think about it.

After a month of games and muck and art projects the final day of summer camp arrived, the day Wins would unhappily come to remember as *'That Day'*. The final day of summer camp was of course Sports Day. The day Wins had most excitedly anticipated since before enrolling. There were four events in all and Wins already knew that he would win most of them, and any he didn't win he would still land a podium place for his performance.

Rish's parents moved to the area from the other side of the country the previous year. Wins was the only kid to have made friends with the slight and skinny outsider when he arrived looking so lost and little. Rish's diminutive frame did not mirror his personality however, quite the opposite was true. For every centimetre of height Rish lacked he made up for with boundless and fearless confidence.

Wins' sports day bib displayed a large bold '7' on his front and back, a lucky number, or so he had been told. As he lined up with Rish and the other kids for the opening event he gave a wave to his Mum, Dad and baby brother, BB, who were watching from the stands nearby.

The first event was the relay race, four lengths of 100 metres, where teams of four kids were equally spaced out; poised to pass the baton on to their teammates in order to race, (or win, as Wins thought of it) as a team. Wins had teamed up with Rish, Raj and Mo. Spread out around the track, Mo was first, followed by Raj, Rish then Wins in the final stretch. One of the summer camp leaders switched on a megaphone, hitting everyone present with a squeal of feedback before counting down to the starter's whistle..... 3..... 2.... 1.... the whistle screeched and Mo chased its call with all his might, pounding his legs down against the turf over and over again. Wins gave a hopeful glance to Rish, the entire playing field boiled to a deafening chorus of cheering, roaring and exuberant yelps with everyone yelling out for their best friends, brothers and sisters. As the names of all the runners rose into a cacophony of encouragement, Mo was quick to reach Raj, Raj falling behind the competition struggled to keep pace but deftly gave the baton to Rish mid-stride. Rish, with his shorter gait, couldn't catch the other runners and by the time he had placed the baton in Wins' frustrated and fidgety outstretched grasp Jamie's team were about to take first place.

Wins tunnelled his vision towards the finish line, and closing the final few metres, was briefly aware of a blur of colours at the edge of his senses. In what seemed like a few short seconds the race was over and was aggrieved to see Jamie, a taller boy, excitedly jumping about with an expression of sheer delight plastered across his face. He turned back to the stands to see his parents cheering wildly for him then back to the camp leader who bellowed through the megaphone that Jamie's team had won the race. "Third place." "THIRD PLACE!" He thought to himself. Why were those other boys so slow? Wins found it indescribably frustrating to have to rely on other people who couldn't pull their weight.

To his surprise, he was almost knocked off his feet as Mo jumped on his back hugging him victoriously, followed by an epic high five from Raj and a gleeful bouncing chest bump from Rish. "Third place Wins!" Mo shouted, "THIRD PLACE MATE!" he continued "I never get a podium place!" "Well in Wins," Raj followed on "you brought us back from the brink, nice one!" Wins faked a smile and slapped them on their shoulders; the group hug enthusiastically enjoyed by his teammates didn't make him feel any better.

Everyone prepared for the next event; the long jump. A sandy strip was freshly filled and had distance markers running parallel to it. A bright white line in front of the strip marked the point at which each participant was to launch himself from after a short run-up. By now, Wins had worked himself into a funk, not a cool funk like people in music videos, but the other kind, the dark, smelly, angry, self-defeating kind where nothing seems to go the way you want it to. He barely noticed the other boys' long jump efforts. The only one he did notice was Jamie who cleared over 3 metres, a full 30 cm more than the next best kid.

Wins heard his name and saw one of the summer camp leaders gesticulating at him. It was his turn, he was up. Wins stretched out his legs, positioned himself at the start of the run-up, got the nod from the leader and burst forwards. Four strides later he leapt high and hard bringing his legs up to his chest, forcing his outstretched arms forwards and bending his knees just enough so that he could land without injury, but not so much that he would hit the sand early and ruin his score. He rolled forwards making sure not to disturb the sand any more than possible, stood up and saw his distance: 3.05 metres! He exploded "WOOOOOOOO!" he had finally beaten Jamie! "I'm not going to lose every game after all!" he bellowed in his head.

His funk evaporated and his blood rose in his veins. Exuberant, he turned to his friends expecting a lavish display of congratulatory applause; his high spirits were swiftly shattered however by one of the summer camp leaders, a bulky bearded man, holding up a red flag. "Over the line," the summer camp leader stated starkly. "What?!" Wins snapped. "Over the line, over-the-line Winston, I'm sorry but your toe was over the jump-off line. You have to try again"

"I was NOT over the line!" Wins protested, "I won, I got 3.05, everyone saw!" "I'm sorry Winston" the bulky bearded summer camp leader insisted. "Fair is fair and your toe was over the line. Would you like to try again?" "What are you talking about, that was the best jump of my life! I don't *need* to try again, I just did it!" Wins countered. "Listen Wins," the summer camp leader replied, "Either you try again, or I mark it zero." "No way!" Wins pushed back. "You'll mark it 3-0-5 coz That's. What. I. Got!" "I'm marking it zero Winston, go to the next event." With his exuberant victory instantly turned to furious anger Wins predictably exploded "THATS! NOT! FAIR!" "Fair? FAIR?" the camp leader snapped back "Am I the only one around here who gives a heck about the rules?" "You were over the line, you didn't want to retry. Now you have a zero, *hero*. Go to the next event." And with that Wins knew that the day was well and truly ruined.

Walking to the third event, dribble-and-strike, Rish wandered up to Wins. "What's up dude?" "It's just not fair," Wins replied "I totally smashed that long jump and that idiot summer camp leader wouldn't let me have it! This day just keeps getting worse and worse." "Come on mate," Rish said with an annoyingly cheery tone "It's just for fun." "For you maybe," Wins suggested, "but that was a personal best and that stupid power hungry idiot probably only denied it to make himself feel better than me." "Wins," Rish encouraged, "let's just do the football thing and see how it goes, yeah?" Wins' mood lifted.

The aim of the dribble-and-strike was to drive a football around a set of cones and blast it into one of the goals which book-ended the field, whereupon the player would receive a new football, dribble it back around the cones to the start and smack it into the other goal. Each participant had three minutes to score as many goals as possible without missing out or knocking over any cones.

First up was Rish. Always the joker and never a footie fan, he wasn't fussed. He took his sweet time and managed to get widely around each of the cones, missing the goal on his first attempt before retrieving the football and scooping it in, using his leg like a hockey stick. He just about got past the first pair of cones on his return before the whistle blew.

Wins, a die-hard LFC fan, had been watching football ever since he could remember and playing from the days he could first walk. He tried to focus his mind on the task afoot but found his funk setting back in. The bulky bearded summer camp leader had really got under his skin and thoughts of how he had been cheated out of his personal best in the long jump crept to the front of his mind. Distracted, he was late to hear the starters' whistle blow. Unprepared he pushed forward with the ball and immediately knocked it into the first cone. Cursing the game, he put the cone up and started again knowing this would set him back at least 10 seconds. He found it hard to control his frustration and reel in his urge to kick the ball harder than was wise but started again, passing the first few cones only to prang his toe in a pit hidden beneath some long grass. He spilled over just managing to catch himself in an uncoordinated press-up, his knees causing the football to ping out sideways. Feeling his rage building, he jumped up and sprinted after the ball. A parent he didn't recognise at the front of the stands picked it up and rolled it back but their aim was awful and it flew right past him, out of his reach. Grunting through his frustration he caught up with the ball, took it around the remaining cones and onwards. Approaching the first goal he let his fury out upon the football, it fired forward with the full force of his furious frustration, hit the crossbar and recoiled straight into Wins' waiting face with a loud resonant slap. Wins didn't know what was worse, the stinging pain of the football smashing into his face or the humiliation of it having happened, by his own doing, in front of the whole summer camp and their families. Then the whistle blew and he realised he hadn't managed to score a single goal.

Anne came running onto the field "Oh Wins! Are you Ok? I

heard that from all the way over there. Let me see." Now suffering the double humiliation of having his Mum rush up to him all a-fluster in full view of his mates, and having just embarrassed himself, was too much to bear. Without a response Wins turned and walked away. "Winston! Winston! Are you Ok?" his Mum called again and again, each time a shudder of sludgy embarrassment caused him to clench his muscles. "How could this day get any worse?" he growled to himself, as he heard Jamie score his sixth goal.

The final event was the obstacle course. Pretty much a free for all scramble over, under and across all the adventure equipment he had come to be familiar with over the last four weeks. No lines, no groups, just a mad muddy dash for the end. Spotting Rish, Wins sheepishly walked over hoping he'd have some quick-witted quip to distract him from his stinging cheeks and forehead, not to mention his stinging sense of embarrassment. "Dude!" Rish exclaimed, "That looked even more painful than it sounded, and it sounded horrendous. How's your face?". "It kills." Wins replied, disappointed that this was all Rish wanted to talk about. "I don't want to talk about it." "No prob, listen this is the best bit of the day anyway, I'm gonna get so filthy no one will even know it's me by the end of the race!"
Wins shoved his way to the front of the pack with all the boys and girls of summer camp raring to go at once. Wins could feel a surge charging through the crowd and his heartbeat rose up to meet it. A voice wailed through a megaphone, 3… 2… 1… and, SQUEEEEE, the whistle cut through the air and everyone charged forward through the mud.

Wins forced his way through the scrambling horde into a waist-high ditch of gloopy muck and clumsily waded through. Some boys were overtaking him in mud-bound slow motion but he seemed to be holding pace ahead of the pack. Pulling himself out the other side he rushed to the camouflaged net tunnels; earthy mulch blanketed by knotted ropes. Wins dove deep into the sludge and crawled on as fast as he could, imagining himself as a great Gila-monster chasing his prey. Exiting the tunnel, only two other boys were ahead of him.

Wins ran up a muddy mound throwing himself on to the climbing nets and was over them in a matter of seconds. Catching up with Jamie and Oliver he saw his chance; the rope swings. Each of the pair of ropes was being held by a summer camp leader. Slipping past Oliver Wins dashed as fast as he could and grabbed the rope Jamie had just used. He lunged with his body's momentum onto the waiting lifeline and plunged into the swing. The mud from Jamie's effort moments before wetted the rope; Wins' grip failed as if he were trying to clutch at a stream of olive oil. He landed face first in the muddy pool between the two stands either side of the rope swings. He sent splodgey gloopy mud far and wide, covering the summer camp leaders nearby. Enraged, he pulled himself up and out of the mud to see half a dozen boys swing overhead to embark on their final sprint to the finish.

Wins ran round to the jumping off point and was forced to wait for the summer camp leaders to pass the rope back to him. He pitched across the gap and landed at the far side, hearing a sploopy wet smack behind him. Over his shoulder he saw an unrecognisable, muddy boy reach up out of the same muck Wins had just escaped and call for help. "No-one helped me," he told himself, leaving the kid in the dirt and making a desperate dash for the finish line. He knew now he couldn't win, and all he could hope for was not to come in last. His clothes were caked in mud, the additional weight slowing him down. Forcing himself on, Wins raked at his clothes to lighten the load, flinging armfuls of soggy dirt at the ground. He stumbled onwards crossing the line in penultimate position. The summer camp leader monitoring the finish line asked him what his number was, "Seven." Wins barked. "Well where's your number then?" the summer camp leader asked. Wins looked at his chest, he had lost his racing bib. He looked back and saw it on the ground, barely recognisable in the mud. He rushed back to it but not soon enough as the unrecognisable mud monster Wins had neglected to help at the rope swings ran over it, trampling it further into the ground. Crestfallen, Wins snatched his lucky number seven from its grave and marched over to the summer camp leader who became the focus of all his anger. "There you go!" Wins snarled, throwing the broken bib at the summer camp leader's feet before storming off.

Rish approached Wins, wary of his mood. "Why didn't you help me Wins?" Perplexed, Wins responded, "What do you mean?" "When I fell in the mud at the swings, you didn't help me, I asked you for help and you just ignored me and ran off!" Rish seemed genuinely upset. "Rish I'm sorry, I didn't know it was you. All I could see was mud." Not only had he ruined his own race, he'd ruined Rish's too. Cooling off, Rish tried to change the tone, "OK mate, OK. I guess I was swimming in the stuff." Wins felt better now he could see Rish wasn't going to hold a grudge, but couldn't shake his sense of failure and frustration which felt like a choking smog around him. "Sorry Rish. Honestly." In silence, they walked back to the crowd of kids now awaiting the final scores and medal ceremony.

With his funk fully descended upon him, Wins watched with

total dissatisfaction as Jamie, having won every event, received the overall winner's medal for the day. The crowd surged forwards with spontaneous applause, leaving Wins feeling hopelessly lost, ignored and insignificant amidst the frantic fray.

Sometime later, making his way to the car with his parents and baby brother, Wins was lost in an infinite cycling loop of gloomy thought. He couldn't hear his Mum and Dad's words of encouragement or feel their pats and squeezes of comfort and reassurance. For his mind was fixed on a single image. The image of his lucky number seven trampled into the dirt. Something about that image hurt him much more than it should have, and he couldn't work out why. Wins squeezed his participant's medal until his hand hurt. "Stupid." he thought, "Stupid loser's medal!" his mind shouted.

His awareness faded back to his bedroom, Wins noticed the damp patch on his hammock left by tears. He remembered how, without a glance, he'd dropped his 'loser's medal' on the playing field and left it to rot in the dirt '*That Day*'.

3: The Aldershot Academy Achiever's Award **AKA**: The Triples

Wins' first week at Aldershot Academy wound onwards and his nerves gradually settled down as he settled into his new school. He'd formed a solid mental map of the building, so didn't feel quite as geographically lost anymore. However, a lingering sense of panic still pervaded his overall outlook. The events of 'That Day' remained raw and tender, causing him to wince inside when his mind went back there. Although the size of the school no longer scared him, the size of its occupants loomed over him like numberless hordes of monsters climbing the horizon. He didn't have the words to explain to himself how he felt. He felt, off-kilter somehow; as if he was sick with a mysterious, malevolent malaise. All he knew was that he didn't like it, and he would do anything to make it go away.

The bigger kids didn't acknowledge Wins or his fellow year 7s except to bark and snap at them, "Move it *shrimps*," or "Outta my way *small-fry*." Wins remembered how he used to feel like the king of his primary school. Well-liked, best at P.E. and adored by his teachers. The strange thing was; he never realised he felt that way until now; until he didn't feel that way anymore.

At the start of his second week at Aldershot Academy the entire school congregated in its enormous assembly hall once again, the thousands of chattering voices in the room blended together reminding Wins of the incessant buzz-buzz-buzz of vuvuzelas at a world cup match. Miss Maude took to the stage draping a quieting chill over the school.

"Good Morning Aldershot Academy," She boomed.
"Good Morning Miss Maude," the chorus of voices replied.

Gazing out over the room Miss Maude addressed her pupils "This year is the one-hundredth anniversary of our school's founding as well as our a hallowed annual tradition; the Three-Fold Aldershot Academy Achiever's Award, *The Triples*."

Miss Maude went on "Each semester; autumn, spring and summer a sporting contest will challenge your determination and perseverance. Every pupil, regardless of age, is invited to take part in any or all of them over the course of the academic year."

"If anyone manages to win all three contests, a rare occurrence indeed, they will be forever remembered and their name engraved on the crest of our venerated school to be honoured in perpetuity…" Miss Maude gestured floridly to the back of the hall where a large brass crest donned the wall over the ornate wooden archway, "as well as on The Triples cup." She held aloft a tremendous gold cup, its two handles sticking out of opposite sides like goofy golden ears, its gleaming girth made it seem unnaturally heavy.

"In recent years, only one pupil has won all three events, and so very proud we all are of him; please stand up Mr Jackson Treehorn." A thunder of feet shuffled around and a thousand heads turned searching the room for Jackson. A tall, broad, hard-eyed teenager stood up in the balcony rows and punched the air victoriously. Miss Maude started a round of applause, the crowds joined in with intermittent whoops and whistles.

Starting to feel apprehensive Wins asked Rish; "Who is Jackson Treehorn?!" "I heard he's year 11, he's always the captain of the track and field teams," Rish said. "But my cousin told me he's really mean, this one time…" Before Rish could finish his second-hand story he was shushed by Miss Hussain from the end of their row.

Once the applause died down, Miss Maude continued "In keeping with tradition each event will be different than the previous year's Triples. Our autumn term's contest will be…" Miss Maude paused for dramatic effect, "400-meter swim." She waited for a moment then continued "Our spring term's contest will be…an off-road bicycle race." Miss Maude, clearly a seasoned speaker waited to sharpen the audience's attention. "To celebrate the special centenary of the Three-Fold Aldershot Academy Achiever's Award we will be concluding the academic year with an appropriately special event; our first triathlon!" Around the hall whispers of anticipation mixed with murmurs and gasps at this new news. Wins felt an idea tingle up from the depths of his mind, he couldn't quite see what it was, but it felt good, it felt like it might be the opposite of his mysterious, malevolent malaise.

Later that day Wins and Rish sat in the canteen eating their uninspiring school lunch. It comprised lots of green stuff, some brown mulch and something that was probably meant to be dessert but had the texture and appearance of a bath sponge. Breaking the hungry silence Wins tapped Rish's lunch tray, "Rish, you know it's my birthday after half term, well, I saw there's a new go-kart racetrack opening up soon. I've always wanted to kart for real, I was thinking about asking Mum and Dad if we could go there for my party- what do you think?" "That would be epic!" Rish said nearly jumping out of his seat, "My 3rd cousin went karting when she was on holiday… said it was *brill-i-ant*."

Without warning, Rish's face turned pale. "What's the matter?" Wins laughed "The food's not that bad." Rish's gaze rose up over Wins' eye line and stopped a high above his head. Wins heard the ruffle of clothing behind him. Slowly, he turned around to see a shirt and tie centimetres from his face, looking up he saw Jackson Treehorn glaring down on him. Wins shot up and stepped back to escape Jackson's space invading presence.

"Well lookie at these two *shrimps* right here." Jackson mocked, inviting his friends to do the same. "It's little shrimp and even littler shrimp, haha!" one of Jackson's cohort commented "What's your name *shrimp*?" he prodded Wins' shoulder. "Wins." Wins' snarled back "Leave us alone, we weren't even talking to you." Jackson burst out laughing "Wins! Wins? Loser more like! Jackson turned his unwelcome attention to Rish "What about you tiny? You got a name?" The whole room was looking at them now, wondering what was going on. "My name is Rish, and you should make like a tree and *leave* you grotesque gargantuan gargoyle!"

Obviously unused to people standing up to him Jackson's attitude suddenly shifted, his expression turning nasty. "What did you say SHRIMP?"

Just then Miss Maude who must have been monitoring the canteen broke in. "What's going on here?" Jackson switched his tone and politely replied: "Just welcoming the new year 7's Miss." With a menacing smile, he let Wins and Rish know it wasn't over yet "See you round *shrimp*." "Time to move on Mr Treehorn." Miss Maude commanded before seeing him and his friends off. Wins looked at Rish and trying to hold back his urge to crack up asked, "Make like a tree and leave?" Rish laughed nervously, "I saw it in a film, it just came to me and I couldn't help myself." They both laughed with relief now their intimidating encounter with Jackson Treehorn had passed. Later that evening Wins' brush with Jackson Treehorn was still playing on his mind, the only thing he hated more than being pushed around by bigger kids was seeing his friends being pushed around by bigger kids. He started to worry, and his worries smouldered into agitation over dinner. His older sister's telling of her recent lectures at university only served to aggravate him further.

Hephzibah was her parent's shining delight, or so Wins often thought. When she was younger than Wins was now, her friends struggled to pronounce her name which quickly contracted to Zoop. Her odd name seemed to somehow fit her zooming wit and science smarts perfectly, she skipped a year of school, took her exams early and worked her way to university aged seventeen. Now she was studying psychology at one of the top universities in the country thanks to an all-expenses-paid scholarship. Wins knew this all too well as it was the only topic she ever talked about, and tonight was no different. "We were learning about *mindset*," Zoop began, "how what we think changes what we do. We are going to do experiments next week to find out why some people give up when things get hard and others persevere."

Wins phased out, he found all of Zoop's university-talk unbearable and had other things on his mind. His run-in with Jackson Treehorn seemed funny at the time, but it was starting to feel like a splinter in his thoughts, something about Jackson Treehorn's attitude really got under Wins' skin and he was beginning to suspect that momentary clash might not bode well for the future. Zoop must have finally finished going on about university because she'd just asked their Mum about her day. Mum was a neuroscientist. As far as Wins could tell she studied peoples' brains, although if he was honest he would admit he never paid much attention to his mother's work.

"It went even better than we'd expected," Anne was saying at speed "So, we are trying to fix broken brains; dementia, Alzheimer's disease but after the success of these trials we reckon it could work for things like brain damage and epilepsy!" Ed was glowing with pride. "What happened Anne? I mean, why did it go so much better than you'd expected?" Ed said, spooning out more supper. "Truth be told, we don't know *why* exactly, and we obviously haven't tried them in a living brain yet, but we took a small sample and they all booted up, responded to commands and networked… they all worked *together* as a whole, not just on their own or in small clusters as we'd planned. That wasn't meant to happen; we never imagined it could happen. Hundreds of thousands of my PSIReNS acted as one! You should have seen everyone's faces Zoop, no-one could believe it. We need to crunch the data, but it looks like it'll work. No one else in the world is doing anything like this."

Feeling smothered by the pressure of what happened at school that day, his Mum's and Sister's baffling conversation only served to rile him up inside. Wins had no patience left so wolfed down his supper and abruptly asked to leave the table. "There's still afters." Anne protested. "I'm not hungry." Wins mumbled before leaving the table, plonking his plate in the kitchen and skulking off upstairs. "Not hungry for afters?" Ed couldn't believe it. "He must've had a really bad day. Oh Well, more pie for me then!" He grinned hungrily. "Not a chance Ed!" Anne said snatching his spoon. "You'll take some up to him in a minute."

Wins heard a knock-knock and turned around to see a piece of pie on a plate appear from behind his bedroom door. "Are you sure you don't want any pie Wins? Its Grandma's apple and cinnamon." "Just leave it on outside please Dad." Wins said reluctantly giving in; in the end, there was no resisting Grandma's desserts. "What's going on Wins?" Ed asked concerned, "You haven't been yourself lately." Trying to shut down the line of conversation he muttered: "It's nothing Dad, I don't want to talk about it." Ed tried to console his son, "I can tell when something's up and I'm worried about you, I really just want to talk… well, not even talk; just listen."

A wail broke the evening's quiet. A yell from downstairs followed "Ed, I think The Whoops Baby needs changing, can you go and check on him please." Wins saw his Dad's frustration at their conversation having been cut short. "I have to sort BB out, but please Wins, it's much better to talk about things than to keep them bottled up, OK." Wins nodded dismissively and Ed went to attend to BB. Wins wasn't exactly sure why his parents often called BB 'The Whoops Baby' when he was causing trouble, so assumed it was because he was so clumsy, always knocking things over and breaking stuff.

A minute later he heard a snowballing giggle explosion wildly race past his bedroom door trailed by his exacerbated Dad calling out: "Come here you little monster, you haven't even got your new nappy on yet!" Next, the familiar sound of his Mum's office door slamming shut, suspicious giggling, an even more suspicious silence, followed by a crash. Wins ran to the office to see a guilty little face staring back at him. Their Mum's laptop lay broken on the floor next to her briefcase, surrounded by her research papers and broken glass. Ed shot in and grabbed BB. Reflexively he shouted prompting BB to let out an enormous toddler sneeze then burst into tears once again. Wiping BB's nose with a wet-wipe Ed admonished his littlest son, "NO BB, you're *not* allowed to play in here!"

Standing in his Mum's office Wins heard his Dad yell from BB's room, "Anne! I'm really sorry, BB got into your office and I think he might have broken your laptop." Hearing his Mum's footsteps running up the stairs Wins turned to leave, not wanting to face the full brunt of her inevitable fury. A sparkle caught his eye, there on the floor, miraculously unspoiled by the ruckus was his plate of apple and cinnamon pie. A thin sprinkling of iridescent sparkling glitter glimmered over its crust. "BB must have nabbed it after escaping from Dad's nappy change." he thought. With Anne's stamping steps rapidly approaching Wins proceeded to scoop up the pie. He rushed to his bedroom shutting the door with his elbow before admiring Grandma's confection. She always made the best desserts and no matter how foul a temper he found himself in they never failed to lift his mood. The sparkly glitter seemed to drift off the crust like silver dust forming an upside-down metallic waterfall, rainbow coloured and constantly changing. He sneezed as the sparkles tickled his nostrils, then slowly savoured every last spiced morsel.

Wins heard his Mum's unrestrained ire from next door, "He broke the jar! He broke the jar!" Knowing there was nothing he could do he made the strategic decision to remain in his room. His Mum's moods could be maelstroms so he'd learned to keep out of her way when she was upset. Having just eaten the enormous wedge of perfect pie, Wins slowly slipped into a subdued stupor. With the trials of his day catching up on him he rubbed his eyes and settled down to an unwelcome night of uneasy sleep and vivid, unsettling dreams.

4: The PSIReNS' song

Over breakfast Wins could see that his mum's mood hadn't improved since last night's disaster. "He broke the jar, years of work blown out the window with the wind. *Gone*! I had all the PSIReNS safe on my desk, and now they are lost." Anne buried her head in her hands. "Can't you just make more?" Zoop wondered. "No, I can't. Its' not like that, it took another team years to make those ones. I only wrote their code, I programmed them but I couldn't make them if I tried!" Tearfully Anne pulled at her hair in anguish.

Moved by her distress Wins started to feel awful, but realising he wasn't to blame for the original accident he considered it a wiser option to keep quiet rather than upsetting her further with a question or conversation. Ed, not so wise as his son, blundered in. "Why did you even bring them home if they were so irreplaceable Anne?" "AAAAGGGHHHH! NOT HELPING Ed!" Anne snapped. "DAD!" Zoop chided. "What?! I just wondered." Ed said, failing to make anything better for a second time. "UUUGGGUUUHH!" Grunted Anne.

After an uncomfortable silence, Anne confessed from behind her hands, "If you must know I was so stupidly proud of my work I just wanted to look at them for a while before they got used up in the experiments." With wide red eyes, she continued; "They looked beautiful… like floating stardust, all pearlescent… they shimmered a million colours and never looked the same for more than a second. I can't believe it's all ruined. *My* work. *Everyone's* work. No one will have me back after this; I'll be a pariah before I've published a paper!"

"Shimmering, sparkling stardust?" Wins remembered the glitter on Grandma's pie. A cold, shameful sinking feeling grew in his guts. "What have I done?" He thought, "What have I *eaten*?!" As quiet as he had decided to stay before mum's explanation, he now resolved to take a vow of absolute silence on the matter. Staring into his cereal bowl he finished his breakfast and set off for school.

The first lesson of the day was P.E. Rugby on the playing field. Whilst Wins had spent many hours watching the game on TV it had never been a sport he played with his friends. Although he wouldn't ever admit it he felt nervous at the prospect of being tackled to the ground and having to tackle other kids too. The summer sun hadn't quite calmed for the autumn yet and the playing field was baked solid under weeks of solar glare. Wins and the other boys lined up and awaited the painful picking of teams. Coach Quintana had set two captains apart and told them to pick teammates, their reversible rugby shirts identifying each side as either yellow or black. First up Kobe, stout and strong, was chosen for the black-shirts followed by skinny Pete for the yellow-shirts. As the numbers of unchosen kids thinned Wins heard one of the kids on the black shirts' side say to his captain: "I was on camp with that kid there," nodding at Wins. "He was terrible, whatever you do, don't pick him." Wins' heart sank, he was always first to be picked in primary school, it felt like a long way to fall to find himself at the bottom of the pack now. Cutting into his shame, Wins was picked last landing with the yellow-shirts.
The two teams gathered as Coach Quintana described the fundamental rules of rugby "Right lads," he boomed "aim of the game is to place the ball…" he held up the elliptical brown ball for everyone to see "over your opponent's line." Mockingly

he continued "This is not *American* 'football', we are not 'slam dunking' the ball in the dirt. You need to be holding the ball when it touches the ground behind your opponent's line for it to count as a try." Wins knew enough about rugby to know a 'try' was the equivalent of a goal in football.

Coach Quintana continued "Today we aren't going to worry too much about points an' that, but we are going to remember only to pass the ball *backwards* or *sideways* to your teammates," he motioned with the ball as if he was pretending to chuck a bucket of water over the kids behind and beside him "AND to work as a team. I don't want to see any showing off today, OK? Right, line up, yellow shirts that side and black shirts over here." Wins aligned himself with his fellow yellow shirts. Despite his year being aged only 11 going 12 there was a stark difference in shape and size between the kids sharing the playing field. Whilst some of his mates were on the skinny side like Rish, others could have passed for 15 at the cinema… and often did.

Coach Quintana flipped a coin before announcing that the black shirts would start the game, he passed the ball to a black shirt clad boy and instructed him to drop kick it as far as he could. With a mighty hoofing whack he did just that, the ball flew towards Wins' yellow shirted team, hit the ground and spun wildly off where Danny caught it and began to run forwards followed by everyone else. Seeing the black shirts running his way Wins noticed something odd; some of the black-shirted team seemed blueish, and some of them seemed reddish. It wasn't that they *looked* blue or red, it was hard for Wins to explain to himself. They just *felt* blue or red. Wins put this down to his fitful night of disturbed sleep and tried to keep up with his teammates.

One of the seemingly blue boys charged at Danny and by bear hugging his waist brought him to the ground. Wins noticed that some of the seemingly red boys became seemingly blue as they got closer to the ball carrying black-shirted boy. The black-shirted team rushed the yellow shirts, closed the field and scored their first try. As the ball was smashed down on the in-goal area Wins felt a bad twinge right between his shoulder blades.

The boys returned for kick off at the halfway line, this time it was the turn of the yellow shirts to drop kick the ball. Danny stepped up to the mark and swung his leg in a messy arc sending the ball much higher than further where it came down on the scrambling black shirts. Wins felt that strange sense of colour flow through the opposing team once more. Like a wave, the seemingly red black-shirted boys changed to seemingly blue amongst those under the falling ball. Wins' teammates ran forwards screaming and shouting at each other, everyone believing they had the best plan of action. The black-shirted ball carrier threw the ball sideways to another player before it left his hands Wins felt a change in his peripheral vision, following the sensation he noticed one black-shirted boy had a blue feeling about him, whilst his black-shirted teammates huddling around him remained constant in their redness. It struck Wins as unfathomable that whilst all the players looked absolutely normal, they also seemed to have developed a quality of colour about them, without actually *changing* colour. He was dumbfounded, unable to comprehend the mixed sensations, finding the whole ordeal utterly disorientating.

The black shirts approached like a herd of stampeding rhinos, Wins felt a sharp prickle down his right leg and instinctively yanked it over to his left, spinning around on the spot. A black-shirted boy tumbled past him, his grasping fingers narrowly missing Wins yellow shirt as he went crashing to the ground.

"Wins!" he heard someone yell. The ball must have been dropped, it bounced chaotically over the field towards him, without thinking he found it in his hands. The black-shirted boys dashed his way so Wins flew towards the red side of the field. Ahead he saw three boys thundering at him from three different directions. Two of the boys had that feeling of blueness about them whilst the biggest boy, Kobe, seemed reddish. Wins opted for a run towards Kobe, he could hear his teammates screaming at him "Pass it, pass the ball, pass it now!" But something made him believe he could make it past. With Kobe and Wins heading for a colossal collision he felt that prickly sensation, this time along his left side, he moved away from it as Kobe leapt at him. Wins rotated his body towards his blind side, away from Kobe's fall and deftly skipped round him. Ahead were two more black shirts, blueish in their seeming, looking back at his fellow yellow shirts he spotted Deano, the tallest kid in the year. He had a reddish feeling about him, he did not appear any redder than anyone else but Wins felt the feeling of red when he saw him running on up behind. Wins spun the ball to Deano, feeling that prickle again, this time above him, pulsing and pushing down upon his head and shoulders. Beginning to trust this sensation now he dropped to the ground and rolled, rapidly returning to his feet in time to see two black-shirted boys collide at the very spot he had stood a split second ago. Deano caught the catch and stormed the field to land the ball on the black shirts in-goal area, triumphantly prompting a rush of excitement within Wins.

"Well played Winston." Coach Quintana announced. "Those

were some sharp moves you had out there son, where did you learn to duck and dodge like that?" "Nowhere sir" Wins replied honestly. "And its Wins sir, not Winston." "It certainly is!" Coach Quintana exclaimed. "Listen up." he pointed at Wins, "That's what I want to see, team-work, team-work, team-work. OK, Let's go guys!"

The black shirts having lost the last point were getting ready to kick off from the centre line. Aligning with his teammates something occurred to Wins; when he had caught the ball he had instinctively run to what he thought of as 'the red side of the field', it all happened so quickly he didn't have time to think about it. It wasn't just the players who seemed like they had a feeling of colour about them, but the playing field too. Wins reflected on what he had felt so far, the blueish-ness, the reddish-ness, those strange prickles, the bad twinge when his team lost a try and the rush of excitement when they'd gained a try. What was going on? How did this all fit together? The prickles certainly seemed to happen before the opposing team were right about to tackle him, but not just when he saw they were about to tackle him, no, it was before he had even *seen* them coming. How could this be? The blueish-ness wasn't just a feeling of blueish colour, it also felt cold, and hard, and sharp somehow, whilst the reddishness felt warmer and softer too. Normally when he lost he felt bad and when he won he felt good, but this time it had been more than a general feeling of badness or goodness, it had been a real physical sensation in his body. That bad twinge and that rush of excitement, they weren't feelings like the sense of colour he felt about the field or the other players, they were tangible sensations *inside* his body. Wins couldn't make sense of it all, but he was starting to see a pattern. It was clear he should trust those prickles, they helped him avoid getting tackled twice, and the seemingness of red-that comforting feeling appeared to surround things he should do in the game, people or places he should go to, whilst the seemingness of blue- that icy feeling was a signal, warning about something he needed to avoid. But why? And where was this all coming from?

A ringing slap snapped him off his train of thought and he became suddenly aware of the ball flying towards Rish. Somehow Rish managed to catch it but the force knocked him off balance. Tumbling over he tried his best to roll the unevenly shaped ball to Wins, a black-shirted boy intercepted the pass scooping up the ball, making a dash for the goal line. Wins felt an urge, a draw to chase him down. He instantly broke into a sprint focusing on the black-shirted ball carrier. The boy seemed to have a changing tempest of bluishness and reddishness about him, as the feeling of reddishness grew more intense it felt as though it was concentrating on the boys left side, between his waist and shoulder. Wins knew what to do, imagining himself an African big cat he sprung out of a sweeping swoop and grabbed the boy's shirt just where it seemed reddest. Wins and the boy crashed into the hard earth, Wins rolled on with the momentum of the fall back onto his feet just as the ball pranged off its pointy end and into his arms. Without losing a step he charted a course back up the playing field, between his fellow yellow shirts and with the furious black shirts in hot pursuit. He could hear the yelling and yowling of both teams behind him, calling for him to pass the ball, shouting at each other to catch him- but he didn't care. He saw the shining goal line ahead of him getting closer and closer until he crossed it with a dive for the ground finding that rush of excitement once more. He was met with a sound unlike anything he had heard before, not obvious at first, but quiet. A swelling sonorous song like a whispering harmonious choir of perfect chiming bells, a profound melody that all at once was clear as glass but slipped away like mist when he tried to focus on it. It was as though he was trying to pick one voice out of a crowd, he could only hear it when he wasn't trying to, and as soon as his mind attempted to look right at the song… it fell mute.

Bringing an end to the lesson Coach Quintana proclaimed "Game goes to the yellow shirts- well-done boys." And addressing Wins offered some advice "Try to remember there's no 'I' in 'team' the next time OK?"

Wins considered Coach Quintana's advice and thought to himself "yeah, that may be true but there is an 'M' and an 'E'."

5: The Shape Of Numbers

Wins' odd and exhilarating experience on the playing field the previous week had not returned since. He assumed it had just been a peculiar symptom of migraine or overtiredness from the night BB had caused such a ruckus at home; that was until his maths quiz. Midway between summer and half term the teachers began delivering a set of quizzes in each subject to gauge how each individual was faring in their education. Today's was maths, a subject Wins never enjoyed, or imagined how anyone could enjoy. It was so removed from actual stuff, real things in the real world that he just couldn't see what the point of it was beyond working out how much money you could spend or how many points a team or player needed to win. Wins worried little about shapes and angles, square routes (whatever they were) or statistics which he found so boring as to be sadistic. Given his disinterest in the subject, he was not expecting to do well.

Having separated the pupils one to a desk, Miss Donnie passed out the quiz papers. "Remember, no talking and no cheating! If you cheat you are only making it harder for yourself in the future. Get your protractors, compasses and pencils ready- this is a 'no-calculator' quiz. When you finish or if you break your pencil put your hand up and I'll come to you. You may begin.... now."

Tentatively, Wins turns over his quiz paper. Twenty questions for a forty minute quiz- so two minutes per question, for the first time in his life he started to worry about maths. The paper was covered in diagrams, shapes and sequences of numbers mixed up with x's and y's. Reading over the first question a curious sense grew in his mind's eye. The numbers on the page began to take form; they quickly developed firm solid shapes in his head. Not regular cubes and spheres but very specific sculptures, spiked and smooth, curved and bulbous. He closed his eyes and found he could spin them around to look at them from any point of view he wished. Not only did the numbers have their own shapes, but vivid tones of colour too. He could compare two numbers, like a 3 and a 33, both of which appeared red, and tell which number was brighter or duller, pinker or purpler. "This is incredible!" He thought. Paying closer attention he noticed some of the numbers struck him as having personalities, 7 was obviously very cheeky whilst 12 seemed to be the strictest number on the page.

As he marvelled at his new numerical friends he saw some of them fitted together to make new shapes with different colours and altered personalities. Lemon yellow spiky 7 cheekily joined up with mauve curvy strict number 12 to form a new shape-cool 19, 19 felt like it was the confident popular kid at school, greenish-yellow in colour, tall and slender in shape.

Reading the first quiz question Wins was amazed to witness himself writing the answer. He didn't even need to check, it was clear to him that 128 − 67 = 61. There was no need to go through all the workings, he just envisioned bulky, lazy magenta 128 and pulled nifty green 67 out of it leaving behind solemn old man 61, grey and beardy in its place. Moving forwards the quiz questions were supposed to get harder.
Next up was algebra, working out the missing numbers 'x' and 'y' in a sequence, but Wins didn't see line of text any more, dancing in his mind he saw numbers as they were, their shapes rotating like colourful works of art, each behaving in its own

way, hiding shyly like little baby blue 4 or boldly showing off like fancy 55. The x's and y's on the page weren't x's and y's anymore because those letters simply represented specific numbers in the sequence. Wins laughed out loud when he thought of 55 adding up with an 'x' to make 150 then multiplying by a 'y' to make 600 because numbers couldn't possibly be added up with letters let alone be multiplied by them- it was preposterous! They could only work with other numbers because that was number do.

"Are you OK Wins?" Miss Donnie asked. Wins suddenly realised that what he thought was a single snigger had been a rolling belly laugh and the whole class was staring at him. "Sorry Miss." Wins apologised. And got his head back down. "Letters!" he giggled to himself, "Who did they think they were!" Wins wrote down the answers to the question; boxy turquoise boring 95 and shy little baby blue 4 and raced ahead with his quiz. Each question was a joy, Wins felt like he was meeting exciting new people at a party, making friends at every turn. The quiz questions weren't questions anymore, the whole affair was more like picking friends out of a crowd of acquaintances. When the quiz asked him which angle was in a shape he simply identified a new pal by his or her shape, colour and personality. 23 degrees jumped out at him like a spritely green grandma playing hide and seek in the park whilst a convoluted series of equations tickled his brain like a conga line of fun-loving friends. Before he knew it Wins was finished, so raised his hand.

Miss Donnie strode up to his desk presenting him with a freshly sharpened pencil. Surprised, Wins corrected the misunderstanding, "No Miss, I've finished." "Don't be silly Wins, we only started eight minutes ago." Miss Donnie whispered dismissively. Wins showed her his worksheet "See miss, they're all correct." Miss Donnie looked over his Wins' work with a measure of scepticism. Passing his worksheet back she challenged Wins, "How do you know these answers are right Wins? You haven't shown your workings. Check them over." Wins passed the worksheet back to Miss Donnie. "Miss, I don't need to Miss, they're all right; I can tell." Miss Donnie took Wins' worksheet to her desk and sat down. He could see her comparing his answers to a proof sheet, her eyes and darting left and right as she scribbled over his answers in red pen.

Miss Donnie sternly returned to Wins desk, knelt down and quietly spoke, "Please stay behind at the end of the class; we need to have a chat." Wins was ecstatic, he'd never beaten a maths test before and whilst this one was meant to be really tough it wasn't the slightest bit tricky; it was fun! He sat back in his chair and drank in the glorious performance of numbers gleaming off wall mounted posters and maths course work before they faded to normality whilst waiting for Miss Donnie to congratulate his 100% score.

The school bell rang, as his classmates left for lunch Wins confidently strolled up to Miss Donnie's desk to receive his first 'well done' from a maths teacher. "Sit down Wins." Miss Donnie said crossly. "Where are the answers, and how did you take them from my desk?" Taken aback Wins stuttered "What answers? What do you mean?" "Don't take me for a fool. You got all the answers right in eight minutes and you couldn't show your workings. It's obvious that you cheated, and as I said at the start of the quiz cheaters only hurt themselves." Wins was flustered, but Miss Donnie went on, "How are you ever going to learn if you just cheat on the tests? Out in the real world you can't cheat at life, you need to know how to solve problems and work things out. Now, I'll ask you one more time, where are the answers, and how did you take them from my desk?"

Having been yanked from the expectation of being commended into the accusation of being a cheat and a liar Wins' upset turned to pain, and from behind his teary eyes he was compelled to defend himself. "Miss, I didn't cheat, I didn't. I didn't take any answers I promise." "Then *how* did you get all the questions right in less time than it took most of the class to do the first two? And *why* didn't you show your workings?" Miss Donnie insisted. "I could just tell Miss, I just knew they were the right answers." Wins tearfully replied. Miss Donnie was unmoved. "I can tell you are lying because you laughed at the start of the quiz! What child laughs at the start of a maths quiz Wins? I'll tell you who, the child who had stolen the answers! You may think you are clever but you can't fool me." She looked at him with an accusatory eye, trying to pierce his wall of words. "Well Wins, you leave me no choice. I'll have to call your parents in for a meeting. Cheating and lying are ***unacceptable***." snapping the word 'unacceptable' like a whip. "This will not stand, you will stay behind for detention at the end of the day and I will discuss this matter with your parents. Now off you go, and rest assured this isn't the end of this." He turned away from Miss Donnie, drew his feelings tightly up into his chest, and leaving for the lunch hall wiped his eyes on his sleeve.

Wins found Rish hadn't gone straight to lunch but was waiting for him inside the canteen near the start of the queue. Seeing Wins' upset Rish asked what had happened. Wins took a breath to calm himself then explained: "I got all the answers right, but instead of telling me I'd done good work Miss Donnie thinks I cheated at the quiz, she put me on detention and is going to call my parents in for a meeting!" "What?! Why?! You wouldn't cheat." Rish was outraged. "Because I didn't show my workings she thinks I stole her answers somehow and wouldn't believe me when I tried to explain." Wins was distraught. Whilst he had always been a bit naughty and wasn't afraid to test the boundaries once in a while, he never ever cheated on tests and never ever *ever* had been in proper trouble at school. Wins considered his predicament; "My parents are going to kill me." They sat down at the tables with their perfectly balanced meal of chips, mash potatoes, sweetcorn, pasta and a healthy portion of custard and cake for afters. "How did you get all the answers right?" Rish enquired. "I mean, you did do the quiz really quickly, I'm not saying you cheated or anything, but you know…. You're not normally the best at maths." Wins pondered the question. He knew that he hadn't cheated, but he also knew that no-one would believe him if he told them he aced the quiz because his friends; the extravagant, colourful number sculptures danced around his brain so he could tell which answers were right! "I don't know Rish. I just knew. I looked at the questions and I just knew the answers. I mean, isn't that how anyone answers questions on a test?" Wins realised this wasn't the whole truth, but hoped it would be enough of the truth to convince his best friend he wasn't a cheat. "I suppose you're right Wins, I mean, that does sort of make sense. But at the same time I can see how Miss Donnie wouldn't believe you too." "More to the point Rish" Wins muttered into his custard, "I don't think Mum and Dad will either."

At the sounding of the end of day bell, Wins dragged his feet to the main hall submitted himself to his first detention where Miss Donnie was waiting for him. "Winston," She tersely greeted him. "You have one hour to write an essay explaining exactly why cheating on tests and lying about it is wrong. In the mean-time, your parents will shortly be arriving to discuss your appalling behaviour today." She handed him a wodge of paper and left him in the drafty hall with a dozen other kids of various ages. Coach Quintana addressed them. "Alright, you all know why you are here, and you have been given your own particular detention essays. No talking. Start writing." Coach Quintana sat at the front of the hall and busied himself with work. Frustrated, angry, insulted and betrayed, Wins forced himself to write what he thought Miss Donnie wanted to hear. Pushing through, a memory came to him, the memory- hard and sore, of the time he became lost in the woods and only found his way back to the campsite after forcing himself through thick thickets of thorny bushes and trees.

Back in Miss Donnie's classroom Wins' parents had arrived. Miss Donnie introduced herself and started to explain "Thank you for joining me Mr and Mrs Winters." Anne interrupted "Please, call me Anne, and this is Ed." "Thank you, Anne. My name is Kera Donnie and I am Winston's maths teacher. Did they tell you why I asked you to stop by?" "Not really," Anne replied. "The secretary said something about a test." Miss Donnie explained "Well, I'm very sorry to tell you this but we had our streaming tests today and I was rather shocked to find that Winston cheated. When I asked him about the issue he denied it outright, despite the evidence." Ed jumped straight in, "He will have denied it outright because my son is not the kind of kid who would even think about cheating on a test, let alone do it!" Anne put her hand on Ed's knee and asked, "How can you be so certain he cheated, it's really not like him, he's more likely to throw a tantrum for failing than try and win by cheating. Surely it must be a simple misunderstanding." Miss

Donnie responded "Unfortunately it's pretty clear he cheated and he couldn't give me an explanation to the contrary. The facts are that a few minutes into the quiz Winston burst out laughing, which seemed odd at the time but in retrospect now seems very suspicious. He then completed his test in eight minutes, whereas the rest of his class took forty. Some pupils didn't complete all twenty questions, Winston got every answer correct but couldn't show his workings." Anne's brow furrowed. Miss Donnie went on, "When I asked him how he knew the answers without showing his workings he told me '*I just knew they were the right answers*'." Miss Donnie paused for a moment. She could see the confusion and disbelief all over Anne and Ed. "I know we all like to think our children are geniuses, I'm as guilty of that as any other parent. But Winston is **not** the strongest mathematician in the class and often seems bored and distracted during lessons. Simply put, there is no way he could have worked out the answers to all the quiz questions correctly in less than ten minutes. It doesn't make me happy to say so, but there is no explanation for it other than cheating. And in denying his cheating he lied outright. He is currently finishing off his detention in the main hall." Ed turned to Anne, "I honestly can't believe Wins would do something like this, I know he's been finding things hard since summer camp, but this just isn't him." Anne, ever the measured level headed partner tried to make sense of things and addressed Miss Donnie directly "I agree with my husband Kera, but I understand your concerns and I can see why it appears like he must have cheated. Rest assured we will be having a very serious discussion with Winston when we get home and I give you my word this will not happen again."

Broken and beleaguered, Wins managed to write about half a

page in the gruelling hour of detention he'd endured. He just couldn't bring himself to put effort into explaining why he'd done something he hadn't. Coach Quintana's mobile phone alarm chimed "OK, time's up. Put your work in this tray then you may leave. I hope I don't see you here again anytime soon." As Wins placed his page in the tray, Coach Quintana didn't bother to look up from his desk. He turned to leave and saw his parents waiting for him at the large wooden archway. Despite the enormity of the hall, a large scruffy looking kid shoved past him giving him the evil-eye. *"Cheater!"* he snapped through a thin grin just loud enough for Wins to hear but not so loud that his parents or Coach Quintana could have heard.

The drive home was awkward and conducted in total silence. When they arrived Anne told him to get washed and changed then go to his room because 'They needed to have a very serious conversation'. Reluctantly he obliged. BB was in bed and Zoop was nowhere to be seen, presumably hiding away in her room firmly stuck in a university textbook. There was a stern knock at the bedroom door and his parents entered. Wins was wrapped up in his hammock, dreading the inevitable emotional discomfort of having to be criticised and pressed about his 'cheating'. "Wins," Ed began, "We spoke to Miss Donnie today, she said you cheated on your maths test and then lied about it. We just can't believe it. We raised you better than that." Ed tried to show he was trying to help "I've told you before; you can always talk to us if you are unhappy. You don't need to go straight to bad behaviour, cheating and lying." "I didn't cheat!" Wins said in desperation. "I just knew all the answers."

Anne tried to calm the tone of the conversation. "No child in your class could have 'just known all the answers'. Miss Donnie said you burst out laughing in the test then got all the answers right in record time and couldn't explain how you'd worked it out. We know you work hard Wins, but you have to admit; maths isn't exactly your favourite subject."

Wins could feel the walls closing in on him now, on one side was the unmoving hard place of everyone's misbelief that he'd cheated and lied, and on the other was the rolling rock of divulging that peculiar and exquisite experience headed his way. He was coming to realise he would have to choose whether he was going to jump out of the way of admitting to what really happened into the hard wall of other people's misbelief, or stand his ground and admit to something that was sure to make everyone think he was a liar; who could believe what he had seen and felt? Wins could hardly believe it himself! They would think he was making up more outlandish lies to cover up his previous ones. Faced with a choice between two untenable outcomes Wins opted for neither. "I don't want to talk about it, I DON'T WANT TO TALK ABOUT IT!"

Ed rushed to put out the fire of Wins frustration, but in typical form added fuel rather than water "Believe it or not we are just trying to help. You mustn't get so frustrated, you can't get so stressed." Wins finally cracked "GGGGAAAAAARRRRHHH!!!! YOU ALWAYS SAY THAT, you always say *'don't get stressed, don't get frustrated'* BUT YOU NEVER TELL ME HOW! How is *that* helping?!" "You're right," Anne agreed. "We do ask a lot of you and it's easy for us to forget you're only eleven. You've started a new school, you're becoming a teenager and there is clearly a lot going on in your life that you probably don't want to talk about. Some people prefer to just think things through on their own…. But…" Wins knew there was always a 'but', "what happened today was serious; your teacher believes you cheated and whilst I don't want to believe it you aren't giving me any other options. Did someone make you do it? Is there some reason we don't understand? We just want to help Wins."

A terrible understanding came to Wins, it was as though he were at the controls of a runaway train heading towards a fork in the track, if he did nothing he would go down one path where everyone would believe he was a cheat and a liar, if he admitted what had happened he would go down the other and they would all think he was crazy too. But, there was a slim slither of a chance that his parents might believe him if he told the truth; if anyone in the world would believe him it would be Mum and Dad. Wins paused, took a long, deep breath and tried his best to explain. "The answers came to me, I just knew them." Ed, trying his best to keep a level head, failed. "C'mon, you can't really expect us to believe that can you?" Wins' emotions began to run away on their own prompting a rising panic to flicker over his face.

"LISTEN TO ME!" Wins lashed, "Please, let me try to explain." His parents reclined and gave him reassuring nods. "I was looking at the quiz, I knew I wasn't going to win. Then, out of nowhere, I started to see the numbers, but... they weren't numbers. I didn't see *'numbers'* I saw what the numbers *were...* *who* the numbers were. It was like they were coloured shapes, but they had personalities. Like they were people, no... friends and family. It felt like I knew them personally. When I looked at the quiz I saw the page but the numbers just spun into view. It was amazing, it was as if they were my *friends*. The questions weren't difficult, I could see who the number was where the x or y was in the question, whatever the question asked I didn't need to work it out, it was obvious. Like... like, if I saw Rish- I wouldn't have to work out who he was; I'd just know."

Ed looked like he was about the murder somebody. "No messing around. Did one of your friends give you something to eat this morning? I'm serious now!" Wins was furious "NO! What? Wait? WHAT?! What on earth are you talking about?! You think I was sick from bad food? See, I knew you wouldn't believe me!" "I SAW THE NUMBERS. I KNEW THE NUMBERS!" Wins threw himself over face down in his hammock and screamed in despair. "I knew you wouldn't believe me."
"Wins." A soft voice whispered, "I believe you." Wins opened his eyes to see his sister standing over him. Gently, she held his hand and spoke with sympathy. "You said you '*saw*' the numbers, is that right?" He nodded, "And you felt them, they had colour too?" Wins nodded again. "And... personalities?" He nodded tentatively. Wins wasn't sure what to expect, Zoop was never normally this nice. She squeezed his hand, "Wins, I think you are synesthetic, I think you have synaesthesia."

"Synes-what-ia?" Wins asked perplexed. "Oh my days!" Ed broke down. "Is it contagious, will he be ok?" As if an expert archer, Zoop whipped her head around and shot her Dad silent with a fierce, hard glare. "NO. DAD!" Turning back to her brother she explained. "*Syn-es-theese-ia* is when someone's senses are scrambled, or well, not scrambled, but mixed up. People can taste colours, or smell music, or feel words. It's well studied in neuroscience and psychology. It's not that rare, most people have a little bit of it and don't realise. But what you experienced isn't common either, its super special Wins." He grabbed his sister, rolling into her. With a warm squeeze, the last of his tears were dried.

Their parents joined the hug. "I'm so sorry we doubted you," they repeated one after the other. Wins relaxed his squeeze prompting everyone else to follow suit. Climbing out of his hammock he showed his Sister gratitude for the first time in as long as he could remember. "Thank you, I thought I was going crazy." Zoop wanted to know more "Synesthesia is genetic, it's there from the beginning. Most synaesthetes show signs of it as soon as they can tell colours apart at a young age. It's unusual for it to appear this late. Do you feel it now?" She grabbed a black pen and some paper from the shelf, wrote a number '5' and handed it to him. "No, not now. It was just in the classroom when I had the test."

"OK…" Zoop said trying to put it all together, "All our perceptions, taste, smell, hearing, touch and vision go hand in hand with emotion. It is basically impossible to *sense* something without *feeling* something too. Maybe it only comes on when you feel stressed and worried? Was this the first time; today I mean, in the maths lesson?" Wins could see where this was going, he wasn't looking forward to the impending car crash that would doubtless arrive at the conversation's destination. But so far Zoop had actually been the only one willing to believe him and she was showing him a kindness he hadn't felt from her since he was little. "I'm going to have to do it." He thought. "I'm going to have to admit what had happened and face the consequences."

"No, it happened last week, sort of, it wasn't exactly the same. We were playing rugby; I was a bit nervous. All of a sudden different players and bits of the field seemed different colours to me; they didn't *look* different colours though, they just *felt* red or blue. I know that doesn't make sense in words but it still makes perfect sense in my head. The colours helped me win, they gave me clues about which way to run or who to tackle. And, as well as that... I kept getting prickles in my body when someone was about to tackle me so I could get out of the way. Also, when we scored it felt amazing and I heard this incredible music..."

His parents, struggling to keep up, were looking to Zoop for more explanations whilst Zoop looked at Wins with sheer astonishment.

Wins knew what he had to do. "Mum," Wins sheepishly confessed, "I think I might have eaten your science project."

6: P.S.I.Re.N.S.

The fallout from the previous night's confession continued into the small hours. Wins explained how he'd gone into his Mum's office to make sure BB was OK and found his piece of pie on the floor, believing the sparkly sprinklings on the crust to be decorative glitter. After her initial explosion of scrambled worry, frustration, fury and remorse Anne cooled off and they all agreed that after such an emotional night they should regroup the next morning to come up with a proper plan.

With BB dropped off at nursery and a call from Ed to tell the school Wins was off sick, which wasn't totally untrue, Anne led the family to her office.

Anne must have not slept a wink. She looked like she'd almost fallen out of a skyscraper's window but pulled herself back in at the last second. A paradoxical expression of shock and determination flowed over her face, "We're all worried about Wins, I don't really know where to begin." She took a deep breath, "I don't like my work to spill over into family time so I try not to talk about it too much at home, but after what's happened I think the best place to start is at the beginning and let's see if we can work this out together." Wins, Ed and Zoop leant in attentively. "As you know both of my parents, your grandparents, have been suffering from the early stages of dementia." Looking to Wins Anne explained, "That means as they've gotten older their brains have stopped functioning properly. In time, like many millions of other people around the world, they will die as a result. Brain diseases are still very difficult to treat and rarely ever cured. My work has been to look for a new maverick approach to this problem. I've been trying to repair people's brains with *technology*, rather than by curing the disease directly with drugs."

Anne's tone subtly changed from saddened to hopeful as she continued. "Imagine the brain was colossal, complex crumbling building; rotting from the inside out. The standard approach would be to try and stop the rot once it had started, or better still prevent it from taking hold in the first place. One day this method for curing for brain disease may be a reality. However, in the mean-time, another approach would be to reinforce the broken building, to support it where it is weak, build in new structures to hold it up where the old bricks and mortar had fallen away. This is what I've been trying to do. Working with our nanotechnology group I've been trying to create a nano-neuro-net, an army of microscopic robots that could sure up the failing structures and rewire the faulty circuitry inside the brains of dementia patients. My partners developed the hardware, the nanobots themselves, millions of tiny robots that can take the place of neurons; the nerves in the brain."

Surprised by how fascinating all this was Wins jumped in, "Like a new leg for someone who lost theirs in an accident?" "Just like that," Anne responded pleased that her son understood, "But infinitely more complicated, these robots don't just take the place of neurons, they have to '*think*' too. In order to help people whose brains aren't working properly to think and function as healthy people would, we needed to make those nanobots communicate with each other *and* with the brain too. That's where my work comes in, by carefully studying how the brain processes information I developed the program, the *code*, which will make the nanobots work. What I am trying to do is mimic the organic brain with technology." Anne's passion for her field of study came through in every gesture and syllable.

"Our brains are like computers, they have the ability to process information in astonishing ways we still don't understand. The brain is the hardware, the machine if you like and the program the brain runs; the software that actually interprets and analyses the information the brain is processing is '*the mind*'. This is what gives rise to our consciousness, our awareness of ourselves and what is going on. This is where it gets interesting…"

Wins was gripped now, "It's already was interesting," he thought "how could it get more interesting?" He always assumed his Mum's work was boring, but this was like something out of a science fiction film. Anne started drawing on her whiteboard, a pink brain shape on one side, with an arrow coming out of it pointing to 'mind' and lots of green dots on the other side of the board with an arrow coming out of them pointing to 'code'. "What we are trying to do is put these nanobots in the brain to take the place of broken *hardware* and get them to run *software* that will mimic our minds' conscious experience, helping patients interpret and analyse information just like anyone else." Anne splattered the picture of the brain with tiny green dots to show the nanobots working inside the brain.

"For instance, when I write words, they are just lines and curves, so your *brain* only sees the lines and curves. It's your *mind* that interprets them and pulls out the information those lines and curves carry; the *meaning* of the words. When I programmed the nanobots with the new code I called the combined hardware and software *P.S.I.Re.N.S.*" Mum wrote her mnemonic vertically on the whiteboard

64

Problem
Solving
Independent
Re-cognition
NanoNeuroNet
Subsystem

"Theoretically, they should work *beneath* the conscious experience of the patient meaning the person receiving the treatment wouldn't even know the PSIReNS were there, independently filling in the gaps in their broken brains to repair their cognition, their ability to *think* and help them regain their full sense-of-self and personhood. So far, we haven't started trials yet…" Irate Ed interrupted. "You haven't tested these PSIReNS on anyone, or anything? Then how do you know what's going to happen to Wins?" Anne looked at Ed with a solemn, serious stare "Honestly Ed, I don't know. Everything was designed *not* to cause harm, but I have no data on how the PSIReNS will interact in a biological system yet. Wins is the first subject to have used them."

Anne went on, "Wins, you told me that you think you ate the PSIReNS a few weeks ago." "Yes." Wins confirmed, "I thought they were just glitter on Grandma's apple pie." Anne probed further. "Right Wins, I don't think the PSIReNS would survive being digested; all that stomach acid would have destroyed them. Could you have breathed any in, or, got them in your eyes?" "Wins thought for a moment, well, I was very tired, and ate the pie with my hands…" Anne sighed one of those motherly-sighs that only Mum's could do when they witness to their children's awful manners. "So, I suppose I could have rubbed my eyes without thinking about it… and I remember sneezing a lot, there was like… a stream of rainbow colours sparkles coming off the cake and it got up my nose." Anne rubbed her temples. "The jar BB broke contained the equivalent of about ten thousand doses of PSIReNS, it is quite possible that you consumed, inhaled and rubbed into your eyes many hundred times a single patient's equivalent dose Wins." Wins struggled to understand what his Mum was trying to get at. "Now, assumption being what it is, I never considered what might happen if a *healthy person* used the PSIReNS; so that combined with the unknown but enormous dose you will have received raises many questions."

Ed and Zoop started to look very concerned. "Zoop, Ed" Anne tried to reassure them, "I promise we will come back to what to do in a moment, I just have a few more questions for Wins." Turning back to her son she asked: "You told us yesterday that you experienced some moments of synaesthesia, could you described what happened?" Wins was happy to have a chance to talk to about his curious turns in maths and P.E. again. "Well, it started the day after I ate that pie, we were in P.E. and I started to feel like different people seemed different colours even though they didn't *look* different colours, and I think if it was the PSIReNS, they must have helped me win for my team because... we were playing rugby and my body prickled when I was about to be tackled, but I didn't see them coming, I just flinched and got out of the way before I knew what was going on."

Now it was Anne who was gripped, her mood swinging wildly. "Incredible, just incredible." Wins continued, "Then in maths, well, you know about the quiz and how I recognised the numbers by their shape and colour and personalities, so I just knew the answers and how I got in so much trouble." "Yes, it was the personalities that got me thinking," Anne said, an idea forming on her face. "OK Wins, last question; are you feeling any symptoms or sensations of synaesthesia right now; colours, tastes, sounds etc.?" "No, like when Zoop wrote some numbers last night, I think it only happens when I'm trying to win at something." he clarified.

Anne brimmed with ecstatic energy, "This is phenomenal, this is paradigm shifting, this is a game changer!" "Steady on Anne," Ed said trying to bring her back down to earth "this is our son we are talking about, not one of your experiments." "You're right Ed, I'm sorry for getting worked up." she apologised. "I can't tell you what all this could mean. I was hoping the PSIReNS could help dementia patients, maybe even people who had suffered brain damage from a stroke or an accident. But this; this is unprecedented."

Zoop spoke up, "Mum, I think you should tell us what we should do or we should consider taking Wins to hospital." Faced with reality, Anne's mood dropped down from sky high to match that of Ed and Zoop's grounded trepidations.
Having sat quietly since they started talking Zoop finally broke into the conversation. "Synaesthesia isn't something that comes and goes willy-nilly. You either have it or you don't." Zoop had clearly digested everything Anne had described about her work and had put it together herself, "What I think is happening is that the PSIReNS have become firmly embedded in Wins' subconscious mind. But given the absence of anything to fix in his brain they seem to be keying in on Wins' personal character traits, his particular deep subconscious motivations *and* are attempting to communicate with him." Zoop held her brother's hand but continued to make firm eye contact with her mother, "Because they are processing and interpreting information on

top of Wins normal brain functions… I reckon they are pinging his senses to give him emotional clues to solve the problems that are most important to him."

Anne picked up Zoop's line of reasoning and ran with it "Yes, that makes sense, take the rugby game for example; Wins didn't see the other boys coming to tackle him, but the PSIReNS must have picked up and interpreted information from all of his senses and processed them with astonishing speed and accuracy, worked out someone was approaching him from outside his field of vision and then prompted him to move out of the way, all in a fraction of a second!" Zoop sat up suddenly. "It must be like *'blindsight'* Mum!" Ed tried to keep up, "Blind-sight?" Anne could see exactly where Zoop was going and broke it down for Wins and her dad. "Blind-sight is a curious condition where a persons' eyes are still working, but information is no longer passed from their eyes through to the occipital lobe, the bit of the brain that processes vision. However, what can happen is that they become *unconsciously* aware of things they can't see consciously… because their brain passes information from their eyes, through a *different* route to be processed in *other areas* of the brain not normally associated with sight."

Ed looked confused so Anne tried harder to explain. "It means that someone with blind-sight can't *see* a thing, a chair, a picture or whatever even though their eyes *are* working… but they will *know* where that something is because a different part of their brain is looking at it. For example, they wouldn't *see* which side of the room a chair is on, but if you ask them to guess which side it is on they will generally guess correctly… They *see*, without being aware that they are *seeing*! I think this is what happened to Wins on the rugby pitch. Sounds, feelings, smells, the movement of other players, I think all of this information was gathered up and processed by the PSIReNS which analysed it all and worked out another player was approaching him from the direction he couldn't see... then they signalled Wins with a false prickly sensation in order to ping his reflex response and make him move out of the way." Zoop took the explanation further "And the same thing with the maths test Mum; solving equations must be simple for an artificially intelligent system like your PSIReNS right? Maybe they solved those sums in nanoseconds, then fed the answers back to Wins in a way that made intuitive sense to him."

"YES! That's *IT*!" Anne exclaimed. "What's what?" Ed asked. Anne was on her feet now rifling through her bookshelves, she pulled down a tattered heavy paperback entitled 'Thinking Fast and Slow'. Zoop's eyes lit up "Of course!" Ed exacerbated asked, "Will someone please explain what the hell it is that you two are talking about!" Zoop moved next to her dad "Our minds have two modes; intuitive thinking, stuff we just know are true, things we assume and so on. Our intuition works super quick to feed our fast decision-making processes by using short cuts like assumptions and estimates etc. It helps us solve problems swiftly... but it's not great for tricky problems involving details, specific figures, numbers and accurate measurements. That's where rational thinking comes in to solve the intellectual 'heavy-lifting' problems; the kinds of things you really have to spend time thinking about. It's much slower, but is essential for things like complex maths problems and planning ahead."

Anne took the lead. "What Zoop and I are thinking is that the fast working PSIReNS have integrated themselves into Wins' intuitive subconscious, *but* they are feeding into his rational thoughts. This means he's been getting specific, detailed and accurate information delivered with the speed of his intuition. It's as if Wins has a supercomputer in his brain. However, rather than repairing broken structures like it was designed to do, it's helping him excel at achieving the goals he wants most of all, deep deep down in his subconscious mind. The potential applications of this technology are, well, nothing short of world-changing." Ed, trying to keep up was visibly concerned, "Are you telling me there's an artificially intelligent robot living inside our son's head?" Anne was quick to clear up the misunderstanding. "No, no, it's not *alive*, it's intelligent, extremely intelligent but it's not self-aware like you and me, and it's not an '*it*' exactly. It's like a colony of ants, no single ant is intelligent or knows what's going on in terms of the '*big picture*' so to speak, but when they work together they can achieve things no individual ant could ever do on its own."

Wins, who'd been largely left out of the conversation, voiced his concern. "Earlier you said we would get to talking about what we should do... so what *are* we going to do?" Anne sat down, pushed her glasses back up the bridge of her nose and made her case. "This is a precarious situation we find ourselves in. Strictly speaking, the right thing to do is report the accident to the authorities and the university. This would mean the entire department would be shut down, all our research gets set back by decades; meaning many more millions of people will continue to suffer with dementia who may not have to, and more importantly, Wins would not receive any meaningful help either. The PSIReNS weren't made to be removed, if we try to get them out we don't know what it might do, best case scenario is Wins returns to normal, worse case... who can know? So, I propose a different idea, and one that poses a significant risk to me personally so please don't think I am trying to persuade you to do anything for my own sake."

Ed leaned in "Go on." Anne put her fingertips together and explained her plan "What is happening with Wins is extraordinary, and it doesn't appear to be harming him. If we can follow his progress we could learn new ways to help people, people who up until now had very little hope of a cure for their suffering. I would like to keep what's happened between us and I'd like Zoop to monitor Wins' experiences. If we can get a handle on what's going on we might be able to find a way to safely remove the PSIReNS from Wins' brain *and* get a head-start, not only in curing dementia once and for all; but maybe even helping people become… I don't know, more… *more* than human. You know I'll put Wins' wellbeing first, none of us want him to come to harm. And to be clear, if any of this comes out I will not only lose my job, I'll lose my reputation, I'll never work again and probably end up in prison. So, if we go down this route, we must make a vow that all of this is kept in the family, no one else can know." Turning to Wins, Anne explained, "That would mean you couldn't tell anyone, not your teachers not your mates, not *even* Rish!"

Zoop was the first to speak "Wins, what do you think?" There was so much to take in, so much to consider, Wins was finding it difficult to stay on top of things. Mulling over the two options, and quietly considering his unsettling encounter with Jackson Treehorn, he came to a conclusion. "I want to go with Mum's plan. If going to the authorities would just get everyone fired and wouldn't help me anyway, then I'd rather see if Mum and Zoop can work out a proper way to help me." Ed was in two minds but could see the consensus was closing against him. "You understand what this means Wins, you understand that you won't be able to tell anyone anything about this, even if you end up getting in trouble at school again, even if something happens and Rish asks you directly about what's going on; you can't tell anyone anything!" "I understand." Wins agreed, silently starting to feel more confident about the fast approaching swimming contest.

"And you Ed?" Anne asked. Ed reluctantly chose a side, "Against my better judgement, I agree. As long as this is what Wins wants and Zoop is involved, I think I will be able to live with it, but only on the condition that the priority is to find a way to safely help Wins, and anything you learn along the way is gravy, OK." "Yes, absolutely." Anne agreed. Ed continued, "Secondly, Zoop is *always* in the loop." "I wouldn't expect anything less." Anne nodded in agreement. "And lastly," Ed concluded, "if Wins changes his mind and wants out, that's it, end of story, game over. OK." Anne showed her approval "I wholeheartedly agree." Looking to her son she galvanised the plan, "From now on I would like you to tell your sister about everything that happens, anything out of the ordinary, anything unusual and especially if you feel sick or unwell OK? And Zoop, I would like you to closely monitor your brother's progress and report back to me regularly in as much detail as possible, yes?" Wins and Zoop voiced their approval, "We understand."

Ed pulled everyone up from their seats and squeezed them tightly with his huge arms. "I love you all." He said. Anne hugged Wins, "This is going to be a fascinating journey Wins, thank you for being brave enough to let us all know what happened." With that, they all shared shimmer of excited anticipation, hopeful happiness flowed among them as they finally felt some sense of security at long last.

7: Error & Trial

After the previous excitement and upset the weekend passed without incident. Wins was starting to think that all the talk of PSIReNS was for nought and that perhaps the problem of what to do about them had solved itself. Coach Quintana previously promised the boys and girls of year 7 something fun for their final class of the week leading up to half term, although to build their interest, he'd refused to tell them exactly what it was.
Wins and Rish sat in the canteen anticipating the potential of the afternoon's imminent activities. Their meal was a mulch of over-boiled broccoli, roasted… burnt, potatoes, cheeseless pizza and some kind of splodged pudding. Rish tapped Wins' lunch tray "What do you reckon it's gonna be in P.E.? I'm hoping for trampolines." Wins, lost in thought looked up "I'm gonna do it." "Do What?" Rish asked. "I'm gonna win The Triples. I'm gonna win all three events, even the triathlon… I know I can do it." Rish wasn't sure how they had gone from trampolines to The Triples "You're mad mate." Rish said in disbelief "I mean, good on yer for going in for it, but there's absolutely **NO** way you can win. No year 7 has ever won it. Only the older kids win, and they don't always win all three events!" With dogged resolve Wins batted Rish's comments aside. "Yeah? Well, that's just your opinion. I'll be the first. I'll be the first year 7 to win The Triples"

Before he got to eat a bite of his lunch a bitter taste filled Wins' mouth. It reminded him of the time he'd sneaked a sip of his Dad's unattended beer and was repulsed by the unexpectedly awful flavour. The colour drained from Rish's face. Wins laughed through the strange sensation, "Don't you believe I can do it, Rish?" His friend's gaze rose up above Win's eye line and stopped when his jaw almost pointed at the ceiling. Wins heard a deriding chuckle grow into a condescending belly laugh behind him. Slowly, Wins turned around to see a disconcertingly familiar shirt and tie at the end of his nose, looking up he saw Jackson Treehorn gawking back down at him. Abruptly queasy, Wins jumped up and sideways to get some space between himself and Jackson. "You? You think you can win The Triples, *loser*?" Jackson mocked, unable to contain his laughter. "You think you can beat *me*?" his voice rising in volume. Wins felt the unsettling stare of a thousand eyes upon him. Inside he envisioned two paths opening up before him. He could sit back down and take it, get used to sitting down and taking it, get used to being a loser, get used to never being popular, never getting what he wanted… never *winning*.

Or he could stand up for himself, push himself harder, push others like Jackson out of his way and be the kid other kids wanted to be around. *Be* the winner. Glints of coloured light glimmered and glistened at the cusp of his wits, he heard the distant inkling of the PSIReNS' victory chorus tease his senses. Emboldened by these new sensations Wins stood his ground "My name is *Wins*." He snarled back, "And I don't *think* I can beat you… I *know* I can!" Jackson's howls of hilarity detonated through the canteen like a supersonic explosion. The whole room was looking at them now, wondering what was going on. Jackson swaggered in a circle addressing everyone there. "This shrimp," he bellowed, "this shrimp thinks he can win The Triples. This little nobody thinks he can beat *ME*!" Jackson turned back to Wins. "Wins! Wins? Loser more like, do yourself a favour *Loser* and give up now before you embarrass yourself in front of the whole school." Jackson tried to poke Wins in time with his taunts; "*Three*." As Jackson said the words Wins felt the PSIReNS' prickles surge before Jackson had raised his arm.

Keeping his feet firmly planted he turned causing Jackson's jab to miss his shoulder. "*Times*." Wins flowed with the PSIReNS song twisting his hips, Jackson's second prod flew past him hitting nothing but air "*Over!*" In his fury, Jackson threw himself into his third attempt to physically intimate him but Wins swiftly switched his feet spinning on the spot causing Jackson to follow the full force of his bullying gesture. Wildly off balance Jackson fell forward onto Wins' still filled lunch tray covering himself in mushed vegetables, ketchup and custard.

Jackson stood up towering over his prey. Wins squared up to his rival, sixteen years strong and hard-eyed. "I am going to win The Triples, Jackson," he grunted through gritted teeth. Then standing on his chair shouted for all to hear: "MY NAME IS WINS WINTERS AND I AM GOING TO WIN THE TRIPLES!" Jackson, scowled straight at Wins with a sharp icy stare, then as if a switch had been flipped, flicked his expression to mirth and walked off laughing loudly. Perhaps too loudly, Wins thought. Rish's mouth was so far agape that his jaw could have been picked up off the floor. Win's sat back down, "I'm gonna do it, Rish, you'll see."

Mixed up with his elation Wins found himself in a grump, all agitated and angry. Why had he let his mouth run away with his thoughts? There was no way out of it now. He'd put himself facing the fork of two inevitable roads. He couldn't back out because everyone in the school would forever think he was a big-headed liar who never followed through on his boasts. But also he knew if he lost The Triples after such a boast the whole school would laugh at him for being such a spectacular failure. "Winning The Triples…" he thought, "Even with the help of the PSIReNS I couldn't possibly beat Jackson Treehorn… could I?"

Wins realised it was all or nothing. Rish yanked his friend's arm. "C'mon Wins, there might still be some food left." he nodded at the remains of Win's lunch smeared over the table, "and there's only five minutes till P.E."

The boys and girls separated to change into their gym gear and reconvened in the sports hall. A towering climbing wall stood before them rising up into the rafters of the building. Various knobbly coloured shapes jutted out from irregular positions of the angular surface of the climbing wall. Wins couldn't wait to get climbing. Coach Quintana drew the chattering crowd's attention. "I see you've found the climbing wall," he joked, "that one is for 'lead climbing'…" Wins had never climbed before, not in a competitive sense at least. He loved to clamber into a tall tree as much as the next kid, but had never seen a proper climbing wall and had no idea what 'lead climbing' was. "But don't worry about that, it's for the older, more experienced students."

Wins felt cheated, if they weren't going to get on that massive climbing wall, then what had all the hoo-ha been about? Coach Quintana reached out his muscular arm and with an outstretched hand pointed everyone towards a craggy crooked strip wrapping itself around the shorter wall of the gym and two of its corners. It looked identical to the climbing wall but was only two or three metres high. It was as if someone had taken the big climbing wall and laid it sideways before squidging it up against the sides of the room. "Isn't that a bit short to be a climbing wall?" Rish shouted out. "Ha. Ha." Coach Quintana laughed sarcastically, "You're right Rish, that's because it's *not* a climbing wall… it's a *bouldering* wall." Not wanting to seem like he'd been gotten the best of Rish piped up. "What on earth is bouldering?" "Bouldering," Coach Quintana began, "is rock climbing stripped down to its raw essentials. No ropes, no harnesses; just climbing. Your challenge today is to climb across, i.e. *sideways* around and over the tricky *bouldering* problems sticking out of that wall. The colour of the handholds indicates the difficulty of the various routes around the course. The green ones are the easy route, that's where you should all start, the yellow ones are a few notches harder and the red ones are only for the most advanced boulderers. Today I want to see you each work on using your balance, strength... and your brain to develop problem-solving techniques to traverse this wall."

Wins noticed a tingle in his brain, specs of bright colour blinked at the edge of his awareness and he felt a growing excitement inside. Coach Quintana continued, "Remember, you don't need to go high, and there are safety mats on the floor in case anyone slips off. Queue up to the left of the wall and get ready to follow one another around the course. Let's go!" Coach Quintana clapped his hands and blew his ear-splitting sports whistle. The whole class ran over to the start of the course where the teaching assistant was passing around a bag of chalk dust for them to rub on their hands, it promptly ended up on everyone's faces, backs, hair and for a few curious kids; tongues and teeth.

Wins approached the bouldering wall, the oddly shaped grips looked like giant pieces of pre-chewed chewing gum stuck under a classroom table, but fortunately didn't feel like it. He reached out for the first green grip and stepped onto another with both feet, it was fun to find himself scrambling again. Not since summer camp had he been given a chance to do anything like this. Ahead of him he watched his classmates trying to work their way along, frequently slipping off, stepping onto the floor or occasionally landing with a loud slap on the safety mats.

Moving around he felt the weight of his sagging bum pulling him off the wall, his arms rapidly got tired as he pulled himself from one green grip to the next. An image came to his mind; he recalled watching a nature documentary on TV. Orang-utans were making their way through the trees with their long arms fully extended. The image began cycling in his mind. His thoughts sharpened, then it clicked; they weren't wasting energy *pulling* with their arms, they were swinging, and when they needed to climb higher they could use their strong legs to *push* themselves up instead. Wins reached for the grips furthest from him. Angling his body he realised he could turn his hip to the wall and use the side of his feet to propel himself from one grip to the next, only bending his arms to take in the slack whilst his legs did the hard work. It wasn't long before he had caught up with the girl in front of him. He climbed up and over her whilst she tried to progress from her tangled stranded spot. "SLOW IT DOWN WINS." Coach Quintana yelled across the gym "I DON'T WANT ANY ACCIDENTS, the paperwork is a nightmare." Wins continued on, once he cracked the problem of how to carry his weight it seemed easy to move forward. It was much like walking, albeit with bent legs and long arms. "What must I look like?" he thought to himself swinging and stepping around the final corner of the course.

Coach Quintana walked over to him. "Wins, that was pretty good for a first try, but please be conscious of your classmates, I don't need anyone getting hurt on the last day of school. Listen, next time around try to stick only to the yellow grips OK?" Thoroughly pleased with himself Wins chippered back, "No prob Bob." and joined the queue. Before getting to the front of the queue Wins was drawn to look at the bouldering wall. As he scanned the scene red vapour appeared between some of the yellow grips. The vapour coalesced from fuzzy clouds into translucent red strands, swooping looping ropes joining one yellow grip to another. A pair of strands now took their place upon the bouldering wall. One was higher up and one lower down, although they crossed and crossed back again in the middle of the course. Approaching the front of the queue his perspective changed and it all made sense. This was the work of the PSIReNS alright, but unlike his previous experiences, it wasn't a nebulous vague 'seeming' inside his head. The translucent strands looked as real to him as anything else in the gym, vivid and vibrant. Now poised to begin, he saw there weren't two strands at all but four; one for each hand and foot!

Placing his fingers and insoles to where the strands emanated he felt a pleasant tingling sensation, like a warm electrical buzz. Following the route planned out for him, he giggled as the undulating strands tickled the areas they passed through. Enjoying the new experience he was in no rush to finish and found the guiding strands brought him to perfect points to rest whilst he waited for the kids in front to proceed. Getting close the middle of the wall he followed the PSIReNS' red song and swung both his feet from their yellow grips near the floor to an high outcrop which was level with his head, in only a few movements he had twisted round and reached past his own feet before releasing them into a second, powerful primal swing landing him back in an upward stance further along the course. Waiting for all the kids in front of him to finish, Wins whizzed through the final stretch, flipping backwards round the last corner and on with the flowing strands to the end of the course.

"Top work Wins." Coach Quintana encouraged, "Seems you listened to my sage advice at the start of the class and my tremendous teaching is finally paying off." Wins grimaced knowing full well it had nothing to do with Coach Quintana's teaching abilities but was still aware of his 'no-talking' agreement with his Mum on the matter of the PSIReNS. Smugly, Coach Quintana suggested Wins tried the red grips this time round. Walking across the hall Wins regarded the new route being laid out before him, thick crimson cables coalesced linking the sparsely placed red grips along the bouldering wall. The other kids were scrambling to move along on the green grips, passing through those translucent strands as if they weren't there… Wins had to remind himself they weren't really there at all, only he could see what the PSIReNS were showing him. Setting off along the red grip route he welcomed the familiar warm buzz as his hands and feet passed along the rolling red ropes, however, despite the solution being laid out before him this third mission across the wall was still physically demanding. He needed to stretch further and grip smaller smoother surfaces than before. Part way along he considered the path presented to him and decided that it was going to be too hard. Instead of following the comforting sensation sent by the serpentine strands Wins reached out for a yellow grip to his side. As though a knife sliced through his palm Wins screamed in pain withdrawing his hand with such speed he lost his balance and crashed down to the safety mat below. Clasping his hand close to his chest, a clash of discordant atonal white noise rang in his ears and the bad twinge returned to taunt his spine.

Looking up he thought his hand was bleeding; rich red tendrils were shooting out of his palm and fingers back towards the bouldering wall. Moving to follow them his pain evaporated with the return of the warm comforting buzz. Wins got the message; no cheating! He followed the PSIReNS' song with fluid flow, realising the more momentum he built up the easier it became, it was only when he stopped that his passage became difficult, when he continually moved where his path was shown to be he streamed and surged over the wall like a river. Dismounting at the end of the course Wins wandered over to the large climbing wall and took in its detail; where each of the coloured grips were fixed and how the upper sections jutted out, overhanging the floor. "Are you OK dude?" Rish must have seen him fall off the bouldering wall earlier. "It sounded like you really hurt yourself. "I'm fine, I just got a shock when I slipped." Wins lied. "That wall is massive!" Rish exclaimed. Wins saw crimson cables coalescing upon the climbing wall. "I bet I could climb it, right to the top." Wins reckoned. Not so easily convinced Rish dismissed Wins' claim. "Yeah, anyone could climb it mate, they do it in year 9, don't they."

Seeing the misunderstanding Wins clarified, "Not with ropes though." "Shut up! That must be 10 meters high!" Rish said in disbelief. Doubling the danger Wins doubled down on his boast, "And I could do it using only the red grips too. What do you bet I can do it, no ropes, red grips only?" "Nothing mate," Rish said, "because there is no way you could do that!" By now some other kids were congregating around them. "What's going on?" Zoe asked. Rish explained, "Wins reckons he can climb the wall right to the top with no rope... using only the red grips!" Zoe turned to her friends and repeated the claim. Excited chatter swept through the crowd "*No* way he could do it." "*Not* a chance!" "*Never* in a month of Mondays could Wins do that." But one comment caught Wins' attention over all others. "Yeah, well that's **Wins** for you..." one boy proclaimed "Wins also reckons he can win The Triples, so of course he *thinks* he can climb that wall; he's delusional!"

Wins didn't wait for the stakes of the bet, he didn't care. He wasn't bothered about anything the other kids could offer him when he won. He just couldn't stand the thought of them doubting him. He looked over his shoulder and saw that Coach Quintana and the teaching assistant were facing away, helping kids who were still on the bouldering wall. With everyone around him deep in discussion regarding why Wins couldn't climb the wall, he began climbing it.

The orang-utan inspired method from the bouldering wall held true on the vertical surface too. Wins moved his hands and feet through the twitching crimson cables linking the red grips in a twisting neon stream flowing up the wall. Each of the four strands suggested a subtly different sensation in his body. Wins felt it to be similar to the sound of plucked strings on a harp, only he heard the sound in his hands and feet, rather than in his head. When both his feet and both his hands each passed through their vibrating strands he felt angelic harmonies build inside him. Within seconds he was halfway up the wall and the doubting crowd beneath him suddenly noticed Wins was no longer among their ranks. "Look! Look!" they cried, "Wins is actually doing it!" Cheers erupted and the whole gym rushed to the bottom of the climbing wall to watch in awe. "WHAT IS GOING ON HERE!?!? WINSTON WINTERS GET DOWN RIGHT NOW!" Coach Quintana sprinted across the room but it was too late, remembering the stabbing pain from when he tried to go his own way on the bouldering wall, Wins knew he couldn't stop now. "MOVE BACK, MOVE BACK. GRAB THOSE MATS!" Coach Quintana hurried everyone away from the climbing wall and started piling all the safety mats up at its base. Wins poured himself up the climbing wall like a waterfall, red grip to red grip, pushing with his legs and taking in the slack with his arms. Approaching the overhang he saw what the

PSIReNS' song wanted him to do. The crimson cables his feet followed met at a bulging red glow adorning one red grip, the serpentine strands for his hands met at another, then each shot upwards past the point he could reach whilst keeping contact with the wall. Pulses surged through the glowing guides above him, urging him to comply. The PSIReNS wanted him to jump *up* the overhang.

Nervously he crouched on the red grip with the glowing aura and clung to the red grip at the crux of the outcrop. The pulses he perceived began rhythmically rolling, telling him when to leap. Below him, Coach Quintana frantically screamed at him: "DON'T EVEN THINK ABOUT IT WINTERS! GET DOWN RIGHT NOW!" Wins knew that wasn't an option, if he tried to climb down now the razor-sharp pain of ignoring the PSIReNS might cause him to fall. Meeting the pulsing rhythm, Wins wound up and leapt using every atom of effort he could muster, legs shooting straight, arms whipping down he launched himself into the air, reaching up along the red ropes around him to catch the pointed red grip being targeted. Gasps and screams echoed through the giant gymnasium. In three more moves, Wins reached the top of the wall where he was greeted with that sonorous song whose ethereal notes formed the melody of his victory.

"WINSTON WINTERS YOU ARE IN SO MUCH TROUBLE!" Coach Quintana was furious, flinging his arms and gesticulating madly. "GET DOWN THIS INSTANT WINTERS!" Having achieved his goal, proved everyone wrong and bested the wall Wins looked down to see… nothing. The PSIReNS song was gone. Silence. No more strands of colour twitching between grips, no path laid out beneath him to show him the way. It had all vanished. A panic washed over Wins. He was ten metres up, hanging on by his toes and fingertips and he had absolutely no idea how to get down! His palms felt slick with sweat, his friends below stretched away from him as he finally recognised just how high up he really was. Even with the mats at the bottom of the wall, a fall from here he would surely break a limb. At least a limb… maybe worse! A frigid fear grew in his belly. Coach Quintana's voice changed; no longer angry, he now seemed to share Wins' anxiety, and it didn't make Wins feel any better. In fact, it was making his panic worse. "WINSTON WINTERS, ARE YOU LISTENING? GET DOWN RIGHT NOW BEFORE YOU HURT YOURSELF!" "I, I, I don't know how sir." Wins stuttered back. "WHAT?" Coach Quintana couldn't hear over the terrified children watching on. "I, I, I DON'T KNOW *HOW*, I DON'T KNOW HOW TO CLIMB DOWN!" Wins yelled. As a rush of butterflies filled his guts and his sweating fingers started to slip. The panic he felt a moment ago was nothing now, now he knew only one thing; he knew he was about to fall. He *knew* he was about to die.

A flash of brilliant white light pulled his vision toward the thick hemp ropes hanging from the ceiling of the gym a few meters away, a burst of laser light exploded from his hands and feet and raced to the nearest rope, wrapped in a halo of silver particles. The beaming vision spun in the air telling him precisely what he needed to do. Without a thought, he sprang backwards away from the wall just as he fingers were about to slip from their grip. A deafening screech blasted up from the crowd below "NNNOOOOOOO!!!!" Wins rotated around in mid-air and grabbed the glowing rope, spiralled around it in and clasped it with his entire body. The friction from grasping the rope as he fell against it burnt the skin from his hands and legs but he was just about able to hold on tight enough to catch his fall, and his breath. Apoplectic with rage Coach Quintana lost what little control he managed to maintain until then, his voice broke and his body convulsed. Wins shimmied down the rope to a cold and uncomfortable silence from his classmates cowering behind the petrifying, hulking fury of Coach Quintana. "MY OFFICE. NOW!"

Coach Quintana found the teaching assistant, "Julie, get the first aid kit and dress his hands." Turning to everyone else he bellowed "You lot, get changed and wait in the playground." In Coach Quintana's office Wins waited without a hope. What had he gotten himself into now? The teaching assistant stung his friction burns with antiseptic and bound them in gauze. Coach Quintana stormed in and slammed the door. "What the hell were you thinking Winston!?" Trying to avoid the question he replied, "Its Wins sir, no one calls me Winston." "You're lucky you get to be called anything at all, you could have died out there! You are *banned*, banned from that equipment for the rest of the year, at *least* the rest of the year, you hear me son?" Coach Quintana picked up his desk phone, "Yes, Its Quintana, I need the I.C.E. number for Winston Winters." He scribbled something on a notepad and dialled a new number. "Is this Doctor Winters? I'm Winston's P.E. teacher, Coach Quintana. I'm very sorry about this but I'm going to need you to come to Aldershot Academy. Yes, we need to talk about Winston." Once again Wins found himself in the back of the car suffering through another painful and awkward silence. "Wins," His mother's upset apparent, "When we get back we are going to talk this over and you will explain yourself, until then I'm giving you the benefit of the doubt. But I just can't understand why you would do something so utterly reckless."

That evening Wins, Zoop and their parents sat in the lounge to talk over what had happened.

Ed began, "Mum says you climbed the climbing wall at school with no ropes and nearly fell off, your teacher told her you could have died. Please, please tell me this has something to do with the PSIReNS and you weren't just being stupid." Confident he could explain what happened Wins calmly spoke. "The PSIReNS showed me how to climb the wall Dad, so I knew I could do it. Rish bet me I couldn't so…" Ed interrupted, "Wait, let me get this straight…" he clasped his forehead between his fingertips, "The PSIReNS didn't *make* you climb that wall? You chose to climb it… for a bet?" Not seeing what the issue was Wins carried on. "Yeah, the other kids didn't believe I could do it but knew I could and it was only when I got to the top that…" Anne stopped him this time, tears were pouring down her face. "You climbed the wall, with no training and no ropes; because YOUR FRIENDS SAID YOU COULDN'T DO IT?" Struggling to understand why they were so upset Wins tried to explain again. "I *knew* I could do it, the PSIReNS…" "Winston!" Ed abruptly halted his explanation "You *chose* to do it, you chose to put yourself in danger for no good reason what-so-ever!"

Wins pondered this point for a moment. "Well, I mean if you want to put it like that…" Ed was furious, Anne was distraught and Zoop wasn't saying anything at all. "That's it!" His dad said firmly. "You are grounded for the entire week of half term!" Outraged Wins tried to counter him, "That's not fair, it was the PSIReNS!" "No it wasn't Wins!" Ed said shooting him down, "It was *you*! You chose to do something so incredibly, unbelievably, *unforgivably* stupid that you might have died, and for what? Just to impress your mates? I Despair!" Zoop quietly spoke, "I'd really like to ask Wins about what happened Dad." "Tomorrow" he instructed, "He'll have plenty of time to talk tomorrow when he's *not* going out and *not* watching films and *not* playing Nintendo! Get to your room Wins, I don't want to see you or hear from you for the rest of the night!"

Ed got up to comfort his wife. Wins, realising he had lost the battle stomped off to his room in preparation for a week of unbearable boredom.

8: Thinking About Stinking

Half term had come and gone. To his Wins' surprise, the most interesting periods of his week were those spent with Zoop who was fascinated by his episode on the climbing wall. Trying to crack the PSIReNS' sensational code to find the pattern that made sense of their sporadic actions, Zoop wanted to know every detail and so Wins told her everything. Well, nearly everything; the one part he kept to himself was the pain. That scalpel slicing agony with which the PSIReNS stabbed him when he tried to go his own way on the bouldering wall. If Zoop knew about that, her sisterly concerns would mean it would all be over; and for what? He was in control after all. All he needed to do was listen to the PSIReNS' song when they sang and he would be sure to win everything, every time. No harm, no foul.

It was the Sunday night before his return to school when the PSIReNS sang for him again, but this time they sang an entirely new song. Ed was off-shift and it was his turn to host his fellow fire-fighters' monthly poker party. Wins' dad was a Watch Manager at one of the biggest fire stations in the city, so when he was on-call he often didn't even come home between shifts at all. However, this also meant when he was at home they always tried to make the most of their time together, but when the evening came the ownership of the hours passed to the grown-ups. Like every fire-fighter Wins ever met, his dad seemed to share a brotherly bond with his work-mates. He told people it wasn't like working in an office where people are fine and friendly but tend to go their separate ways at the end of the day. Fire-fighters needed to rely on their buddies to keep them safe, or even save their life if it came to it. Being a fire-fighter meant Ed could be super paranoid about everything being switched off at night, testing smoke alarms and never lighting candles in the house, unless they were on a birthday cake. He freely admitted he was paranoid, but it was because of the things he had seen over the years, and he'd only seen those things because he was so brave.

Wins was ready for bed when the first of his Dad's mates turned up. Raising four overflowing carrier bags above his head Steve announced his arrival: "The snack-man cometh!" "Another healthy night in then?" Anne joked as she left with Zoop. Jealous that he didn't get to go to the cinema with them, Wins was still grounded after all, he reluctantly said goodbye. BB was tucked up in his cot and Wins was of the understanding that once his Dad's friends arrived he was going to have to spend the rest of the night in his bedroom. Ed must have seen the forlorn look of misery on his face because once Anne and Zoop left his Dad's week-long temper seemed to soften "C'mon Wins, help me set up the table and maybe you can stick around for a few hands." Wins didn't know much about poker but he knew that a 'hand' meant the cards each player played. The thought of watching his Dad play, combined with the prospect of getting into all those crisps and treats lifted his spirits. By the time Jeff, Bruce, Matt and Rob arrived Wins had divvied up the various crisps, nuts, sweets and savoury snacks into bowls around the table. After Ed put the drinks out there was barely enough space left for the cards, chips and green felt mat required for the game to be played.

A great gregarious laugh rumbled across the room "Well if it isn't wee Winston, our very own wall-crawling *spider-man*? You gonna join us tonight laddie?" Bruce's thick Scottish accent filled the autumn evening's air. Wins looked at his Dad. "Sure, just for a few hands though, OK," Ed said ruffling his son' hair. Wins beamed, this was going to be the most fun he will have had all week. Wins perched on his Dad's lap "Right boys, let's have a practice round so we can show Wins how the game is played." Ed put aside the first card in the deck, then starting on his left, passed a card to each player around the table then repeated the deal a second time leaving each player with two cards placed face down in front of them. Ed lifted the corners of his two cards just enough for Wins to see that he had a jack of spades and a queen of hearts.

"We play Texas Hold'em." His Dad explained, "We each get two cards the others can't see." Wins looked around the table to see the other players secretively eyeing their cards "Then we take turns betting based on how good we think our chances of winning are." Ed pointed to his chips, neat little piles of circular plastic discs, their colour indicating their value. "After each round of bets, the dealer puts more cards out on the green felt in the middle that everyone can share. Whoever can make the strongest five-card hand wins. Then we do it over and over again until only one player remains; the winner. Got it?" "Sort of." Wins tried to keep up, the game seemed complicated, "How do you know which hands are better than others?" "Well Wins," his Dad said rummaging in the table draw "after you've been playing as long as we have you just remember, but, ah, here it is," he pulled out a scrunched up sheet of old paper "you Mister, can use this list." The sheet of scrappy paper was printed with a list of poker hands from weakest to strongest.

"Can you see," Ed said pointing at the different hands "the less chance of getting the hand, the more powerful it is. So, it's pretty likely that between the two cards I have and the five we will lay out on the green felt I could get two the same, like two Jacks or two Queens." "You'd be lucky," Jeff joshed, "your Dad isn't the best poker player I've ever met Wins, sheesh, he isn't even the best player I've met at this table!" "Haw Haw Haw Jeffrey." His Dad poked back. "Let's see how you fare after you've had a few drinks, joker. Anyway Wins a hand like that, a pair, is pretty likely so a few of us could get one, but a less likely hand like a straight or a flush even is rarer." The practice round continued. "So now these guys to my left would put in '*the blinds*' that's just a few chips to make sure there's some '*in the pot*'." Wins was aware there was no actual pot. "Then we each take turns betting if we think we might have a good hand, or folding, err, putting our cards out of the game if we think there's no chance we'll win the round. But this is just for practice, so we won't bet for real."

Ed discarded another card from the top of the deck "Burn and turn, you gotta get rid of the top card each time you deal to show you aren't cheating with the deck of cards." then laid out three cards on the green felt at the centre of the table. "This is the flop Wins, the first of the community cards." Everyone around the table was now eyeing their cards as if they had forgotten what they'd been dealt a minute earlier and regarding the 7 of hearts, jack of clubs and an ace of diamonds his Dad just placed on the green felt.

"You've got a pair, Dad!" Wins shrieked. "Thanks Wins," A Scottish voice blurted, "Can you tell me what ol' Ed had in the hole there when we're betting for real son?" "Shut it, Bruce!" Ed admonished his mate. "Don't listen to him Wins, but, yeah, let's keep our cards secret OK. The name of the game here is working out if the other players actually have good hands, or if they are

just *pretending* to have a good hand; that's called bluffing."
Fascinated by this turn of events Wins asked: "So, you *have* to
lie to win in this game?" Wins had never played a game where
you needed to pretend to win if you couldn't win for real. "Not
exactly Mister." Ed discarded a card then dealt the fourth card
on the green felt "Its best just to win outright, but, some people
have a good *'poker-face'* and you can't tell what they're thinking
when you look at them. Other people have *'tells'* like big-
mouth-Brucie here." Ed raised a glass to his embarrassed friend
"He always covers his mouth with his drink when he's bluffing."
A groan of disbelief circled the table "What? Is that true?" Matt
asked. "Thanks a lot, Ed!" Bruce said taking an exaggerated,
long sip from his glass. "You asked for it brother," Ed said
batting the banter back to Bruce.

Wins was rapt to see his Dad like this; he was always so
composed and polite at home. This was the first time he'd seen
his Dad getting loud and leary. It dawned on Wins that there
must be a whole other side to his father he never knew, the side
he only shows when he's at work maybe, or just when Wins and
his siblings weren't around? Either way, the strangeness of his
behaviour didn't seem so strange now. It felt like his Dad was
letting him in on a secret, trusting him enough to show him a
bigger part of himself. It made Wins feel grown up to be
included by his Dad whilst he was doing real grown-up stuff.
The fourth card was down "This is the turn." Ed said pointing
at the 2 of clubs. "We'd all do another round of betting here then
burn-and-turn." Ed discarded the third card from the top of the
deck and placed the final card on the green felt. "So, how we
doing boys?" The Ace of hearts shone back at them all.

Various voices cluttered the conversation "I got nothing." "Not me." "I would have folded ages ago." Followed by a happy declaration from Rob, "River-Rob has it again!" as he presented his jack of hearts and ace of clubs.

Ed sighed "I'm glad this was just the practice round Wins, Rob always wins on the final card, that's why we call him '*River-Rob*'." Wins grabbed a handful of crisps and poured himself a fizzy drink whilst his Dad reshuffled the cards for the first real hand. Quietly taking in the game Wins picked up the process and proceedings, he saw how some of his Dad's friends bet on every hand regardless of what cards they might have had whilst others were more cautious, only betting when they thought they had a good chance of winning. He observed the numbers of cards, thirteen in each suit, and four suits making fifty-two cards altogether.

The game went on whilst Wins lost track of time. He began to perceive patterns in his fathers' friends' behaviour, Rob would be quiet most of the game but right before he won a hand would start joking and messing around. Matt was quiet all the time but tended to start eating nuts one after the other before he made a big raise with his chips, and he *only* made a raise when he had a good hand. Steve was harder to track, he was constantly making enormous bets and seemed to only have gotten this far by luck alone. His Dad had the worst poker face at the table, whenever it looked like he was going to get a good hand he started grinning and *everyone* noticed, so much so they called him '*Ear-To-Ear-Ed*'. After a dozen hands, four players remained in the game, Steve's luck ran out whilst the overly cautious Matt didn't take enough chances to win a single hand and ran out of chips.

Ed dealt the cards out to Bruce, Jeff, Rob and finally himself. Each fire-fighter carefully inspected their two cards, holding them close to their chests and chins. Wins leant into his Dad to check which cards he had and a waft of foul smelling air assaulted his nostrils "Ugch Dad, what's that smell?" Putting his cards down Ed asked, "What smell Mister?" "It's awful Dad, smells like bad drains or something, can't you smell it?" "I don't know what you're talking about Wins." Ed protested. Bruce, never missing an opportunity to find humour in a situation piped up "He who smelt it, dealt it, Winston." Ed came to his son's defence "Shut up Brucie, are you in or out?" The horrendous smell was overpowering, but Wins couldn't tell where it was coming from. Ed held a 6 of hearts and a 10 of diamonds.

"Burn and turn," Ed said heralding the three card flop on the green felt; 9 of clubs, 7 of clubs and the 2 of diamonds. Ed broke a grin. Wins regarded the three others still in the game while Matt and Steve watched intently as the first round of betting drew heavy investments from all four fire-fighters.

The fourth card, the turn, was dealt; a jack of diamonds.

The sewery smell got worse, so much worse that Wins thought he might be sick. Another round of betting saw the remaining four players raise the stakes again. Ed discarded the top card from the deck and slowly turned over the final card, the river. He placed it down on the green felt as if it was made of gold and weighed as much. The 8 of clubs; Wins' dad had a straight!

Ed rocked about in his chair, then came to a halt not wanting to give his game away. Wins rushed out to the toilet and gagged over the sink prompting Ed to put his cards face down with his drink on top and rush after his son. "What's wrong?" Ed asked. "That smell, I think I'm going to be sick." Wins coughed. "Catch your breath Wins, I'll get you some water." Ed ran off to the kitchen and returned with an icy glass of water. "Thanks." Wins said, gulping it down, "I think I'm alright now." "Ok, well, if you feel sick again, don't hang around, your mother will kill me if you puke and she finds out how much junk I let you eat tonight." Returning to the table Wins walked into the foul stench as if it were a wall circling his Dad's chair. Rancid and revolting, Wins couldn't bear it. His face must have shown his repulsion because Bruce commented "Too much pop and chocolate son?" Not wanting to draw more attention to himself Wins tried to deflect Bruce's suggestion "No, I'm OK Bruce." The bets were in and it was time to show their cards, Jeff laid his two cards down first, "Just a pair of Jack's boys." showing a jack of clubs in his hand to match the jack of diamonds on the green felt "Anyone beat that?"

"Two pair!" Bruce announced showing an 8 of diamonds and a 2 of clubs in his hand, matching the 8 of clubs and the 2 of diamond on the green felt."
"STRAIGHT!" Ed said triumphantly. He pulled out the 7 of clubs, 8 of clubs and 9 of clubs from the community cards on the green felt and placed his 6 of hearts and 10 of hearts in sequence to make 6-7-8-9-10.

Reaching for the copious collection of chips on the table Rob poured water on Ed's fire. "Not so fast Ear-To-Ear-Ed…" Rob pushed his glasses up the bridge of his nose and placed the queen and king of clubs next to the three other club cards from the green felt and whispered "*Flush.*"

Ed let out a groan of disappointment *"River Rob* strikes again, huh Rob?" "Too right!" Rob said gathering up his new chips, putting him well into first place. "Let's go, guys," Rob said, a smug smile polluting his face. "You gotta be in it to win it." Jeff agreed.

The four friends settled back down for the next round, Wins noticed the awful smell had passed, the evening air drifting in from the windows seemed fragrant and fresh once again. This time it was Steve, no longer in the game, who offered to deal the cards. He discarded the first card and spun each player his cards in two quick cycles. Jeff, Bruce and Rob slyly sneaked peeks at their own hands. The moment Dad lifted the corners of his cards and Wins saw the two aces, diamonds and spades, Wins was hit full in the face by the same putrid stench that had nearly made him lose his supper a few minutes ago.

Wins looked at the other players, then at his father's creeping grin and instantly understood what was going on. The PSIReNS were trying to tell him that his Dad held a losing hand. The nauseating smell was their way of warning him that they held a bad hand. But how could they know? Wins couldn't see the other cards, and the flop hadn't been dealt yet. Then it struck him, whilst he couldn't see the other players' cards... he could see their faces. Could it be that the PSIReNS saw something on the faces of his father's friends he didn't? Wins knew there was only one answer to that question. Wins leant into his Dad for a hug and braving the disgusting pong whispered, "Dad, you have a bad hand, you should fold now." "What are you talking about Wins?" He said lifting his stinking cards again to show Wins the two aces. "No Dad," Wins whispered, "you should fold *now.*" Not listening to what Wins was trying to tell him Ed whispered back "Don't be daft." Seeing that his Dad wasn't going to change his mind Wins played a risky hand of his own;

covering his mouth he bolted to the toilet.

"Wins! Sorry boys, give me a minute here." Ed said running after his son. Shutting the bathroom door Ed asked, "Are you OK Mister? I think maybe we should get you off to bed with a bucket if you're not feeling well." Wins stopped pretended to be ill and looked his Dad in the eye. "Dad, listen to me. That horrible smell, I think it was the PSIReNS. I think you have a losing hand and you should fold." Misunderstanding, Ed questioned Wins' advice "What do you mean, are you saying my cards smell bad?" "No Dad, your cards don't smell bad, the whole game smells bad. That nasty sewer smell; the PSIReNS are trying to tell me that you are going to lose." Ed understood what his son was saying but couldn't bring himself to believe it. "But I have pocket aces, I have *two aces* Wins! That's the best hand I've had all night." Getting annoyed now Wins pushed his point home. "Dad, just trust me OK, fold on this hand and you'll see, alright." "OK, OK, I'll fold this time. But I'm telling you, this is just about the worst poker tip I've ever had Wins." "We'll see Dad." Wins said assuredly and they returned to the table.

"Feeling better Wins?" Jeff asked concerned. "I'm OK Jeff, think I'm past the worst of it now." "Right, blinds are in the pot, who wants to raise?" Jeff said looking around the table. Bruce threw in a large stack of chips "I'm in it for the win lads!" Rob met his bet. "I fold," Dad told them straight, pushing his cards face down to the middle of the table. "Already?" Jeff sounded surprised. The moment Dad folded his hand, the awful stench evaporated. "I see you Brucie," Jeff said matching the other players' chips in the pot.

The flop came down on the green felt. The 7 of diamonds, 7 of spades and the ace of clubs

Dad glared at Wins. He would have had three of a kind already, and the pair of 7's would have made a full house. "I raise." Bruce upped the ante. "I see you and raise again." Rob countered. "I'm in." Jeff said, following suit. The turn was dealt; jack of clubs.

Bruce took a long sip of his drink "All. In." He pushed all his chips into the pot. "Woah, someone's going out," Matt predicted. Not perturbed by Bruce's aggressive tactics Rob nodded his agreement to meet the bet. Jeff looked like he was going to fold, but he had put so much in the pot already, he wouldn't be able to carry on the game anyway "Like I said- You gotta be in it to win it." And he pushed his chips into the middle of the table too. "Time to burn and turn and see who's going home," Steve said as he discarded the top card and laid the 7 of hearts down for the river.

"What have we got boys?" Ed asked, frustrated that he might have missed out on such a large pot of chips. "I hate to say I told you so Jeffrey, but ... Full House!" Bruce chuckled revealing his own pair of kings to accompany the three 7's on the table.

Ed immediately saw that Bruce's hand was almost identical to the one he would have ended up with, although having the two ace's he would have beaten Bruce. Jeff revealed his hand, making an even better full house with his own ace hearts matching the ace of clubs on the green felt along-side the three 7's and Bruce quietly sank into his chair.

"That's the same hand Dad would have had!" Wins thought to himself, looking up at his Dad he could tell this turn of events hadn't been lost on him either. Dad whispered, "I'd still have beaten them Wins, my full house would have been three aces and two sevens, even better than Jeff's two aces and three sevens."

"What about you Rob, ready to send us down the *river*?" Jeff Joked. Acting as if it were nothing Rob turned over his first card, a 5 of diamonds "Nothing much here…" he muttered, "Oh, apart from this little 7 of clubs." Rob dropped his 7 of clubs on the community cards like a bomb with a burst of laughter.

"Four of a kind! FOUR OF A KIND! How on earth did you manage that Rob? And on the bloomin' river too, you sat on that 5 and 7 the whole game and won on the river, AGAIN!" Bruce couldn't believe it. No one could believe it. No one except for Wins and the new believer he'd made of his Dad.

Only two players remained. Rob turned to Ed "It's just you and me Ed, ready to lose?" Steve shuffled the deck five times then the other ex-players also each gave it a quick shuffle just to make sure and Matt passed it to Wins for a final shuffle. Wins inspected the cards and shuffled them as best he could before handing the deck back to Steve. Rob and Ed were dealt their cards. Wins pressed in against his father's side pretending to be shy so that his Dad's friends wouldn't suspect anything. After all, they all thought he'd been sick twice in the last hour. Rob lifted his cards and stared into them stony-faced. His winning streak must have clouded his judgement because without a second thought he greedily tried to draw Dad into a trap. "OK Ed, it's the last hand, all or nothing, let's lay out those cards, flop to river, right now!" Ed discreetly lifted his cards so Wins could see them.

The most delectable scent of freshly baked cinnamon cake and lily flowers filled his senses, delicious and delightful. Seeing his Dad's two cards, the ace of hearts and the 8 of clubs Wins' mouth began to water as his world sprung to life with scrumptious scents and incredible odours; cooking cookies and the smell of sweet popcorn. Wins tugged on his Dad's shirt. "Do it Dad, go all in," he whispered. Wanting to avoid the risk of going all in from the start Ed suggested otherwise "Well, I mean, I don't know if that's such a good idea." "C'mon Ed." the other men tried to push him into the challenge." Ed looked at his son, Wins nodded. "OK, all in it is," Ed said, seemingly persuaded by his friends' peer pressure.

The four previous players huddled around, everyone was taken with the intensity of the moment. "Deal it Snack-Man!" Ed said to Steve, squeezing Wins tightly. The tension was palpable, you'd be forgiven for believing they were watching the world cup final for all the electric excitement in the air. Steve burnt the first card and dealt the flop; queen of hearts, king of hearts and 2 of clubs.

Mumbles and murmurs grew as the four watching firefighters speculated on the outcome. The dealer discarded the top card and placed the fourth card, the turn, in its place; the jack of hearts.

"Holy Mole!" Jeff said astonished, "Someone's gonna get a flush, or even a straight flush!" With haughty anticipation of the river card's treasure, Rob began to smile his smug grin once again. Steve discarded the penultimate card and dealt a devastating 10 of hearts.

Rob exploded into victorious laughter and turned over his cards, "I have it on the River boys! My 9 of hearts makes it a *straight flush*!"

Shouts of disbelief burst out among the friends. "I just don't believe it! How does he keep pulling this off?" they argued, throwing themselves about in fascination and fury. "Hold your horses there Roberto," Ed said interrupting the riot round the table. "You might want to see this..." he turned over his cards to show them his winning royal flush.

"A bluff works both ways..." Ed instructed his son "Just as you can pretend to have a winning hand when you don't, you can also pretend to have a losing hand and draw a fool to the fruit of his folly." Dad cracked his famous ear-to-ear grin, flashing it at Rob, "It's not just you who likes to ride the *river... Rob*." Ed winked at his best friend and scooped up all the chips from the table.

"WINNER WINNER *CHICKEN DINNER*!" Ed laughed, gulping down a great glass of his dark drink. Everyone at the table fell about, their uproarious mirth and merriment drowning out Anne and Zoop's arrival home from the cinema. "Sounds like you've been having fun." Anne said walking into the mayhem "Shouldn't you be in bed Wins?" Zoop wondered, grazing on the chocolates and sweets from the table. "Your uglier, hairier half just wiped the floor with us, Anne." Rob admitted. "And what did he win for his troubles?" Anne asked. Ed slid open the drawer under the table and pulled out everyone's contributions, it turned out that the price of playing became the prize for winning. "Sixty English pounds!" Ed announced, fanning the cash like a peacock displaying its feathers. Zoop wasn't impressed, "That doesn't sound like much." "Sounds like a lot to me." Wins thought, he didn't get pocket money the way some other kids did, and was still too young for a job. "Alright chaps," Ed said winding up the evening's amusements, "time for me to tidy up." "Aren't you going to see them out?" Anne scolded Ed. "They know the way." Ed smiled. Bouncing his smile back at him Anne apologised, "I can only say sorry for my husband guys... and I often do."

As the firefighters shuffled out the front door Ed called his children over. "Zoop, you'll want to go and have a chat with Wins... if you know what I mean." He gave her a meaningful look. "Wins, this is for you son. I know you had a dull half term, maybe this will make up for it." Ed put the winning cash into his son's pocket "Dad?" Wins wasn't sure if he could take so much money, he'd never had that much cash at one time before. "You earned it Mister. Now off you go, Mum is still working on a solution for the you-know-what so make sure you tell Zoop *everything*."

And that is exactly what he did.

9: Redline

In the weeks following half term, Wins became more and more familiar with the PSIReNS new perceptions. As his Mum predicted, they only asserted their influence when Wins was faced with a challenge or some form of competition. His encounter with his numerical friends only occurred again when he was sitting a test, so, for the most part, he still had to learn in maths class just like any other kid. But when a quiz came around his colourful, charismatic chums returns to show him who the answers were. Wins' solution for the problem that landed him in so much trouble before half term was simple. Systematically he would answer each of the quiz questions one by one in just a few minutes then spend the rest of the quiz trying to show his workings as if he had written them out first. On the few questions where he couldn't actually get to the bottom of the full explanation, he would scribble out the correct answer and put a wrong one in its place to ensure Miss Donnie didn't suspect he was cheating like last time.

P.E. became much easier too, although he was still banned from using the climbing equipment, including the bouldering wall. P.E. lessons either ended up in a sporting contest or were completely competitive from start to finish so it was there that Wins always felt the PSIReNS' song, the more time he spent under their influence the better he got at following their flow. Their guidance never failed to show him the path to victory and as long as he didn't ignore the call of the PSIReNS song he never felt their painful fury. Wins had become the best in the year at P.E. now, so much so a few kids were starting to say he might just manage to hold his own in The Triples, even if they didn't think he could actually win all three outright. So far, whether it was rugby, gymnastics, badminton, or track and field Wins was always top of the class, thanks to his secret helpers. Soon the year group would start swimming sessions in preparation for the first of the three Aldershot Academy Achiever's Award competitions which would take place in the school's pool at the end of the autumn term.

However, all of this was far from Wins' mind as today was his 12th birthday and he was all set for his long-awaited go-kart party. Wins, Rish and four of his other friends, Deano, Neet, Benji and Oz arrived at the newly opened Redline Racetrack for a ten lap race in real petrol engine go-karts, followed by cake and Mario Kart 8 on the huge TV in the party room. Wins was a champion at Mario Kart, he knew every trick, hidden secret route, all the ways to out-smart the non-player-characters and how to power-slide round corners for extra speed boosts. But this time the karting was for real, as they gathered for the instructor's induction Wins could hardly concentrate for the noise of the go-karts screaming around the track and the smell of petrol in the air. Once they saw the safety video and were shown how to drive the vehicles (one pedal to accelerate and one to break, thankfully there were no gears) the six friends took to the starter's position on the track. Each driver got their own go-kart. Redline Racetrack only opened a few weeks earlier so all their go-karts were still shiny and new. Sleek spray-painted designs adorned each boy's vehicle; fire and flames, lightning, super-heroes and electricity covered their roofs and side panels making the karts look like something out of a Hollywood racing film. The instructor walked around each go-kart making the final checks and pulled the cord to start each engine. Wins was at the back of the waiting pack when his go-kart came alive. He felt the roar and rumble of the engine shake his bones and as if called by the starter's whistle, the PSIReNS awakened.

The thumping rhythm of his engine's pistons and the fluctuating whining pitch of its mechanics came together in his mind as music, a driving, hard, exhilarating tune turning his blood to gasoline. Wins' foot slammed down on the accelerator pedal and he burst off the starter line shooting ahead of his friends. Almost by his command, a translucent red tunnel rose from the racetrack to guide him, showing him the fastest lines to cut round corners and between bends. The roaring music in his mind pushed him to go faster still on the straights and feathered his foot on the brake pedal as he approached the corners. Wins tore around the track hitting the corners with such speed his rear wheels swung out causing him to slip sideways. The colour of the mechanical music directed his hands upon the steering wheel. He fed it between his fingers turning back into the direction of the slide and drifted round the curves like a street-racer. It was sublime, his mind melded with his machine until his wheels and chassis were indistinguishable from his hands and feet.

In full flow, he saw Oz's car ahead. Wins realised that he must have sped around the track and caught up with the driver in last place. The red tunnel lead his line between Oz and the wall of the track, it was tight but he knew he could make it. His accelerator pressed to the metal of his chassis and he rushed forward, his wheels squealed as he powered sideways round the bend lapping Oz, then ripping past the unsuspecting Benji. With only three laps to go the hot idea popped into his head; when he lapped all the other racers he would come in *double first place*. First place for being first overall, and first place again for overtaking every one of them a second time.

Next was Neet and Deano, both boys were blocking the racetrack as they tried to overtake one-another in a back and forth battle for third place. Stuck behind them, Wins slowed down as the pounding music in his head slowed its tempo. The red tunnel narrowed and pulsed in waves targeting the slender gap between both his friends. Wins knew what to do, he hardened his heart and rammed ahead, **BASH**, he glanced of Deano's go-kart and into the side of Neet's, zig-zagging between them then out in front. Only two laps remained, Wins could see Rish a quarter of a lap ahead, rounding the approaching hairpin turn and zooming back past him. It dawned on Wins that there was now only one way he could catch him, he had to conserve all his speed, all his momentum on every turn… for the rest of the race, he couldn't use his brakes if he was wanted to win.

Wins stormed on taking each bend like he was on a rollercoaster ride. Strips of rubber peeled off his tyres like autumn leaves falling from trees, the scent of engine oil and petrol fumes making him drool like a hungry dog. Gaining on Rish in the final lap Wins saw his chance; if he hit the bend at just the right angle he could overtake on the inside of the curve and power out the other side to win by half a kart-length. The screech of his wheels slipping and spinning over the tarmac was deafening to everyone but Wins. For him, it was the apex of his engine's overture, the climax of his mechanical music. Crossing the finish line he was awash with excitement and elation. Skidding to a halt he heard the PSIReNS ethereal song sound his victory.

The Redline Racetrack instructor rushed up to Wins' go-kart with his hands on his head "WHAT IN THE…. Just look at the kart… We've only had them two weeks…My boss is going to be so mad… The new paintwork is ruined and, and, how did you do that to the tyres? That's like the thousand miles of wear in ten laps!" The instructor wasn't the only one who didn't seem happy about Wins' double-first-place victory. Deano and Neet looked positively furious. "What were you doing Wins?!" Neet accused. "You ran me and Deano into the sides of the track!" Crashing down from his winning high Wins realised what he'd done, "I'm really sorry, I didn't notice at the time. Are you OK?" Deano didn't seem any more forgiving than Neet, "Not really Wins. It actually hurt a lot when we crashed into the barriers then we had to wait for the instructor to come and turn our go-karts around."

Wins felt awful. He was so consumed with winning that he completely neglected his friends, and now he didn't know how to make it up to them. "Guys, honestly I'm so sorry, I guess I just got carried away." Turning to Oz, Benji and Rish Wins tried to show concern as best he could, "Are you guys OK?" Rish answered first, "Well, you didn't run me off the road or anything, but you scared the hell out of me undertaking on that last bend like that." Oz and Benji agreed, "Me too" "And Me." Ashamed and seeing himself under the spotlight of his friends' stares Wins apologised again and suggested they all went to the party room where they could have their cake lunch and play Mario Kart 8. Ed and Anne were waiting for them with Zoop and BB. BB was looking out over the next group taking to the racing course whilst playing with his toy cars and sneaking handfuls of crisps from the table when he didn't think anyone was looking. Wins was pleased to find his parents had made him a towering chocolate cake covered in white icing with a huge '12' candle on top. "Who wants a go at multiplayer Mario Kart?" Wins prompted walking towards the huge TV displaying the start screen. "I'm alright." Deano shrugged. "Yeah, I'm more of a PlayStation fan," Neet admitted. Missing the hint Wins asked Rish, Oz and Benji. "Sure, we'll play," Rish said speaking for all of them. "C'mon guys." The four friends played through on the toughest settings, Wins was so familiar with the game that he didn't have to try too hard to come out on top in each race. After the game, Deano sheepishly shuffled over, "Err, me and Neet have to go early, Neet's Dad is downstairs now, so we'll see you at school yeah?" Neet murmured, "Happy birthday." from across the room before both boys said their thank-yous to Anne and Ed and headed off.

"What's their problem?" Wins asked Rish, annoyed that they'd left his party before the gigantic birthday cake was cut. Rish took a breath, trying to think of the most diplomatic way to explain the obvious. "Well, I mean, you were pretty nasty on the racetrack mate, you ran them right of the road and think it really upset them." Feeling accused Wins dug in to defend himself, "Yeah well I didn't mean it *and* I said sorry. They shouldn't be so sensitive." Seeing room to lift the mood Rish tried to make his best friend feel better, "Hey, just means more cake for us right!" Wins grinned and the four friends made their way to the lunch table for their wholesome meal of pizza, chocolate and ice cream.

After the boys ate their fill Anne and Ed set about tidying whilst the four friends enjoyed another round of Mario Kart. Benji and Oz left and Ed began taking everything to the car. "Hold up Ed," Rish shouted, running over to the bag of birthday presents. Rish pulled out a poorly wrapped rectangular box. "I wanted to give this to Wins now." Running back to his friend he gave him his gift, "Go on, open it, dude." Wins managed to find the one spot on the package that wasn't sealed in tape and prised off the wrapping paper. "Oh, nice!" Wins was thrilled to find a boxed pair of stylish sunglasses. Rish was bouncing up and down with excitement. "Yeah, they're so cool…" He turned the box over in Wins hands and pointed to the back, "My 2nd cousin got a pair in the summer; it comes with a set of different lenses so you can swap out the colours. There are red ones, and blue ones, green ones, and yellow ones and paranoid ones too." Ed was intrigued, "*Paranoid* sunglasses? Let's have a look." Ed chuckled, "That word is *polarised* boys. They are great for sunny days, it makes colours look saturated- you know; extra rich, and also gets rid of reflections on water and stuff. Me and Jeff use polarised lenses when we go fly-fishing." Laughing, Wins thanked Rish, "Mate, they're amazing I can't wait to try them on."

On the journey home Wins couldn't help pondering Neet and Deano's oversensitive upset earlier. Seeing his pensive expression Zoop asked, "Did you enjoy your party Wins?" He nodded, but there was something he wasn't sure about. "Yeah, it was brilliant, I loved the go-karts. I felt like an F1 racer out there." Ed interrupted jokingly, "And you looked like a demolition derby driver out there!" Anne tried to bring the conversation back around. "You look deep in thought Wins, what are you thinking about?" Convinced he was in the right Wins did his best to articulate his thinking. "I was kinda annoyed that Neet and Deano left early. Rish reckons they were upset because I smashed into them on the racetrack, but, I'd already explained that I got carried away and I did feel terrible *and* I already had said sorry about it. So, why were they still so angry at me? I didn't mean it." Zoop saw the gap of his misunderstanding instantly, "Well Wins, Sometimes… to be honest *all* the time, it's never about what you meant; but what people *think* you meant." Wins was perplexed, "What do you mean?" Zoop expanded her explanation. "So communication isn't just about what you say, it's also about *how* you communicate what you say. The most import thing is it doesn't matter *what we* mean when we try to communicate with someone, but what that someone *thinks* we mean. It's no good saying something that means one thing to you, but something else to the person you are talking to; that's not communication, that's confusion." Wins thought Zoop had missed his point "OK, But I said sorry, and I told them I didn't mean it, that I just got carried away." Being the expert she was Zoop spotted Wins' error, "Did you tell them you didn't mean it, or that you got carried away? Because those are two very different messages." Wins tracked back through his memories. "I think I said sorry and told them I got carried away." Zoop could see Wins was starting to put it all together. "Can you see now how they could have got a completely different message from you than the message you were trying to send? What you meant was *'I'm sorry, I didn't mean to be so rough on the racetrack, I feel terrible.'* But what they heard was *'you're sorry, you were having so much fun you didn't care if you hurt your friends.'* Do you understand now how that would have upset them, *even though* you apologised?"

A cold dread sweep over Wins upon the realisation that he'd been horrible to two of his closest friends and again another flush of discomfort washed over him when he realised that hadn't even noticed that he was doing it when he had done it. "What should I do Zoop? I feel awful." Zoop could see the sincerity on her brother's face. "I think you need to find Neet and Deano at school on Monday and apologise again…" Wins broke in, "But I already said sorry and it didn't work." Patiently Zoop carried on, "You need to say sorry again, but this time explain to them how you hadn't realised how much you upset them and that you really want to earn their trust again because you value their friendship." "That's a lot of apologising." Wins remarked. "Well Wins," Zoop said raising an eyebrow, "I guess that just depends on how much you want their friendship. If you are really their friend then a genuine apology is a small price to pay for the value of two good friendships." Wins mulled over Zoop's point, "Thanks Zoop."

Happy he now had a plan to resolve the problem, Wins put his worries behind him, and admiring his new sunglasses settled back into his seat looking forward to his imminent birthday dinner and family film night.

10: What is it like to be a bat?

When describing his racing escapade at the Redline Racetrack to Zoop she was particularly interested in how his senses reached beyond his body and into the go-kart itself. At the time it happened Wins was so caught up in the moment he hadn't appreciated how strange it was to perceive the wheels and chassis of the go-kart as parts of his own body. Now the moment had passed it was as if he could recall two separate memories of the same event, one where feeling the racetrack beneath his tyres made perfect sense and another where it seemed so outlandish an idea as to be incomprehensible.

For now, Wins needed to face the toughest task of all; he needed to say the hardest word and make sure his friends knew he really meant it. He spotted Deano and Neet when all of Aldershot Academy's pupils congregated in the playground before registration. Wins could see both boys were deep in conversation as he approached. "Hey guys." he greeted them. Looking past him Deano dismissed his greeting, "Oh, hi Wins." whilst Neet turned half sideways as to not make eye contact with him. "Listen," Wins said trying his best to edge past their obvious discomfort, "I just wanted to say, Well, I realise I was pretty horrible at my party and I am really sorry for what happened on the racetrack." Neet considered his apology, "Yeah, you said that on Saturday." "Look, I didn't realise how mean I had been until afterwards, I felt awful that I'd treated you two so badly. If it had been the other way round I'd be just as angry with you as you are with me. I was out of order and I'm really sorry. I promise I won't do anything like that again." Neet turned back toward Wins and Deano's demeanour started to relax. Neet commented first. "Yeah, it wasn't much fun getting smashed off the Racetrack like that." Deano nodded in agreement. "But, OK, if you say you're sorry I guess we can forget about it, what do you think Deano?" "Yeah, I think so… We're playing 5-aside against some kids from 7K at lunch break," he paused for a moment "…if you want to join us." Thoroughly relieved Wins secretly sighed. He'd started to think they weren't going to accept his apology at all "Definitely!" Wins enthused, "I'll see you there."

Later that week when all the tumult of the weekend's upset had long passed Wins, Rish, Neet and Deano were debating the best stroke for the upcoming 400-metre swimming competition on the way to Miss Walters' science lesson. "It's got to be front-crawl." Neet insisted, "You look at any of the professionals and its always front crawl that's the fastest." Rish wasn't convinced, "What about butterfly?" "Well yeah, "Neet admitted, "but you have to be so strong and have so much stamina to make that work, normal people can't do butterfly, you probably have to train for years to make that work." "Backstroke?" Deano suggested. "Nah." Neet said with undue authority, "It's a bit like butterfly; you have to really know what you're doing to pull that off, one wrong stroke and you're smashing your head backwards into the end of the swimming pool. I'm telling you, its front crawl all the way, it's the only stroke that a regular person can learn well enough in time to win the competition."

Wins had come to enjoy his science classes more than he expected at the start of the year, especially since everything that had happened with the PSIReNS. Miss Walters always had something interesting for them to do. A lot of the other classes he went to seemed to mostly involve remembering things rather than actually learning stuff and working things out. When it came to Miss Walters' lessons he got to solve puzzles and find patterns which he found increasingly satisfying. There was the first challenge when they had started in September to mix up salt, sand and water then find a way to separate them back out again into their pure forms, then later using batteries and coiled copper wire to send magnets racing round a table top race track and to his surprise he'd loved growing plants under different conditions.

Miss Walters began, "Good Morning 7Y." "Good morning Miss Walters." They sang back. Miss Walters wrote across the board as she explained the goal of the lesson. "As you know, biology is the science of living things, plants, animals, fungus and micro-organisms. Today we are going to try to answer one of the hardest questions in all of biology; what is it like to *be* a *bat*?" "A bat Miss?" Wins wondered. "Yes Wins." Miss Walters continued, "We often imagine animals see the world much as we do, but that's not the case. Every species of animal perceives the world differently, very differently from us, and from each other." Miss Walters passed out the biology textbooks and brought up the smart screen on the main board. She played a looping slow motion video of a flying bat turning in mid-air and catching an insect between its pointed jaws.

"Does anyone notice what's odd about this video?" She asked. "Is it the colours miss? " Rish questioned, "They're all green and black." Miss Walters was pleased with Rish's question. "That's right, does anyone know why?" Thirty blank faces gave her their answer. "This video was filmed in pitch darkness, the camera is using night-vision technology to see when the bat cannot. So, how does the bat know to turn and catch its prey?" "Can it smell it miss?" Someone speculated. "Well, it probably can, but that wouldn't work quickly enough to catch it." Miss Walters said, trying to tease the idea out from the class. "Can it hear the insect miss?" Wins suggested "Closer." Miss Walters encouraged the class. "The bat uses '*echolocation*'." She wrote the word on the smart board and clicked onto the next video. This time the same video was animated with curved coloured lines spreading forwards from the bat and then smaller curved coloured lines bouncing back from the insect towards the bat. "The bat sends out high pitched squeaks which bounce off things up to three metres away." Miss Walters narrated. "The bat can hear these sounds bouncing back to it and use those sounds to build a picture of its immediate surroundings in its *mind*. If a lot of sound bounces back the bat might '*see*' those sounds as a tree or a cliff side, but if a little slice of its squeak comes back to it, it might see that sound as an insect worth eating for its supper." "So bats see with their ears?" Deano asked, "Not exactly." Miss Walters tried to clarify the details "Bats, like us and all animals see with their *minds*, but when they can't use their eyes; the paint they use to produce their picture of perception comes from hearing the sounds they send out echoing back to them. Now, they can't see colour with their echolocation, but they can tell if something is coming towards them, flying away or staying still. This information gets put together in the bat's brain and built up to make a picture so detailed that the bat is not only able to fly in the dark, but hunt too! Like us, bats are mammals, they give birth to live young, breathe air and raise their babies on milk. But these mammals see the world very differently to us, and so they can go out flying at night by *seeing* in sound." "What about whales and dolphins miss?" Noah noted, "Don't they do that in the ocean?" "Yes Noah, that's true. Toothed whales like dolphins and orcas use aquatic echolocation to envision their underwater world.

Some dolphins have even been known to pay special attention to pregnant swimmers; it seems they can see the babies growing inside their mothers."

Miss Walters changed the picture on the smart board to a video of a dog sniffing around in a park. "Hands up if you have a dog?" Half a dozen hands went up. "Does your dog ever perk up before someone comes home, before you knew they were about to come into the house?" The same children all voiced their own stories of their dogs' amazing abilities to know when their parents were coming home minutes before they arrived. "Dogs, another species of mammal, have *super-senses*. Whilst they can't see the colour red like us, they have extra rods-cells in their eyes so they can see better at night. They also have hearing that is four times more sensitive than ours *and* can hear much higher pitched sounds than we can. For a dog, hearing noises in high definition detail is easy. Your dog at home can pick the noise of your parents' car out from all the other traffic by the particular sound of its engine... and when it's four times further away than you would be able to hear it at all." Given Wins' recent experiences he paid close attention. "Miss, my Dad says they have a dog in the fire brigade for sniffing out petrol." Thankful for the segway Miss Walters picked up the prompt. "People have befriended dogs for thousands of years because of their astonishing senses. Dogs have a special apparatus in their snouts to isolate and examine the air they breathe. It allows them to smell more than *ten-thousand* times better than we can and on top of that, they can close their nostrils individually to sniff in different directions." She darted her head left and right triggering a ripple of giggles from her class. "Now, imagine what it must be like to be a dog, your canine world would appear very different to our human one. For a dog, there is little by way of colour, but their image of what is going on around them extends beyond what they can merely see with their eyes. They can hear and smell things far far away, or sniff out what happened days or weeks earlier; like the dogs who work with the fire brigade Wins; they can smell the tiniest whiff of petrol weeks after a suspicious fire has been extinguished. A dog's world is alive with sensations we cannot comprehend."

Miss Walters changed the slide on the smart board again, this time to a photo of the strangest looking creature Wins had ever seen.

"This is the star-nosed mole." Miss Walters used her laser pointer to point at the mole's face "Those aren't its eyes, those are its nostrils, this subterranean mammal is blind; it has no eyes at all." "How does it see miss?" Noah wondered. "It doesn't see like we do at all. But it does paint a picture in its mind's eye, only it uses its super sensitive star-shaped nose as the brush. Its tiny twenty-two tendrilled nose has twice as many touch sensors as your entire hand. The star-nosed mole lives its whole life underground, by feeling around the tunnels it digs it builds up a detailed mind map of its world. The sounds and vibrations carried through the soil and scents permeating the earth guide it to its food- worms mostly, and never having needed vision it lives quite successfully in its native world of touch."

"Now, we've spent quite a lot of time talking about mammals, but before we finish off for the day, I want you to push your imaginations even further. Try to imagine now, what is it like to be a snake, a shrimp and a spider." Wins and Rish looked at each other, they had been used to be called 'shrimp' by the bigger kids since they started at Aldershot Academy in

September, but neither of them had thought about actually being a shrimp. "Snakes are reptiles; they don't have warm blood and need the sunshine to warm their bodies up before they can fully function. But like dogs, they can smell in directions. Each time they flick out their forked tongues they taste the air and can tell which way a scent is coming from, if it's a predator they can flee, if its prey they can pursue it. As well as this, some snakes have special sense organs on their heads which let them '*see*' the body heat of their prey, so like bats; they can hunt in the dark."

Miss Walters returned to the front of the classroom. "Some animals see more than we can. Certain species of eagle can spot their prey from *two miles* away and some chameleons, dragonflies and squid have 360-degree vision." Wins tried to imagine being able to see in all directions at once, the thought gave him a headache. Miss Walters brought up a picture of a butterfly sitting on a flower glowing with otherworldly colours. "Most animals see fewer colours than we do, but a few lucky creatures see *more*."

Many insects see 'ultra-violet' light, a colour of light which is invisible to humans. But that's not all; one species of Mantis Shrimp can see up to *sixteen colours* compared to our paltry red, green and blue colour vision. What the world must look like to them!" Miss Walters exclaimed. Wins put his hand up. "Miss, I don't see three colours though, I see loads of colours." Wins noticed most of the other children in the class were thinking the same thing. Miss Walters answered his question for the whole class, "You're right Wins, we all see many colours, but our vision is based on only three colours; red, green and blue- from those three colours our brains extrapolate thousands of in-between shades from the mix of those primary colours, but Mantis

Shrimps can see even more colours than us, so their tiny bug brains can perceive thousands of times more colour than we can. Not bad for an underwater invertebrate!" Wins and Rish looked at each other, trying to imagine how they would appear to a magnificent mantis shrimp.

"Before we finish I have one last experiment for you all to explore. We are going to find out what it is like to be a spider." Miss Walters passed out shoe boxes and blindfolds. "Spiders spin webs to catch their prey, but, those webs become more than just a net to the spiders, when a fly falls into its trap the spider feels its panicked protests and rushes out to bind it up in its silky thread for its supper. For the spider, its web becomes an extension of its body. It feels *through* its web." Wins was reminded of his race at the Redline Racetrack at the weekend when he perceived the wheels and chassis of his go-kart as extensions of his own body. "Now, each pair of students is going to take turns putting on their blindfold and trying to work out what kind of object their partner has put in front of them, except, you aren't going to use your hands to feel each item, you are going to use the flat end of your pencils. "What? How are we meant to tell what something is without actually touching it?" Neet protested. "A fine question Neet." Miss Walters replied, "How indeed is the question. And the answer is for you to work out. Each box has a different item in it, so once you've had your turn swap your box with someone from another table."

Wins put on the blindfold and picked up his pencil by its pointy end. "Go on Wins, I've put it right in front of you," Rish said moving Wins' wrist forward. Wins felt a hard surface as his pencil pinged on contact with the unseen object. Moving his pencil side to side he realised it was curved and smooth and had a loop sticking out of one side. Sliding his pencil upwards he slipped forwards into a hollow horizontal alcove. Holding his pencil vertically he probed the inside of the object and gave it a light flick which produced a quick high pitched ringing sound. Sure he knew what he had been inspecting he made his conclusion. "It's a mug isn't it Rish?" "Sure is, my turn now," Rish said excitedly. Wins passed him the pencil and blindfold' once Rish put it on Wins pulled out a tennis ball from the next shoebox and held it in front of him on the table. Rish moved the pencil forward in waves until he found the tennis ball. "Oh, it's kind of rough, no furry. I can feel that it's round too." he pushed the flat end of the pencil down on the tennis ball. "It's hard but it squishes a bit if you push down on it, it's too round to be a fruit. I think it's a… tennis ball right?" "Spot on dude!" Wins said helping him untie the blindfold. Around the room the two boys saw the other children had been inspecting all kinds of oddly shaped objects, shoes, pears, sunglasses and teddy bears were amongst the items Miss Walters had collected for the experiment.

"How was it feeling like a spider? Did everyone find their spider-sense?" Neet was first to shout out, "It was a bit tricky at first Miss, but after a minute it was like I could sort of imagine the sunglasses even though I couldn't see them." Wins joined in, "Miss, it's a bit like having whiskers isn't it miss? Feeling things without actually touching them." "That's absolutely right Wins." Miss Walters agreed. "Just like rodents, we can sense things we can't see, even if we don't touch them directly." Miss Walters collected up the boxes. "We don't use *only* our eyes to *see*. None of you actually touched the items you were examining with your fingers but most of you still managed to get a sense of what they felt like and work out their shape and texture. We see with our minds, and so it is for animals of all kinds too. Their world is very different from our own. Some animals see with touch, some with sound, some with temperature and some with more colours than we can imagine. But they all *paint a picture* of their world in such incredible definition and detail that they don't just survive; they thrive!"

The bell rang and Wins cluttered out to the playground with his classmates. He felt the mist of an idea coalesce in his head. Something about Miss Walters' lesson had planted a seed-crystal in his mind and he could feel it gradually growing into a hard-edged, clear concept. He couldn't quite make it all out yet, but he knew it would be something special, something new… something truly tremendous.

11: Winner Swimmer, Swimmer Winner

When the details regarding the first of The Triples' events were announced two weeks before the end of term, two weeks to the day before the much anticipated aquatic contest the news landed like a bomb. Some people were beyond excited at the novelty, others outraged by their shattered plans for victory. Many people had been training only one swimming stroke for months and were furious at the last minute change to convention. Against all expectations Miss Maude had explained the new format; instead of a 400 metre swim as previously promised the new contest comprised a quadruple medley. A four-length swimming sprint... but the kicker was each twenty-five-metre length must be swum in a pre-specified stroke; butterfly, backstroke, breaststroke and finally freestyle-although it was understood everyone always went for front-crawl whenever freestyle was allowed as it was significantly faster than other strokes. The entire school had only two weeks to consider and prepare for the contest, many potential participants had dropped out in the belief that if they couldn't win they shouldn't even try, maybe out of fear of embarrassment or maybe a fear of failure. Truth be told, Wins might have been one of those kids in the past but after all the surprising strangeness since the summer he immediately saw the advantage the medley would give him. Miss Maude's changes to the expected format levelled the playing field, or the swimming pool at least. Everyone would be brought down to the same level of preparedness and even if some kids had a special skill for one or two particular strokes, they wouldn't have time to match those skills for all four. It was a perfect opportunity.

The final P.E. classes of the year gave everyone a basic introduction to butterfly; most people struggled with the complex rhythm of timed breathing between the froth and foam generated by the huge symmetrical swinging arm movements. They also got a good overview of backstroke, breaststroke and front-crawl too. Wins picked up the fundamentals and was starting to feel like he could just about hold his own in his class, but the reality of the situation hadn't escaped him. A lottery would be drawn on the day and he would likely wind up battling much older kids, kids with longer legs and stronger arms. He knew his secret singers would assist him, but he was under no illusion; he also knew they couldn't guarantee his victory. When the day of the medley arrived all classes were cancelled. The whole school crowded into the Aldershot Academy's swimming pool spectator stands, the atmosphere was electric. After the unexpected dropouts and last minute no-shows, only sixty students of over twelve-hundred possible participants turned up on the day to compete. Most were year 10 and 11, there were a few year 9's but only one year 7 among their ranks. Names were being ceremoniously drawn from The Triples' giant gold cup. Wins searched the crowd for his family and spotted them high up in the guests' section waving wildly at him. He drank up their warm encouragement and braced himself waiting for his name to be called. Wins' ears pricked up as the speaker system crackled across the great room, "Winston Winters, race 5, lane 12." "The end lane, the lane right next to the wall of the pool." he thought, his mood dipping. Everyone said the lanes next to the wall were the worst due to the other swimmers' chaotic choppiness crashing into the sides of the pool. The choicest lanes were those in the middle of the pool as the chop tended to emanate outwards rather than accumulate inwards towards the centre.

Wins felt a shove as a large scruffy looking kid pushed past him giving him the evil-eye, "Cheater!" he snapped through his thin grin. It was the big kid from detention, Wins had completely forgotten about him although it seemed he hadn't forgotten about Wins. "Jackson Treehorn," the speaker system bellowed, "Race 5, lane 6." Wins flinched. "Jackson Treehorn is not only in the same race as me, but he has the best lane too!" He became aware of a sinking lull in his belly and a fogginess wrapping around the back of his head clouding his previously triumphant thoughts. Wins picked up his towel and moved to the competitors' benches to await the fifth race. Walking to the reserved area he heard a loud bullish man ranting at one of the older kids. "You're the best around, nothing's ever gonna keep you down son. You're the *BEST*." Wins could only see the back of the bigger boy but the man, presumably his dad was almost screaming at his son, his face blazing as if had been sunburnt. He continued to rave "Fight 'til you drop, never stop, you can't give up! You're going to be the new Michael Phelps, son. Failure is *NOT* an option Jackson!"

Wins froze. He'd have to walk straight past Jackson to get to the competitors' stands and would then need to wait within metres of him whilst the preceding races took place. But Wins was prepared for this, he knew that it was all-or-nothing and if he couldn't even walk past a bully and take his own rightful seat in the competitors' stands then how could he hope to achieve anything at all? He passed Jackson, who was so engulfed in his father's pep talk he didn't notice him walk by. Jackson was repetitively clenching and unclenching his fists, shuffling about on the spot whilst panting and huffing himself into a frenzy. Wins had never seen anything like it, it looked like some kind of superstitious ceremony. Wins heard his name through the cacophony of the crowd and followed it back to Rish who was sitting with Oz, Neet, Deano and Benji. They were clearly excited for him and began chanting his name. The speaker system interrupted their cheering to call the first race. Wins watched carefully as twelve kids mounted the stands at the end of the pool and poised themselves to dive as the buzzer counted down; *buzz, buzz, buzz, BBBUUZZZZ* twelve boys and girls leapt into the pool, crashing under the surface to burst out a few metres on in a tsunami of splashing chaos, the resulting riotous waves smashing against the sides of the pool. Not one of them had mastered butterfly. The toll on some of the kids was obvious, one boy seemed to be stuck in the same spot spinning his arms around like a broken paddleboat, another slipped into breaststroke and was instantly disqualified. Those who made it to the end of the first length rushed back in backstroke. Despite the ceiling flags designed to signal to the swimmers when they were approaching the end of the pool, two still managed to swing an arm into the corner of the concrete lip and one poor girl swam headfirst into the wall. By now there was an enormous separation between the remaining swimmers with some starting their breaststroke length whilst others were already into their final freestyle front-crawl. Minutes later only half of the original competitors were able to complete the race with the winner coming in at 5 minutes 46 seconds.

This pattern of injuries and incomplete innings repeated itself over the following three races. The fifth and final race was being called, Wins felt his heart start pumping and breath shorten. He was nervous and he knew it. Ahead of him Jackson Treehorn's huge frame filled the path to the pool. Intimidated, Wins noticed his nerve slip. "WINS! WINS! WINS!" Rish, Neet, Benji, Oz and Deano were chanting his name "WINS! WINS! WINS!" More kids joined them, as the chant grew louder it sounded like the whole of year 7 were calling his name and cheering him on. The call echoed off the hard walls of the swimming pool's hall drowning out the hub-bub and chatter of the crowd "WINS! WINS! WINS!"

His spirits lifted. The ferocious roar of his friends and fellow year 7's bolstered his belief and repaired the cracks in his confidence. He took his place on the mount at the top of lane 12, looking to his side he saw Jackson Treehorn deep in focus, flexing his body in preparation. At first, Wins thought he was stretching but on a second glance, he realised Jackson was repeating the same strange superstitious ceremony as before; stretching out and touching his fingertips together in a very particular order. Jackson must have noticed Wins' curious stare as his concentration cracked and he shot him a deathly glare. Their shared moment was shattered by the buzzer, *Buzz buzz buzz* **BBBUUZZZZZ.** Wins jolted forward...

...Slicing through the surface of the still water, his mind smashed through the doors of his perception. The split second his fingertips entered the water Wins saw the totality of the pool and everything in it, its edges and fluidic moving mass as one. He was above himself, outside of his body looking down, or in, or through. No, it was more than that, he could *see* everything as without needing a single point of view; he was looking at everything at once. "360^0 Vision!" He thought. The rapid realisation came to him; it was more than just 360^0 around a horizontal plane, it was 360^0 perception in *all* directions! His vision was gone, replaced with something else; he saw everywhere simultaneously. Wins observed his body sliding down into the choppy waters whilst witnessing each individual swimmer's movement in this tremendous colourless vision. "The PSIReNS," Wins thought, "what's happening?" The urge to breath bore down on him, he pictured himself in the pool like a video game avatar on a screen, only this screen wasn't in front of him, it was everywhere. He focused on his avatar and willed it up for air and as if he were playing that game, his avatar broke the surface gasping. A numbness wrapped him like a winter blanket, he couldn't feel the coldness of the water nor smell the chlorine in the air. He'd become unstuck from his body. Willing his avatar forward he kept pace with Jackson Treehorn, the two swimmers already ahead of the pack. Wins hadn't got the hang of the counter-intuitive butterfly stroke in P.E. but his avatar surged forwards with effortless ease, powered by the force of his will alone. Wins felt the urge to draw air once more, making his avatar exhale into the water and pull in lungful's of air as it breached the surface near the end of the first length. Wins saw Jackson was transitioning to backstroke as he met the end of the first length. He desired his own transfer from butterfly to backstroke and drove his avatar into the wall of the pool using his elastic momentum to blast backwards into a torpedoing backstroke. Colourless ripples caught his mind's eye. The crashing, splashing waves stirred up by the other eleven swimmers were interfering with each other; when a peaking wave met a troughing wave they cancelled out for a moment before reappearing on separation. By the same measure when two peaks met they formed a fleeting peak of doubling height just as two combining troughs formed a double deep dip in the surface of the water. Wins' avatar bore the brunt of these chaotic patterns as he was racing in lane twelve next to the concrete side of the pool. The double deep dips and twice high peaks developed a texture amid his visionless picture of the pool. An inkling occurred, tickling along the train track which carried his thoughts. Wins pushed his avatar into the textured troughs to ride the resulting peaks. Timing each stroke to match the appearance of these waves of chaos on the surface of the pool he found he could gain ground… well, water, on his rival. The difference wasn't much but he knew it was incrementally building to a fighting chance. Not needing to regard the ceiling flags to find his place in the pool Wins executed an expert turn and rushed into his penultimate lap. Breaststroke allowed Wins to draw huge gulps of air on every stroke whilst powering into the tiny variations of the rough frothy waters. He was ahead of Jackson now although he could tell Jackson didn't know it yet. In seconds he'd used his momentous force to perform a flawless switch into his final freestyle length before Jackson had found the wall at the end of his third. Wins forced all his will up, down and into his avatar, mentally shrieking his own name he watched it shred through the waves "WiiiiinnnnNNNNNSSSS!" The advantage of the final length had fallen to Jackson with his indomitable front crawl, who was quickly catching up. Wins twisted his wish to win into a diamond-hard piercing spear and shot it through his avatar, he surged forward spiralling like a dolphin, once, twice, three times. His hands found the end of the pool and …

…Wins was yanked back into his body hailed by the crowd's ecstatic applause. His muscles were on fire, he scrambled for the lip of the pool only to drop beneath the water whilst frantically trying to pull himself up and out. A fully clothed body collided with him from above and wrenched him onto the pool-side. The spectators were on their feet, a hush fell over the onlookers and a small familiar crowd surrounded him, his parents, Zoop and Rish were by his side. He couldn't make out what they were saying.

"...did...OK...you...it...three...are...dude... oh-two..."
Wins found his Mum's face, holding an excitable BB in one arm
she touched his cheeks with her free hand and kissed his
forehead. Soaking wet, Coach Quintana rolled Wins onto his
side. "Let him breathe. Let him breathe." Coach Quintana
spluttered. Sideways, Wins saw Jackson Treehorn distraught.
He was screaming at Coach Quintana, "YOU CANNOT BE
SERIOUS!" he was flexing his muscles and whipping his towel
on the seats and stands. "WHAT WAS THAT HE DID?! THAT'S
NOT A STROKE, YOU CAN'T ALLOW IT!" Coach Quintana,
the pool water still rolling off his tracksuit, was trying to calm
him down. "Jackson, you need to relax right now. It was the
freestyle section Jackson, he didn't break any rules. He won fair
and square." Jackson Treehorn's father stormed up to Coach
Quintana, "What the hell is this? That waif cheated, what was
that corkscrewing nonsense he did there? That can't be allowed,
my son won by default!" "No, Mr Treehorn." Coach Quintana
purposefully stepped closer to the obnoxious man, soaking his
trousers and shoes with his own slopping wet clothes. "Today
your son didn't win because that boy over there, that boy who
pushed himself so hard he nearly drowned, beat Jackson by one
and a half seconds." Jackson Treehorn's father was livid and
looked like he was about to punch Coach Quintana. "Mr
Treehorn," Coach Quintana cut, "That boy there *deserved* to
Win, I know this because he won. That's how sports work sir.
Now if you'll excuse me I would like to get dry." The PSIReNS'
song welled up within Wins, the ethereal sound of their success
thickened and a blissful delight washed through him, easing his
pain. Ed carried him, wrapped in his towel, to the competitors'
stand. Wins sat up, Rish was pointing at the digital board, and
right up there in yellow on black Wins could see what had
happened.

WINSTON WINTERS: LANE 12: 3:02.10

And below it

JACKSON TREEHORN: LANE 6: 3:03.60

Wins had won. He'd beaten Jackson Treehorn in the first of The Triples. It nearly killed him, but the PSIReNS once again led him to triumph. Wins stood up to see the crowd, on sight of him rising a riotous roar erupted and his name sang from their lips. He staggered out and Rish came to his side to help support his weight. Coach Quintana, now wrapped in a towel of his own greeted him. "Well Winston, there's just no doubting your grit is there son?" Wins was speechless, literally. Even after resting he couldn't quite catch his breath. "I've never seen anything like that Winston, I watched you win against children twice your size, I saw it with my own eyes and I still can't explain it." Coach Quintana saw Wins was trying to speak, "Go on son, say what you need to say." Wins pressed his feet down on the cold concrete floor and took his own weight from Rish's shoulders. "No one calls me Winston sir, its *Wins*." Coach Quintana let slip a skinny laugh and relief seemed to flow after it, "Well Wins, it certainly is now!"

Wins and Rish sidled over to the top table where Miss Maude waited with his medal laid out on a green felt cloth. "You are one to keep an eye on, young man." She asserted. Picking up the microphone she called for everyone's attention. "Please join me in congratulating one of our newest pupils as well as our newest addition to the Aldershot Academy Achievers' Award winners' board; Mister Winston Winters!" Coach Quintana lent over and whispered into Miss Maude's ear, she raised the microphone to her lips one last time, "Mister Winston '*WINS*' Winters." The ovation was epic, Wins finally felt as though he was onto a winner, "I can do this now." He told himself. Winning The Triples to secure his place, his future, his friendships and his sense of self was all within his grasp and he knew it. He was on the right track alright.

12: The Game of Kings

Christmas break was a welcome refuge from the tumult and turmoil of the autumn term's odd events. As well as not having to think about schoolwork, Wins was able to catch up on various video games left uncompleted. It used to be his favourites were the racing games and first-person-shooters, all that excitement became addictive over the years. Although the PSIReNS didn't join in with his imaginary adventures Wins now found himself drawn to the puzzlers and role-playing-games which featured long, complex quests filled with esoteric brainteasers and tricky challenges. The epic Legend Of Zelda series occupied much of his free time and he spent hours trying to find every last secret and item hidden in Hyrule. When he wasn't questing for collectables he enjoyed playing board games with his family, before they started to get bored of playing with him. It became impossible for him to lose, and thus impossible for his parents, brother and sister to win. Whilst Zoop, Anne and Ed found this boring rather than annoying, bright BB's development from baby to toddler prompted increasingly frequent bouts of frustration when he lost to his brother meaning the two-and-a-half-year-old was now the one who threw awful tantrums and became inconsolably upset if he didn't win. By new year's eve, it got to the point where his Mum and Dad locked the board games away in an effort to keep the peace.

The next day the Winters set off for their annual family reunion hosted by Anne's Great Uncle Quentin Quiggins. Each year the entire extended family would descend upon Great Uncle Quentin's palatial home for food, conversation and the occasional argument. Ed said Great Uncle Quentin was 'A Character' which over the years Wins worked out was a polite way of saying he was eccentric, arrogant and could put his Dad to shame when it came to clumsily trampling other people's feelings. Great Uncle Quentin was a mathematics professor by profession and a Chess-Grandmaster by reputation. He made a name for himself many years ago defeating rival chess champions thrice his age whilst he was in his teens and twenties. He went on to gain worldwide fame not for his undeniable mental prowess but by becoming the first grandmaster to be defeated by a computer; a fact he never managed to put behind him and one that forever skewed his view of information technology. Indeed, it became a tradition that their annual new year's family reunion was a phone-free affair.

As they'd come to expect the catered spread was extraordinary. Great Uncle Quentin took immense pride in providing all manner of exotic delicacies presented to look like a work of art. In keeping with his enormous ego, the huge, lengthy oak table was crowned with an intimidating and intricacy carved ice sculpture depicting a gigantic chess piece. "Look," Ed said sardonically, "who could have guessed the centrepiece would be a *king*?" Anne chided him, "Shhh Ed, we've only just arrived!" Approaching the table Wins saw one of the waiters climb a set of folding stairs to pour whisky through the ostentatious ice sculpture. It spiralled through a thin channel inside the body of the frozen king flowing out into a chilled crystal tumbler at its base. "Edward! Anne! Hephzibah! Winston!" Great Uncle Quentin lifted his iced spirit and raised it to them. "No baby brother today?" BB peeped out from behind his father's legs. "Oh, there he is!" Great Uncle Quentin observed, causing BB to cower behind Ed once more. Anne greeted her uncle, "It's wonderful to see you, Uncle Quentin, you're looking well." "I am, I am." Great Uncle Quentin replied. Zoop was unsure if he meant he was well, or he was *looking* well but assumed it was the later as Great Uncle Quentin's pride and arrogance went hand in hand with his vanity. "That's quite some sculpture you have there Quentin." Ed commented, "Mind if I take a tipple too?" Great Uncle Quentin paused to regard Ed. Wins always felt like Great Uncle Quentin looked down on his Dad because of his job, although quite why risking his life to save other peoples' lives was anything to look down upon, Win's could never work out. Great Uncle Quentin reluctantly offered his treasure to Ed, "Certainly Edward… it's a discontinued run, I bought up the last of the distillery's stock." "Great!" Ed enthused "Where's the coke? I like mine mixed." Great Uncle Quentin nearly choked on his drink. "Ed!" Anne exclaimed. Ed paused to let Great Uncle Quentin's exasperated expression settle in before deliberately leaving his clarification long enough to be too late. "I'm joking Quentin, I'm joking. I'm not a philistine." Great Uncle Quentin forced a smile and spotted someone else he needed to greet over Ed's shoulder. Zoop sniggered, "What?" Wins wondered. "Never mind Wins, let's go and say hello to our cousins."

As the afternoon rolled into evening the customary chess boards were laid out in the low lit library. Everyone was invited to test their skills whilst Great Uncle Quentin slipped between games observing and offering advice to the players. A few of Win's extended family were semi-professional chess players, following in their Uncle's footsteps although none had reached the same heights as he had. Wins was aware of the fundamentals, how each piece moved and the goal being to place the opponent's king in 'check-mate' whereby it was under threat from your pieces and could no longer manoeuvre. Zoop encouraged him "Come on Wins, let's play a game. Maybe *you-*

know-who might make an appearance." They found one of the round tables with wooden pieces already set up and ready to go. Zoop made a knight's move up and over her defensive line of pawns. Wins, without a plan, lifted a pawn releasing a weak yet wonderful whiff. "Mmm." "Is it them?" Zoop whispered. "I can smell the moves." Wins whispered back. "What does it smell like?" she asked. "It's like cinnamon, but, it's faint, I can only just smell it." They played on, Wins whispering his olfactory experiences. As the game progressed the scent of cinnamon became stronger when he lifted the pieces that furthered his game until at last, he placed his sister in check-mate delivering a delicious deluge of magical flavour and an accompanying victory chorus. "I can taste it Zoop!" He said. "Shhhh." Zoop motioned with her hands, "Keep it quiet." "Sorry," Wins said under his breath, "It's the first time they've given me such a strong smell, I can taste it too. I wasn't expecting that at all." He gathered up the pieces, "Let's play again."

They reset the board and started a new game, Zoop's eyes brightened. "I've got an idea, let's see what happens if you try to lose the game." "I'm not sure Zoop, it normally isn't very nice for me if I lose." "Come on Wins," Zoop pressed, "We're meant to be finding a cure after all, how can we learn everything if we only look at what happens when you win." and with a wry smile she pushed her idea, "It's for science!" Persuaded, Wins acquiesced. "Alright, but if I want to stop you have to let me OK." "Of course," she said moving the pawn in front of her king. Wins brushed his fingers over all of his pieces. The ones he couldn't move felt ordinary, some smelt pleasant as before but a few felt slightly rough, like fine-grained sandpaper. He picked one of those ones, a prickly pawn, and moved it forwards onto the square that felt most uncomfortable. "There, that was the wrong move." Wins told his sister. "What did it smell like?" She asked. "Nothing yet." Wins explained, "It just felt rough and itchy, but the game is still early on so it might get worse later." Time after time Wins felt for the worst move and made it, after eleven moves, purposefully placing his pieces in positions to be taken the rough sensation had grown to pin pricks and a gentle stink wafted off the squares where he was putting his most valuable pieces in vulnerable positions. "It's starting to smell really bad." Wins whispered, "It's like rancid drains, the same as at Dad's poker night that time."

"No, No, No." A condescending voice asserted. "It's almost as if you are trying to lose the game, Winston." Great Uncle Quentin remarked from the other side of the room. The stout sentinel glided over to their table. "You have a lot to learn Winston…" Wins interrupted, "Its Wins Uncle Quentin, no-one calls me Winston anymore." Taken aback Great uncle Quentin showed his indifference to his nephew's favoured moniker. "All it takes to prove you wrong young man is for one person to call you by your given name, *Winston*. Now, come and join me for a game and let's see what you're made of." "But I'm playing with Zoop." Wins protested. "You will have plenty of opportunities to *play* chess Winston, now come along and let me *teach* you chess." Great Uncle Quentin insisted. Wins looked at Zoop, she nodded her consent so Wins followed his Great Uncle to the centre of the room where a grand golden set lay untouched on a silver board. Unlike the other chess sets in the room, his great uncle's personal set differentiated its parts by its sheen and shine rather than colour. Thirty-two of the silver squares on the board were polished to a mirrored finish whilst the rest were matt and muted. Similarly, the golden pieces were distinguished by their lustrous gleam for one player and their deep dull exterior for the other. Great Uncle Quentin took the shiny set leaving Wins to sit aside the lustreless set.

"So Winston," his great uncle began, "I hear you won a *swimming* contest at school recently." Ed was listening nearby. "He did Quentin, against teenagers twice his size too." "Well good for you Winston." Great Uncle Quentin said pointedly, although from his tone Wins knew he didn't really mean it. It seemed to Wins that Great Uncle Quentin didn't think much of anything that wasn't chess. "Well my lad, chess is known around the world and in all cultures. Many other games, older games, have come and gone but chess remains. It has been said by cleverer men than me..." he waved his hand in the air perhaps indicating that he meant people in the past, although Wins was starting to feel like Great Uncle Quentin didn't really think there was anyone smarter than himself, "...that no city, sea or civilization could hold this immortal game. They were right of course, Chess is over one and a half thousand years old and do you know why it survives to this day, Winston?" Wins shook his head. "Because my boy, there are more moves to be made on a chessboard than there are atoms in the universe!" Wins couldn't believe it, there were only sixty-four squares on the board and just sixteen pieces for each player. "Surely that's not true Uncle Quentin, it can't be that many." The mathematics of chess could be studied for a thousand lifetimes and there would still be more to learn, in just the first few moves there are trillions of possible combinations to be made. The whole cosmos can be explored here Winston, the infinity of the universe sits before us; reduced to two dimensions, captured and condensed upon these sixty-four squares. This is not a game to be played or a contest to bested like a brute playing at sports..." Great

Uncle Quentin raised his head, sneering at the very idea of a physical contest, "...chess is a war of wits Winston. The complexity of the infinite combined with the cunning of confrontation. Minds are created... and crushed here Winston, this is *The Game Of Kings*!

Great Uncle Quentin moved the pawn in front of his king. "The king's gambit, I offer you a pawn and open my front line, do you attack? Do you respond with caution? Whatever you chose the resulting repercussions will resonate throughout the rest of the game."

Wins moved the pawn in front of his leftmost rook two squares releasing the slight scent of sweet cinnamon. "A cautious move Winston." Great Uncle Quentin commentated, pushing his queen into the middle of the board. Wins felt more now, more than when he was playing against his sister, the periphery of his vision dimmed as though he were viewing the board through a tunnel. He passed his fingers over his pieces, each had a sense of pale colour about it and its own unique but vanishingly vague aroma. Some scents were pleasant and others made Wins wince. He found his right most knight and placed it to the right side of the board. "Winston," Great Uncle Quentin prompted moving another central pawn forwards, "I see you have tactics... you can clearly see the appropriate moves you need to make. However, I wonder if you have a plan for the long game. Where is your *strategy* young man?" Blooming from the board, a great tree appeared before Wins, the brightness and gleam of gold burnished its branches. "The PSIReNS!" thought Wins, "But what are they trying to tell me?" Wins picked a cinnamon scented rook and moved it to his front line, before him branches broke away from the golden tree whilst others brightened, pulsing with potential above him. Great Uncle Quentin aggressively shifted a bishop into the middle of the board causing more branches to break, falling out of infinity. "This is the game." Wins realised watching the golden tree stretch on forever up and outwards as an unrestrained rainforest. "These branches must be *all* the games to be played." He touched his pieces one at a time, some prickled, whilst others smelt of elderflower and ginger. With each touch a corresponding branch trembled with luminous potential or revolting rot, indicating the path that move would open. Wins found the cinnamon bishop and moved it to the edge of the board causing a chunk of the golden tree's trunk to evaporate. Great Uncle Quentin continued to dominate the centre of the board whilst Wins cautiously set his pieces to defend his king from attack. "I'm surprised young Winston, I thought you didn't have the gumption for a game such as this." He took a long sip of his whisky, "You're doing well to keep up son, but sometimes the best way to learn… is to *lose*." He launched a bishop across the board threating Wins' queen.

A choking stinking cloud descended upon him, he covered his mouth and grimaced whilst vast swathes of the PSIReNS' gleaming forest defoliated before him. Zoop could see his discomfort "Are you OK?" "I'm OK, it's nothing." Wins coughed, trying to deflect the question. But he knew it wasn't nothing, it was definitely something serious. A crowd had gathered, it was rare for Great Uncle Quentin to play a game of chess with anyone, more often than not he would observe from a distance, giving the impression that it wasn't worth his time to actively engage with lesser players. Mutters circulated the library, no one expected this game to take place, let alone a young boy such as Wins to hold on so long. Wins instinctively moved his queen out of harm's way, immediately regretting it. The move bit into the PSIReNS' infinity tree tearing almost all of it down. He felt dark thorns wrap his ribs and spear his spine. His Great Uncle's net was encircling him, he realised no matter what he did next his defeat was inevitable. Be it in three moves or thirteen he simply couldn't win. All his pieces lost their delectable appeal and each produced varying extremes of disgusting, foul stenches. Wins wretched, he felt the vomit rise in his throat and forced it back down. Picking up the least prickly piece he moved it to the square where the stench wasn't at its worst. "A noble effort Winston, but... did you forget about your queen?" Great Uncle Quentin asked rhetorically. He took Wins' queen and in doing so encroached on his king, restricting its sphere of freedom. Wins stifled a scream, the barbed thorns felt as though they were piercing his skin now and the reek of his pieces made him nauseous. Wins jittered his hand out to move his king, reflexively recoiling at the stabbing pain he was given for touching it. Again he forced his hand to move the painful piece away, the limbs of the PSIReNS' golden tree dimmed and disappeared leaving only one winding dead end to travel toward. Wins grimaced, seeing the walls closing in on him. Great Uncle Quentin moved his rook, "Check..." Wins held his nose, closed his mouth and endured the pain of a million needles through his fingertips to move his king one last time. Great Uncle Quentin slid his queen into position trapping Wins' king. "...And mate."

The pain was electric, instant and unbearable. Wins jolted up, the claustrophobic cloud of failure's stench forced itself up his nostrils to the back of his throat and down into his stomach, burning and making him gag. In his haste to run away his shirt sleeve snagged on the corner of Great Uncle Quentin's prized personal silver board tipping it off its round table, landing on the ornate mosaic tiled floor with a crack and sending its solid gold pieces skittering across the room. "WINSTON WINTERS!" Great Uncle Quentin bellowed as Wins rushed out of the library and locked himself in the toilet.

Wins lost his supper, lunch and breakfast but couldn't stop convulsing over the toilet bowl. There was a knock at the door. "Wins, are you OK? What happened?" "Go away, go away." Wins pleaded. "I know you're hurting, please let me in, let me help." Reluctantly he unlocked the door for his sister. Zoop saw the regurgitated mess of bile and Wins disquieting distress. "What's going on? There's something you've been holding back isn't there?" He considered his options; if he told his sister how the PSIReNS could hurt him, what might that mean for his Mum? He didn't want her to get in trouble and more than that, he didn't want to lose their power when he was on his way to winning The Triples. But, as their power to help him win grew, so did their punishment for his failures, he couldn't do this by himself. He needed help. He needed his sister. Wins washed his face in the sink "Zoop, there's a side to the PSIReNS I haven't told you about." He dried off and looked up at her, "They don't like it when I lose Zoop, they really don't like it when I lose and they make sure I know about it."

"Are you two OK in there?" Ed asked from the hallway. "I think you need to come out and apologise Wins."

Wins found his feet and stood up straight. Zoop held his hand. "Everyone out there thinks you flipped the chess set on purpose, they think you threw one of your tantrums again." Wins thought for a moment. "If I say sorry, do you think we can just go home? I don't want to hang around any longer. Everyone was watching... I'm so embarrassed." They unlocked the door to find their Mum, Dad and a curious BB waiting outside. Zoop explained, "Wins isn't feeling very well, he says he needs to tell us about *you-know-who*. Will it be OK if he apologises then we make our excuses and head home?" Anne and Ed looked concerned, "Is it something we should be worried about?" Ed asked. "I'm not sure." Wins replied recognising how his desire for victory had gotten the better of him yet again. Cowed, he looked at his feet and admitted his secret, "But, I do need to tell you some stuff that maybe I should have already told you." Anne sighed, "Well, at least it wasn't a tantrum after all, we can talk about it at home. Come now, it's time to say sorry to your Uncle Quentin."

Wins walked tentatively back to the lavish library, the whole room turned to look at him as he timidly approached his Great Uncle. The imposing patriarch composed himself. "Well, Winston, what do you have to say for yourself?" Wins tried his best to calm his nerves, the crowd of on-looking extended family were making him anxious and he felt his voice waver. "I'm sorry Uncle Quentin, Honestly, I didn't mean to knock your board off the table." Wins saw how this excuse wouldn't quite pass for the truth without an additional reason behind it, "I was just really upset that I didn't win so I ran out. Honestly, it was an accident." Great Uncle Quentin's taut stance transitioned to one of ease, he put his hand on Wins shoulder and looked him in the eye. "A spirited player!" he announced cheerily turning about to address his guests. The atmosphere, previously pregnant with tension, abruptly exuded jovial cheer. "Winston, you played well, very well my boy. Much better than anyone expected." Wins didn't know what to say, his memory of the game was bitter and fretful, fraught with feelings of failure and hurt. "Two weeks from now I'll be hosting a charity chess tournament. I just had word one of the scheduled players has fallen ill leaving a space open on the roster. You should try your skills young Winston, don't be upset when you don't win there though, these are some of the best players in the country. They will be trying to get through the knock-out rounds for their chance to battle a *Grandmaster*." Great Uncle Quentin gave a flourishing gesture from his cravat to his waistcoat. "But, I think you may well find your taste for the game develops... in the *proper* environment." He glanced at Ed. Wins pondered the proposition, the results of last game ravaged him but he wanted to know what lay at the top of PSIReNS golden tree. Whilst the suffering of loss made him sick to his stomach, his longing for victory had not waned one grain. Wins stood tall, "Yes, Uncle Quentin. I would like to come along if it's OK with Mum and Dad." Anne stepped in, "Thank you, Uncle Quentin. Let's see how you feel in the morning, Mister."

After saying their goodbyes, a waiter brought their coats to the front door and with them a brown paper bag. "Professor Quiggins asked me to give this to you Master Winters." Wins opened the bag to find a hefty book entitled 'Chess; a guide to tactics & strategy'. He turned it over in his hands and saw a picture of his Great Uncle staring back at him. That familiar tingle twitched up his back, threading itself into his thoughts. "Perhaps all is not lost." he considered, "Perhaps there is a way to win after all."

13: The Octogenarian Chess Champion and The Unexpected Temper Tantrum

After Wins described the full extent of the PSIReNS' growing influence over him his parents were initially upset. Along with Zoop, they had no idea how intensely the PSIReNS could inflict devastating discomfort and distress upon Wins when he didn't fulfil or follow their synesthetic songs. He'd kept this part of their power to himself for fear of losing the advantage they gave him, but having explained it he only wished he'd told them earlier. He felt like the incrementally increasing weight of that secret was now lifted. For his family, some of Wins' more compulsive behaviours like sprinting out of a crowded room or finding himself stuck at the top of a climbing wall, made more sense too. In the end, they all felt some relief now that more pieces of the puzzle were falling into place.

One problem remained, however; despite all the information gathered by Zoop and Wins' discussions over the previous months and all the insights and theories that followed, Anne was no closer to proposing a solution. It was obvious that the PSIReNS forceful sway over Wins was growing with each event. But avoiding every eventuality that might provoke them into a response for the rest of Wins' life was impossible. Thus everyone agreed that simply waiting to see what would happen was no longer an option and they needed to formulate a plan. If they couldn't physically remove the PSIReNS from Wins' brain, they would need to find a way to render the PSIReNS inactive, or better still, turn them off for good. Anne supposed in light of this new information she could re-examine the PSIReNS artificial intelligence programming for flaws which might lead to a hypothetical 'off-switch', Zoop and Wins agreed to keep a closer record of events in the belief that even the tiniest detail may provide a valuable clue.

Ed was not so sure that his son should still take part in the chess competition proposed by Professor Quiggins. Nevertheless, Zoop and Anne both believed that chess, being an intellectual rather than physical pursuit, would be the safest way to garner in-depth insights into the inner workings of Wins' secret singers. Wins spent the next two weeks reading and re-reading Great Uncle Quentin's book 'Chess; a guide to tactics & strategy'. As well as investigating various schools of playing styles such as romantic, classical, hypermodern and so on, the book also contained an appendix detailing Professor Quiggins' greatest victories. Wins replayed all of his Great Uncle's games on the family's chess set dozens of times, yet couldn't shake the feeling that some invisible information was missing from the whole picture. Wins suspicions led him to an online forum where *all* of his Great Uncle's chess games were recorded move for move, not just his winning games. After many hours of re-enacting his Great Uncle's losses and draws the faint sound of the PSIReNS' song called to him from far off shores, their spine-tingling tickle returned and Wins envisioned a purposeful plan crystallising in his mind; sharp-edged, clear and as intricate as a cut-glass labyrinth. It was then he knew he had the missing piece of the puzzle.

The Winters arrived at the town hall early on the day of the charity chess tournament and made their way to the registration table. Wins signed himself in and was presented with his official ID on a lanyard. Zoop helped him find his table for the first round whilst Anne and Ed looked for Great Uncle Quentin. The charity tournament was sponsored by the watchmakers 'Knox-Harrington' who donated one of their most expensive watches as the winner's prize. There would be seven rounds, the winners of each round would go on to play similarly ranked winners in the next round with one point being awarded for a win, half a point for a draw and zero for a loss. Those players who drew would get a chance to regain points and remain in the runnings by duelling with other players who also drew in their games. After six rounds the two players with the highest scores were set to play each other on the top table's electronic chess-board on stage. Every move would be relayed onto a projected screen for the whole hall to watch, whilst simultaneously being webcast on various chess sites worldwide. On the far side of the hall, a staggered chart displayed the names of each player for the first of the knock-out rounds followed by a triangular flow of blank nameplates finishing at the final round's apex.

"What a pleasure to see you here Winston." Great Uncle Quentin's refined voice startled Wins. "I trust you were able to read my book?" "Yes, thanks Uncle Quentin, I read it cover to cover." keeping to himself the specific number of times he'd read it cover to cover. Professor Quiggins' tone shifted to a more serious timbre, "Now listen young master Winston, please don't be upset if you don't do so well today. I remember my first tournament... whilst I won, of course, I still recall those nervous shakes sitting down for those first *real* games. It can be an intimidating place to find yourself; there are no age categories today you understand." He snorted a little laugh, "The rules are such that theoretically even *we* could end up at the same table." Professor Quiggins gestured towards the top table on the stage at the head of the hall. Wins felt like he never really knew what to say when an adult told him things he already knew, so just nodded along and thanked his Great Uncle when he stopped talking. A young woman in a sharp blazer took to the stage and announced the first round. Wins was set to play a lower ranked older boy named Ethan, although it seemed all the participants were older than he was. Ethan's opening move brought the PSIReNS to life with a tangible tingle in his head. He felt over his pieces taking in their scents, seeking the softest textures, picking his piece prompted the golden infinity tree to sprout before him shooting high and wide beyond the periphery of his senses. After four moves Wins saw his opponent's strategic flaw; he focused only on defence. Even his body language, sat behind his crossed arms and legs, screamed that he was too scared to take a risk. Considering this Wins opted to pursue the moves that smelt and tasted like hot ginger developing the more aggressive and assertive positions available to him. After five more exchanges Wins had Ethan on the run, he pushed harder and put his opponent under checkmate in short order. The PSIReNS whispered their ethereal victory song in celebration of his first victory.

Wins' name moved up to the second round and he awaited his next opponent. Once all the first round games were finished Wins was surprised to see Ethan sitting across from him once more. Wins' look of confusion must not have come as a surprise to the other player as unprompted he said, "I'm Joel, Ethan is my brother." Wins acknowledged his understanding and they began. Unlike his brother, Joel mounted an attack from the start. Urgent, eager moves designed to put Wins on the back foot. Examining his options Wins saw an opportunity. If he needed to push when his opponent pulled back, as he had done with Ethan, then he should pull when his opponent pushed. Wins needed to make him think that Joel was winning, whilst all the while he was secretly laying a trap for his older opponent. Wins closed his eyes and pictured the board and its pieces. The PSIReNS played out thousands of games in his mind's eye until Wins recognised the winning game. It required some uncomfortable sacrifices of primary pieces but lead to a sure victory. Having seen it through in his head Wins felt as though the game was already played, all he needed to do was calmly follow the predetermined steps. The smell of moving his pieces to vulnerable squares made him gag but in under twenty minutes, he scored his second full point and was feeling confident once more.

With the help of the PSIReNS Wins bested the following two players swiftly, sniffing out their strategies early and mounting the tastiest counter attacks. When met with a tricky tactic Wins sought out an even trickier response and with each victory, the PSIReNS' song grew louder, as with each point won the crowd cheered more excitedly. Being an unknown entity on the chess circuit Wins was been initially matched with lower ranked players, but having won four matches in a row he was moved up a tier to play a red-haired woman who seemed as old as his mother. "Cynthia Sobchak." she introduced herself and offered her hand. Her hair seemed to blaze under the lights. "Wins Winters," he replied, shaking it. "Seems you've caused quite a stir Wins, how long have you been playing?" Cynthia asked sincerely. Without considering his answer Wins told her the truth, "About a fortnight." Cynthia's eyes widened, she took a slow sip of water. "Well then, I look forward to seeing what you've learned."

Wins opened his frontline to allow his queen out on his next move, sweet cinnamon drifted off the board. Cynthia matched his move and the game picked up pace. The sprawling golden tree pulsated and flourished around him, stretching off into infinity. Cynthia's dynamic moves cast a net around the outside of the board, her bishops stalked the diagonals and her rooks marched around his pieces, Wins started to smell the rotten tells, the scent of failure's approach. He took a moment to search his tree of possibilities and saw none that won, he should have looked harder and earlier instead of assuming he could win again. Wins noticed some sour branches that didn't lead to a loss. The taste of earth and autumn's decay began to fill his mouth as he opted for the routes less likely to bring defeat. Wins made his designs on Cynthia's king but could see one of her pawns creeping up the left side of the board, he knew what this meant. Once she had her pawn on his rear row she could swap it for any piece she liked, no doubt a second queen to dominate him from the back of the board and attack him from the front. He had to act fast. His brain felt like it was being cooked, a terrible heat bloomed from inside his head and streams of sweat poured off him. This wasn't imaginary pain like the stabbing prickles, this was real. This was now. Branches and limbs fell away from his golden tree, the forest was swiftly shorn leaving only one path. Wins could taste the stale bitterness of the inevitable outcome ahead. Whilst not as repulsive as the smell of failure, it wasn't a pleasurable sensation as victory either. Wins saw the pieces and the flickering places they needed to be. He could see that Cynthia saw it too. They both moved towards their inevitable end and met in a squalid, sticky, stalemate. Wins shivered as prickly tingles raced over his body. "That was quite a game for a beginner young man," Cynthia said. "I doubt anyone else here would have survived it, well except for Professor Quiggins." Wins head was spinning, he tried to compose himself. The stalemate draw felt like someone had pulled the rug out from under him. "Thanks, It was the toughest round I've played." Cynthia looked at the board on the wall, "That's my second draw, so, I'm on 4 points for five games and you… Wow, 4.5 Wins. Well done!"

Coming through the less experienced players, Wins had performed better than anyone had expected. Most of the higher level games ended in stalemates meaning only one player had five full points for five outright wins. Zoop rushed up and hugged her brother, "You're through Wins. You're going to play Uncle Quentin!" A cold dread filled his belly as the blood drained from his face. "I, I, don't know if I can lose again Zoop." "You can't think like that Wins, if you think you can win, or you think you can't, you'll find out you were right." He considered his sister's advice. He'd come this far and he'd studied all his Great Uncle's losing games. "You're right Zoop, I'm not about to back out now." Their parents spotted Wins and Zoop in the crowd and beckoned them over. BB was in his father's arms holding a king in one hand, a queen in the other gleefully sucking on a rook. "I can't believe it," Anne was beaming. "This is incredible Wins, it normally takes years of practice to achieve what you've managed in two weeks!" Ed interrupted, "How are you feeling Mister?" "I'm pretty overwhelmed, to be honest Dad. That last game made my head hurt." Wins answered honestly, although it seemed like nobody quite understood what he meant.

The young woman in the sharp blazer took to the stage to describe the details for the final match. "Good afternoon chess-nuts!" A mixture of giggles and groans sputtered through the hall. "What a day, what an unexpected turn of events." She pointed to the staggered name board on the wall which revealed the two players who had come through to the final game. "After winning five consecutive rounds Professor Quiggins has gained his place at the top table here on the stage. Joining him, a dark horse, a new player who we understand is Professor Quiggins' very own great-nephew; Winston Winters!" A round of applause grew and dwindled. The young woman in the sharp blazer continued, "As we are outside of official competition rules for our fundraising event today Knox-Harrington timepieces have suggested something a little different for the final match." A hush fell over the room "Breaking with the traditional format the final round will comprise a *'blitz-hourglass match.'*" Wins looked at Zoop with questioning eyes, Zoop shrugged back, "I've no idea either." The young woman in the sharp blazer explained, "The timer for the final game has been set to allow for one minute per move... however, every second a player takes will be added on to their opponent's time allowance." The great hall buzzed with excitement. Wins whispered to Zoop, "So if I take thirty seconds to play my move Great Uncle Quentin will get a minute and a half for his?" Zoop nodded. "That's right, but remember, it goes both ways. You'll get his time too." The woman in the sharp blazer held up a box containing an elegant, angular, silvery timepiece. "The winner will be awarded an engraved Knox-Harrington Platinum Stargazer Chronograph. Now, I'd like to invite to the stage our own venerable *Grandmaster* Professor Quentin Quiggins and his young nephew Master Winston Winters."

Wins felt a chill in his stomach, apart from his family he didn't know anyone in the room and his Great Uncle seemed unbreakable ascending the steps to the stage, he looked like he knew he belonged there. Ed bent down to his son, "I know you're nervous Mister, but just remember it's OK to be scared; you can *only* be brave when you *are* scared. Do you understand?" Wins took in his Dad's cryptic message and nodded once. "Whatever happens we are proud of you and you have already surpassed everyone's expectations; you have nothing to lose alright." Ed hugged Wins and sent him on his way to the stage. Climbing the steps to the stage Wins was greeted by his Great Uncle's stern stare, which he quickly swapped for a practised smile. Uninvited, Professor Quiggins took the microphone from the young woman in the sharp blazer. "What an honour it is to be here today and can I say... what a delight it is to see my young apprentice ready to prove his worth this afternoon. This young man only started playing in earnest two weeks ago after I gave him a copy of my book *'Chess; a guide to tactics & strategy'*," he talk-whispered into the microphone from behind the back of his open hand, "(signed copies are available in the atrium.)" A smattering of chuckles crackled amid the crowds. Professor Quiggins put his hand on his Wins' shoulder and squeezed too hard. "Are you ready Winston?" Wins spoke softly, "What's that young man?" His uncle asked. Wins pulled the microphone down so he could speak into it "Its *'Wins'* Great Uncle Quentin, no one calls me Winston." There was a brief moment of silence broken by gentle applause from the audience. Wins calmed, the quiet support of the onlookers made him feel like he was no longer an imposter in someone else's world, but he belonged on the stage as much as his uncle did.

They each took their seats beneath the projector screen, the electronic board was connected to a computer that was webcasting their game over all the popular chess websites and would show their game live on the screen behind them with their 'hourglass' time allowances at either side of the projected board. Professor Quentin opened his front line moving the pawn in front of his king. Wins touched his pieces prompting the PSIReNS to come alive once more in a halo of hot sparks. Their glowing golden tree sprouted out of the board and he saw for the first time the true extent of infinity. Wins felt dizzy with vertigo standing on the precipice of its endlessness, but drew himself back to his body, focusing his mind on his pre-planned strategy. Wins lost ten seconds to his Great Uncle simply trying to get started, but that was all part of his plan. He moved up the leftmost pawn, its elderflower scent smelled like magic and its soft texture was like fur under his fingertips. Wins awaited his rival's response and just like the last time they played his Great Uncle developed his strongest pieces into the middle of the board. Wins returned his uncles provocations with cowering, desperately defensive manoeuvres whilst surreptitiously creeping his pawns up the outer edges of the board. The stench of moving his pieces to vulnerable squares made him gag, but he continued with his ploy, castling his king with a rook to give the impression he was on the back foot.

The hourglass slipped in his uncle's favour now, and in the rush of the blitz speed game, Professor Quiggins made a fatally erroneous assumption. Even though he only needed the half a point a draw would earn him to win the contest, Professor Quiggins believed that deploying his comfortable tried and tested strategy would beat a weaker player outright and gain him a full point win. But what he failed to consider was Wins was no longer a weaker player. Wins saw beyond. Wins saw his familiar friends, those numerical companions of his; colourful and countless filling his golden tree like rainforest fruits showing him which branches to harvest. Hidden in the complex labyrinth of his forever forest they drew Wins towards the most beautiful problem and its luscious solution; how to win. Wins knew what to do. He swept a bitter bishop over the board and threatened his uncle's queen, instinctively his Great Uncle took Wins' piece. With the rival queen drawn out of the way Wins brashly placed his uncle's King in check with a pawn. Startled, Professor Quiggins went to take Wins' attacking pawn with his king but found it was protected by Wins' second bishop. With Professor Quiggins' time slipping away he rashly moved his king backwards toward his rear line. Wins brought another sweet, chocolaty pawn forwards to take a forgotten rook. Wins saw creeping panic fill his Great Uncle's eyes. "He can't have forgotten that everyone expected him to win and that the world would be watching, *again*." Wins thought. Professor Quiggins stuttered, he went to move his queen, then his knight, then his king again. He couldn't make up his mind. It was as if he had forgotten how to play altogether and was a beginner again. The young woman in the sharp blazer cut through his confusion. "Ten seconds remaining Professor Quiggins." He moved his queen to take one of Wins' rooks leaving his rear defences open. Wins' plan was working, using his pawns as a single organ of stealthy attack he'd set his trap, distracted his Great Uncle by leaving his stronger pieces near his back line whilst incrementally pre-positioning his imminent endgame's finishing blow. Wins put a pawn on His great Uncle's rear line and swapped it for a queen placing his rival's king in check releasing the spiced flavour of burning ginger upon his tongue. With only a few seconds to respond Professor Quiggins shifted his king off the diagonal line of Wins' attack to the square adjacent to the queen's horizontal line of attack. Dropping his axe on the PSIReNS' pulsing probability tree Wins pushed a second pawn onto his Great Uncle's rear row and swapped it for a knight; a tornado of sweet scents filled his head. "CHECKMATE!" The pulsating golden branch he ascended burst into bloom. Vivid fire flowers flared up around him, he drank deep from the flavours of his winning game and the euphoria of the PSIReNS triumphant chorus washed over him; a deluge of tingling delight. The crowd unanimously erupted in riotous applause.

Professor Quiggins started muttering to himself, "No, no, no, inconceivable!" Growing more agitated he started to yell and yammer "NO! NO! NO! IT'S NOT FAIR! NO ONE SWITCHES FOR A KNIGHT!" He slammed his fist down on the corner of the board, flipping it and sending the pieces sailing into the thunderstruck crowd. Wins backed off, he had no idea his Great Uncle would react this way. "He looks like a toddler throwing a temper tantrum, he looks like... he looks like... is this what I look like when I lose?" Wins thought to himself.

The whole hall stared in silence whilst Professor Quiggins' composure nosedived. As though a blanket lifted from over his face Professor Quiggins noticed the hundreds of onlookers, jaws wide open, staring at him. Speechless with embarrassment he turned in an uncoordinated stumble and stormed off the stage through the middle of the crowded hall and out of its front door. The flustered young woman in the sharp blazer walked to the centre of the stage. In stunned shared silence she considered her words and raised the microphone to her lips. "Winston '*Wins*' Winters!" She announced. The spectators cheered in spontaneous applause whilst Wins grinned from ear to ear, the sound of the PSIReNS victory song ringing in his mind. The woman in the sharp blazer pulled a box out of her pocket and passed it to him with the lid open. The Knox-Harrington Platinum Stargazer Chronograph watch weighed heavy in his hands. It felt like it was made of lead, so much heftier than it looked. She leant down to him, "Well done young man, that was truly astonishing!"

Wins spotted his family in the bustle, Ed pushed his way to the stage and lifted his son down onto his shoulders. Joel and Ethan squeezed through to shake his hands and Cynthia offered her congratulations. "Those were some maverick moves Wins," she said sincerely, "I'd like to know how you managed to pin him down so swiftly." She gave Wins a thoughtful smile "I'm going to keep an eye on you young man." Ed put him down, "My son the chess champion!" BB wriggled out of his Mum's arms and ran into Wins, "My brother!" he said squeezing him. Wins saw his mother's beaming pride. "Mum, I just needed to learn how to control them. I don't need to be afraid anymore, I just have to listen more carefully and make sure I don't let them do whatever they want." Anne hugged her son tightly, "Enjoy your moment, let's talk about it later." Hugging his sister Wins passed her the box "This is for you." He handed her the new watch. "I can't take this!" Zoop protested. "You earned it." "No Zoop," Wins maintained, "I wouldn't have got close to being here if you never believed in me. I don't know what would have happened, I would have thought I was going crazy. *You* deserve this." Zoop rubbed her eyes and kissed her brother's forehead.

For the first time in a long time Wins saw the fog lift, he felt like he wasn't blindly stumbling through. This time he set the strategy, this time he chose *how* to win. He could make this work, he was no longer adrift on an ocean of chaos. He was captaining his own ship towards his own destination.

14: #BoyGenius

Wins never expected the events of the charity chess tournament to have as far-reaching a fall-out as they did. After the video footage of his lightning-fast game and Professor Quiggins' astonishing temper tantrum went viral on social media the national news got wind of the extraordinary game and the Winters woke up the to swathes of reporters hoping to interview the trending '#BoyGenius'. The house phone rang off the hook and Wins' parents were forced to turn off their mobile phones so they could get through the day without being pestered by unsolicited callers desperately trying to get an official quote for their articles. Zoop and Anne stayed home from university and the Station Manager at Ed's fire station was forced to tell the reporters to leave because they were getting in the way of the fire engines' emergency exit bays. The local news tried to record a piece outside Aldershot Academy's gates right when everyone was arriving for registration, asking the school kids what they knew about Wins. Seeing this, Miss Maude stormed out of the building and told them to "GO HOME!" and to "STOP BOTHERING MY PUPILS OR I'LL CALL THE POLICE!" in her most intimidating headmistress voice which promptly put a fear in the reporters so severe they all scarpered.

Great Uncle Quentin was even more averse to speaking to the press than the Winters. Unfortunately for him, TV news crews aren't allowed to show footage of a child without their parents' permission, so the few bits of footage they scraped together for the news articles featured video of Great Uncle Quentin losing his temper after the chess game, and ten seconds of him standing at his front door screaming about how he'd been tricked by the blitz hourglass format into losing a game he should have won. Poor Professor Quiggins was the only person who knew that the reason he'd screeched at the cameras was because they'd been ringing his doorbell for hours and wouldn't leave him alone. Anyone else watching would just assume he always answered the door that way.

Zoop suggested they sat down together with Great Uncle Quentin and gave a short interview to BBC breakfast news to set the story straight and get everyone off their backs. Anne struggled to convince her uncle to take part in a televised interview but in the end, he agreed on the understanding he could say Wins had been studying his own Grandmaster's guide to chess. Wins saw this suggestion; that he'd only won because of his Great Uncle's own intelligence, as somewhat disingenuous but eventually agreed with the proviso that his Great Uncle called him 'Wins', not 'Winston' on camera. This seemed a fair compromise to Wins as he would have the final word. Professor Quiggins went agreed as it was more important for him that people thought him an intellectual, rather than a raving lunatic. Anne saw an additional advantage; pushing focus onto the book was a good idea as it simultaneously placated Great Uncle Quentin's enormous ego *and* gave people a believable reason as to how a young boy could have beaten this particular grandmaster. Once the interview aired the press seemed satiated and moved on to the next viral craze, but Wins won himself a reputation at school. The Nickname #BoyGenius was a double-edged sword; whilst he became more popular with the kids in year 7 the name made him more noticeable to the older kids who seemed to resent him for it. It also didn't help that the Jackson and his friends were perpetually shouting jibes and accusations at him whenever they crossed paths. "He must have cheated!" they would yell scornfully, and sarcastic shouts of "*HASHTAG-BOY-GENIUS*" were often hurled across the playground or lunch hall.

Walking home with Rish one evening Wins finally cracked. "I always thought that being well known for winning something would mean people liked you more than they used to, not less." He blurted out after a particularly trying day. "What do you mean?" Rish asked, a bit baffled by Wins' spontaneous statement. "All this hassle Jackson's lot keep giving me. I was, I am… really proud of myself for winning that chess tournament, honestly it was the toughest thing I ever did. So much harder than that freestyle medley before Christmas." Rish stopped walking, "So what's the problem?" Wins tried to choose his words before speaking. "It's embarrassing that all these people know me now. I hate the idea that people might be talking about me behind my back and I keep wondering what people are saying about me when I'm not there." "But they don't know you dude, they just think they know you because of one thing you did one time," Rish replied. "People get '*known*' for some viral video or post online that bounces around for a while but no-one new actually '*knows*' them." Wins wasn't convinced. "Yeah, but this is all anyone will ever know me for, it's like Jackson's crew have turned something brilliant into something horrible. I feel stuck in a rut, I'm so tired of it." Rish tried to lay it all out. "Listen; haters, bullies, cruel kids- they never *need* a reason to be mean. It's not like you *did* something so they pick on you. It's exactly the other way around; they *decided* they don't like you, so whatever you do they will pretend that's the *reason* they don't like you." Wins had never thought about it that way. "Really? I mean, I thought I should try to keep a low profile and stay off their radar." "Not at all." Rish insisted, "It was like this at my old school before I knew you. These kids used to bully me every day and I always thought it was my fault. I tried to change what I did, what I said, I tried to turn myself into someone else so they would leave me alone. But it didn't work. That's why I ended up moving to Mont primary in year 5." Wins listened carefully. "But after I moved schools I realised that it wasn't me who had the problem, it was them. Whatever I did or didn't do- they would use it against me." Wins was starting to understand, "So what should I do then?" Rish continued, "You have to *own it* Wins. If they call you 'Boy Genius' smile and say thanks, show them that whatever they say it doesn't bother you because it's those guys who are wrong, not you." Wins' thoughts lifted, he saw the cloud of his mood drift apart. "Yeah, yeah I see what you mean." Wins enthused, "If whatever I do they're going to hate me for it anyway I should just get on with enjoying myself. If my doing well aggravates them, then there's all the more reason to do it!" "Exactly!" grinned Rish. "I wish I worked this stuff out whilst I was still at my old school... but then we'd have never even met." The notion of something bad leading to something good left both Wins and Rish lost for words, it didn't add up the way they'd been taught life ought to.

Rish broke their silence. "Did you see the funfair is in town first weekend of half term?" "Yeah, I wasn't sure about going before but... now I'm well up for it." Wins replied. "I'm skint." Rish explained, "So I won't be able to go on much..." Wins cut his friend off midsentence, "Dude, don't worry. I still have a load of cash I haven't touched since last year so it's my treat." "Really?" Rish asked. Wins nodded slyly. "How much cash exactly?" Rish probed. "Sixty quid." Wins answered coolly. "SIXTY QUID?!" Rish couldn't believe it. "How the hell did you end up with sixty quid?" Wins tried to pretend it wasn't much to talk about, then changed his mind. "I won it in a game of poker." "SHUT UP!" Rish laughed "You did not." Wins laughed along with his friend, "It's a long story, but it's mine to spend how I want and I want to spend it at the funfair; so are you in or not?" Rish didn't miss a beat. "Damn right I'm in!" The two friends headed home riveted in speculation over which rides and spectacles they might find at the funfair, made their plans and parted ways.

Saturday's early evening air carried the sounds and scents of fairground excitement. The roaring rides and stalls spread out over the parkland blared their discordant clash of songs and clamouring buzzing sirens unashamedly calling for attention. Drawn in by the tantalising smells of candy floss and roasted nuts Wins and Rish eagerly waded through the thick festival atmosphere and loud crowds of punters. "What do you want to do first, Rish?" Wins asked. Rish looked around for the tallest, fastest ride he could see. "That one," Rish pointed to an enormous white ring rising high in the dusky sky, "the Wonder Wheel." "Whoa!" Wins exclaimed, "What is it? "You'll love it, dude. It spins so fast you stick to the wall, then it turns ninety degrees up into the air, more likely than not someone will puke on the ride; it's hilarious." Wins was unsure but didn't want to let his friend down. "It'll probably be me that throws up… let's do it!"

They made their way through the hustling stalls following the screams of exhilaration to the Wonder Wheel. Wins paid for them both and they followed the queue to their places on the ride. A bar came down over their chests, Rish shouted over the music "Hold on there." and motioned to the vertical bars either side of Wins. A siren sounded, lights atop the huge wheel began cycling colours and the wheel started to spin. Wins felt his body press against the wall behind him, it was like gravity had shifted sideways and was pulling him backwards rather than down toward the ground. The wheel jolted up then began to tilt, they were lifted up and their ride changed from a round-a-bout to a Ferris wheel only much, much faster. Although Wins could see they were now spinning up and down, up and down over and over it felt like they were being held heavily against a wall and it was the world which whirled about them. Wins heard a kid screaming and wasn't sure if the kid was ecstatic or terrified. After a minute Wins realised it was he who was screaming, and it was both sheer terror and utter delight that was making him do so. Wins turned his head to see Rish in uncontrollable fits of laughter, the ride tilted back down to the ground and slowly came to a halt. The bars lifted and Rish doubled over giggling. "What? What is it?" Wins wondered. Rish pointed to the other side of the ride where a teenage girl looked mortified. Next to her a bunch of older kids were covered in vomit; one of them was Jackson Treehorn. "Wins turned around so the bigger kids couldn't see his face. "Rish, that's Jackson." he urgently whispered. "Let's get out of here while he's distracted." Rish couldn't stop laughing as Wins dragged him off the ride and round the corner.

"That was amazing," Rish gasped, "just seeing Jackson get puked on was worth it." "We're lucky he didn't see us." Wins said, "He must've been furious." "Don't worry about it dude" Rish reassured him. "There's plenty of funfair to go around, he won't even know we're here. "So what's next?" Wins considered his options. "Food, let's get some terrible hotdogs and too much candy floss." Rish enthusiastically agreed so they went to find somewhere to fill their bellies. Night fell from the dusk, the two boys tried each and every ride until there were no new ones left to try. Wandering through the stalls something enticing caught their eyes. On a stand under a spotlight stood the most incredible mountain bike they'd ever seen. The two boys cut a line directly through the thick throng of fairground-goers to the intriguing stall. Rish didn't wait to get the stall owner's attention, he shouted over the noise, "Mate, mate, what's the deal with the bike?" Below a pyramid of prizes ringed by all sorts of fairground games leant a wiry man with an engine oil stained cap. He turned around. "The bike?" Rish was quickly losing patience, "Yes mate, what's the deal with the mountain bike?" The wiry man lent back and explained, "That young man, is the Continuum Stump-Jumper mk8." The bike gleamed under the changing colours of the LED spotlight.

"21 gears, rim brakes and dual suspension." The two friends let out a unified gasp "It looks incredible!" Wins exclaimed. "You want a chance to win it?" The wiry man asked "Absolutely!" Wins jumped in, "How do we play?" "It's easy." the wiry man pointed to a large sealed glass jar on a rotating pedestal. The jar was filled with hundreds of wrapped sour sweets. "All you have to do is guess how many sweets are in that jar." Rish spat out his guess, "502." The wiry man laughed, "Its £2" per guess son." Rish looked at Wins.

Wins paused, "Let me try this one mate." Rish gave him a quizzical look. Wins looked back "Trust me, I can do this." Wins stood up against the counter and focused on the rotating glass jar, concentrating he tried to take a moving mental image of the sweets and the spaces between them. He felt the PSIReNS sparkle to life and take notice of his problem, they built up a picture in his head, recreating each of the outer items and extrapolating what must be behind to hold them against the glass walls of the cubic container. Wins actively watched the jar rotate twice, three times, four times and finally a fifth. With each turn, an image of the interior of the jar developed in his mind like a map. In his head, he reached in and picked out each sweet one after the other, faster and faster counting as he went. The numbers spun before him, their colours, shapes and personalities announcing the ongoing tally until they rested on brown-purple patterned and confident 876. Wins pulled out a £2 coin. "Eight-hundred-and-seventy-six." He told the wiry man. "Are you sure son? You can make more than one guess if you have the money." "One go is enough mister, and it's not a guess. There are exactly eight-hundred-and-seventy-six sweets in that jar." Wins insisted.

No sooner than he'd placed the money of the stall a prickle ran over Wins' skin, behind him a familiar voice spoilt the moment. "Well lookie what we have here!" It was Jackson Treehorn, a faint stench of vomit wafted with him on the wind. "If it isn't the little *cheater* and his tiny friend *Fish*." Jackson's cohort of hangers-on forced out their laughter. "Do you smell something Wins?" Rish asked sarcastically. He exaggerated his repulsion, "Smells like puke." Wins tried to hold in a chuckle, Jackson looked embarrassed then tried to cover it with anger. "Shut your face you little liar." Rish wasn't dissuaded, pretending he couldn't see Jackson he started pacing around to find the source of the stink. "No, I can definitely smell it Wins." he maintained, "Something round here smells like it got puked on." Rish raised his eyes slowly up to Jackson's face. "It's this thing Wins," Rish turned to Wins as if Jackson was an inanimate object, "This gargantuan gargoyle smells like puke!" The prickles rippled over Wins and Jackson grabbed Rish by his jacket's collar.

"Play or leave!" The wiry man yelled. Jackson looked at him and let go of Rish. "What?" The Wiry man adjusted his oil stained cap. "Leave that tiny kid alone, there's four of you and you're all twice their size. Either you play one of my games or you leave right now." A sly smile crept over Jackson's face. "What were they playing?" The Wiry man pointed to the jar, "Guess how many sweets are in the jar for a chance to win that bike." Jackson seemed like he wanted to make a point of it. "OK, OK," he said sauntering over to the stall, "How much?" "£2 a go." The wiry man replied. Jackson pulled a £20 note out of his pocket and slammed it on the counter. "I'll have ten goes then." Jackson looked at the jar for a second and reamed of a list of numbers, counting them on each finger as he did so. "302, 390, 425, 536, 555..." Jackson seemed like he was just picking numbers out of the air, he stared at Rish and Wins alternating between them with each count. "661, 672, 717, 786 and 808." The wiry man made a list of Jackson's numbers on a note pad and read them back to him for confirmation. "And you kid, your number was 876 right?" Wins nodded. The wiry man climbed a ladder and lifted the jar. "Well, we actually have a winner tonight!" Wins and Rish couldn't contain their excitement. The wiry man carried the jar down from its pedestal and placed it on the counter. He turned the jar on its side revealing three digits writing in permanent marker on its base. '7-8-6'. Jackson burst into self-satisfied laughter. "WOO!" he gesticulated wildly at Wins and Rish. "Can't cheat your way out of this one *loser.*" Jackson mocked. Wins felt strange, an odd and uncomfortable sensation stuttered across his belly and back. "No, that's not right." Wins told the wiry man. "That's the wrong number." The wiry man looked genuinely apologetic. "I'm really sorry kid but that's the number, my dear old Dad wrote on the bottom of the jar after we counted the sweets in last year. No-one's won 'til now." Jackson's friends were congratulating him whilst he made his plans for taking the bike out over half term. They raved and riled, revelling not so much in their victory as in the two boys' loss."

Wins knew something wasn't right. "Listen, I know that's the number written *on* the jar, but that's not the number of sweets *in* the jar." The wiry man gave Wins a funny look. "As I said, I'm sorry kid, but that guy paid his money just like you, it wouldn't be fair if I didn't let him take the bike. After ploughing through his poker winnings Wins was left with a twenty-pound note and some change. "Wins plumbed his pockets, teased out the crumpled cash and offered it to the wiry man. "What are you doing?" Rish looked confused. "I told you dude- trust me." Wins replied, and turning back to the wiry man leant forward with the confidence of his number said, "There are *exactly* Eight-Hundred-And-Seventy-Six sweets in that jar. I will give you this twenty quid right here to count them again. If I'm wrong you can keep the cash. If I'm right you can take the money for your trouble... and I get the bike." The wiry man considered Win's offer for a moment, he turned his cap backwards and rolled up his sleeves, "You're on, kid." Rish pulled on Win's arm. "Dude, are you crazy, you're just throwing your money away." Wins gave a wry grin, "Dude, twenty-two quid for a new mountain bike *and* the look of losing on Jackson's face; it's a bargain!" Rish seemed unsure at first, then thinking of Wins' unbelievable achievements at the chess game and the swimming contest conceded "Okay, Okay." He said sneakily, "This is going to be interesting." The wiry man lifted a large steel bucket onto the counter next to the jar, the metallic clunk caught Jackson's attention. "What's going on? I want my bike mate." The wiry man didn't bother looking up. "The kid reckons you and me are wrong, so I'm recounting the sweets." Jackson was furious "YOU WHAT?! I won that bike, it says so on the jar!" "Well, seeing as how nice you were to these two kids earlier I thought you wouldn't mind if I check the result, you know... just to be sure." The wiry man emphasised his tone so that Jackson would know he wasn't going to take any more trouble from him. "Why don't you come and count with us young man?" The wiry man tapped a space at the counter to the other side of the jar and bucket than Wins and Rish were standing. "UNBELIEVABLE!" Jackson complained as he walked over to the stall.

Grabbing handfuls of sweets the wiry man began counting them out into the big steel bucket, marking on his note pad every time he got to a multiple of ten, then circling his figures each time they reached the next hundred. As they hit seven-hundred became clear that Jackson's figure of '786' was not going to be correct. Counting past his number the wiry man's face broke into a subtle smirk and Jackson let loose another tirade of fury and frustration. "What the hell?! I guessed the number on the jar, doesn't matter if it's wrong, I won and I deserve that bike!" The wiry man finished counting to 800 and stopped. "Nope. To win you have to guess the number of sweets *in* the jar, *not* the number on its base." Jackson changed tact and pretended not to care, "Whatever, I have three bikes at home anyway and it's not like this little **Boy Loser** could have guessed right." He scowled at Wins. "I'm gonna hang around just to watch you lose, loser." The wiry man counted out the remaining sweets, placing them in groups of ten. "I don't believe it," he said laying out the 7th row, the two boys started to feel the thrill of their triumph approaching. The wiry man placed the final six sweets down one by one. "How on earth did you do that kid?" Rish wailed with excitement, "Oh my days! I can't believe it, but I do, I do believe it Wins!" Rish jumped on Wins' back and hugged out the victory like it was a winning goal. "786, 876?" The wiry man said to himself. "My dear old Dad must have got the numbers mixed up when he wrote them on the jar!"

Jackson seethed, his friends picked up on his mood and chimed in, "#BoyGenius? Cheater more like!" One lad thoughtlessly suggested, "No one could have won that, that guy must have been in on it with them." Forgetting that minutes ago Jackson was down for the prize. The wiry man looked at Wins. "You're that kid aren't you? The one who won the chess game with the maths professor right?" Rish stared down Jackson and his mates, "That's right" Rish said to the wiry man, "the **Boy Genius**." Wins planted his feet hard in the ground pushing his shoulders back and his chest out. The wiry man drew breath. "Now ain't that a thing? No wonder you knew how many sweets there were in the jar." "This isn't over loo…" Jackson started to say but before he could finish his sentence Wins cut him off. "*Wins*, Jackson, my name is *Wins*." Rish shook Wins by his shoulders, "But if you don't like that, **Boy Genius** is just fine too." Wins finished. Together the two friends stood proudly. "Jackson leant forward with a pointed finger. "You're lucky he's here." He said nodding towards the wiry man before storming off with his rabble. The wiry man climbed up the pyramid of prizes on a ladder and brought down the Continuum Stump Jumper mk8 mountain bike. "Honestly kid, we've had that bike up there for ages and no matter where we set up shop most nights nothing much happens at my stall. But that was something to behold, I'll be telling the story of tonight for years, lads." The wiry man shook their hands and rolled the bike out from behind the counter. "Listen, keep your money. It was worth it just to see that bully get his comeuppance." Wins took his £20 note back and thanked the wiry man. They turned to leave and the wiry man called them back, "Aren't you forgetting something?" The two boys looked at each other not sure what he meant. "I can't very well use all these sweets again, can I? Their luck is all gone. You two need to take some." The boys' eyes lit up "How many can we take mister?" Rish asked. "As many as you can carry lads." Wins and Rish rushed back to the stall and filled their pockets. "Thanks again." Wins said gratefully. The wiry man tipped his cap and the two boys wheeled their new bike off into the night. Heading home the shared experience of the evening filled their conversation, they couldn't wait to tell Deano, Neet, Benji and Oz about what happened. With the second of The Triples approaching Wins was glad to have a solid trail bike to share with Rish. Already he knew this was a good sign, after all the dour worries that plagued his previous weeks, things were on the up again.

15: A Moment Of Connection, A Moment Of Clarity

For the most part, Rish was right. The first few days at school had been much like the last few weeks before half term as far as things went with Jackson Treehorn's unpleasant crew. However, whenever they lobbed a jibe or insult at Wins he reminded them he didn't care one bit by keeping his cool and changing the subject to the new bike he and Rish won at the funfair. After a while the bullies realised no matter what they said or did, it just didn't bother Wins what-so-ever and their nastiness tailed off. Almost. Jackson still seemed to hold a special hatred for Wins, he didn't get drawn into out-and-out bullying as before, but would still hold a vicious and unhidden scowl for Wins on crossing paths. Winning the chess tournament and freestyle medley taught him that no matter his expectations, there's nothing you can do to *make* some people like you. He realised that there was nothing wrong with this either. People don't have to like anyone if they don't want to and so long as people who didn't like him left him alone he could get on with being himself. And if they didn't leave him alone... well, it was like Rish said; 'You just have to own it.'

A few weeks before Easter Miss Maude announced the details for the second of The Triples; the bike race. It would be an off-road cycling scramble through Oxhey Woods. Not far away, the woods were a popular spot for outdoor sports with its various tracks and trails. Wins begged his parents to take him down there with the new bike so he could get a feel for the place before the competition at the end of term. Anne said she would, but only if she could come with on her bike too. Reluctantly Wins agreed. The weekend was one of the rare kinds that fall between spring and summer, crisp and clear with a bright chill in the air.

It had been his Mum's turn for music on the way to Oxhey Woods, her old rock stuff. Some Spanish song about a hotel in California was reaching its peak as they drew into the car park. "I'll get our bikes off the rack, could you go and have a look at the map over there get an idea of which trails we can try?" his mum suggested. Wins bounded over the engraved map of the Woodland, it showed suggested horse paths, walks and bike rides. Winding through the peaks and troughs of the nature reserve green, amber and red lines intertwined and were peppered with symbols for various levels of accessibility. Wins found a shortish green bike trail and memorised its route before returning to the car. He grabbed the sunglasses set that Rish had bought him for his birthday and their interchangeable coloured lenses. He hadn't found much use for them in the winter months and was glad to have an opportunity to try them out for real. He opted for the green lenses, casting his view under an emerald tinge and put the rest of the set in his backpack. "There's an easy one that starts over here Mum." He pointed at a green wooden pole behind them "Shall we try that one first?" They walked their bike to the start of the trail and fastened their helmets before setting off.

The green route wound on easily enough, gentle rises and shallow slopes, it wasn't too trying but it felt good to be out in nature. Oxhey Woods were predominantly a pine forest so the morning air was saturated with the fresh, clean scent of its fragrant oils. Wins and Anne continued on their way to the end of the loop back at the car park. He enjoyed the ride but didn't feel like he'd gained much and wanted to to experience the Continuum Stump-Jumper mk8 at its fullest potential. "Mum, can we try the amber trail next?" he asked, "Yes, but please don't get too far ahead from me OK." Wins nodded. Just before pushing off again he realised he'd forgotten he was wearing his sunglasses. The emerald tinge no longer seemed to be in effect so he decided to swap his lenses out for the yellow ones. "Woah!" the moment he removed his wraparound shades his world turned purple. "You OK?" Anne asked. "Yeah, no it's nothing." Wins explained. "I just took off my green shades coz I thought they had stopped working and everything went purple for a minute. So weird!" Anne smiled. "Your brain is a strange thing Wins. Well; your brain especially! But everyone's brain tries to adjust and adapt to the information it receives." Wins wasn't sure what she meant which must have shown on his face. Anne tried again, "When you put your green shades on, what did the woods look like?" "Green." Wins replied. "Then before you took them off what did everything look like?" Anne asked again. "Nothing, I mean, normal. I forgot I was even wearing them." Wins told her. "Exactly," Anne enthused, "Your brain compensated for the green lenses, your eyes were only getting the greenish colours of light that got through the lenses, but after a while, your brain began to adjust your perception to make up for the lack of blue and red light." Wins remembered his science class from way back when Miss Walters taught them about vision in different animals. "So, my brain added lots of blue and red into the mix?" "You could think of it like that." Anne granted. Wins clicked, "So when I took off my green shades, my brain was still adding blue and red to my vision which is why everything looked purple?" "Pretty much." Anne confirmed, enjoying the moment they were sharing. "Our brains are incredible anticipation machines, they are perpetually trying to find patterns in the information they receive through our senses so they can guess what's going to happen next." Wins pondered this idea. "So if our brain sees things are wrong it makes corrections, like with the green glasses?" Anne gave him one of her 'it depends' looks. "Sometimes... Our brains are so complicated no-one really understands exactly how they work, we've learnt so much in the last few decades, but nowhere near everything. One day we may well understand everything there is to know about how brains *know* things and create the world we experience." Anne leant up from her handlebars and moved her hands around her head. "We have a really good idea of which bits of the brain do what, and are starting to work out how. But it's a bit like examining a 'black-box-computer' at times; we can see what goes in and what comes out but not what *work* actually gets done on the inside." Wins considered the idea, he assumed scientist like his Mum knew all the answers, being told they didn't was quite a shock.

She continued, "It's not so simple as 'our-brains-know-to-make-corrections'." What do you mean?" Wins wondered. "Unfortunately, a lot of the time our brains may not realise they are getting bad information at all so don't compensate for it, or think good information needs adjusting so make corrections when we don't need any; like when you took off your green glasses and everything appeared purple to you."

Wins was starting to think he couldn't even rely on his own brain anymore. "So, how can I trust anything my brain tells me then?" Anne relaxed on her bike's saddle and took some weight off her feet. "Remember when I told you that the brain is like the hardware of the computer and the mind was like the software, and that's how the PSIReNS work; physically filling gaps in the hardware and helping to run the software of people's broken minds so they can function again?" Wins nodded. "Well, that idea is a nice way of explaining things but there's more to it than a straight-forward-binary '*brain Vs mind*' difference. The fact is, the brain *is* the mind, and the mind *is* the brain. They are completely inseparable." Wins remembered the picture she had drawn all those months ago, with the PSIReNS dotted in green all over the pink brain. "Whilst the brain can make errors, and our mind experiences these errors as misperceptions and misconceptions it can also process information in astonishing leaps of understanding and insight." "Like when I realised how to win at the freestyle medley and the chess tournament!" Wins said. "*Exactly*," Anne said, pleased that Wins was grasping these complicated cognitive ideas. "Whilst the PSIReNS were helping you make those leaps, your brain was also working to build connections, find patterns, spot contradictions that didn't add up and seek out curious coincidences to try and build a new story, a new way to explain what just happened and predict more accurately what was going to happen next."

Wins felt an inspired relief breeze past him. "So it's not all broken brains and bad information then?" "Not at all!" Anne said happily "It's a balance; the cost of using the most advanced, complex and amazing anticipation machine in the known universe is that there *will* be errors. But the *benefits...*" Anne let her arms flow through the forest air, "are everything we enjoy about being alive; experience, expression, arts, science, smell, taste, touch, sight and sound, imagination, emotion, relationships... all the joys of life and so much more." Anne's eyes sparkled with zeal as she spoke. "We humans can solve any problem, and the most striking example of this is when we have an instantaneous insight; the '*a-ha*' moment. Our brains run through all the data and spit out a solution so maverick, so simple and so marvellous that we could never have come up with it by sitting down and deliberately *thinking* about it. That's the beauty of the brain Wins; It can do things nothing else in the *universe* can, and we each get our own unique one to last us a lifetime."

Anne hugged Wins affectionately. "Wins, I never said sorry for what happened and I'm so, so sorry it did." Wins saw her eyes well up, "Sorry for what Mum? You don't have anything to say sorry for." Anne knelt down to meet Wins' eye-line. "For exposing you to the PSIReNS Wins. It was so utterly reckless of me to bring my work home like that, I was so caught up in my research I didn't even consider the risks. You should never have even been in the same building as the PSIReNS, let alone the same room. Our home is meant to be a safe place and now *they* are in your head." Anne's eye shed a tear, "I feel awful about it and, and I just need you to know that and to know it was my fault, not yours or BB's OK?"

Until then it never occurred to Wins that it was anyone's fault he was exposed to the PSIReNS. The realisation that it could have been prevented stirred him up inside. He hugged his mother without a word and felt the tremor of her tears. "Its OK Mum," he said trying to reassure her. After a few minutes, she let go of him. "Wins, why don't you... why don't you go for another ride... I'll catch you up." Anne stuttered. Wins saw she was more upset than she was letting on and needed some space to herself. "Sure," Wins remembered the woodland map, "I'll take the amber course next OK." Anne nodded tearfully and walked her bike over the viewpoint on the other side of the car park.

Wins was mixed up inside. Until now he hadn't thought anyone needed blaming for what had happened to him, but he also knew that his mum would never intentionally do anything to harm him. She had messed him up, but she hadn't meant to. It was a lot to think about. Wins swapped out his green lenses for the yellow ones, a golden glaze fell over him matching the amber bike trail and he set off. Over rocky rises and tight turns Wins tried to take the measure of the mountain bike, feeling for its limits, pushing it to find the points at which it would no longer respond the way he wanted it to… needed it to, if he was going to win the off-road woodland race at the end of term. Peddling faster, gripping the contours of the trail flickers of scintillating light and sparks of song sprang up at the outer edges of his senses. He noticed the shift inside himself, the change of gears, the realignment of sensational awareness that he'd come to know as the moment when he and his PSIReNS had internalised a new skill set.   Although the intense synesthetic trappings of those exquisite experiences remained absent, he felt the allure of the Triple's golden cup tugging at his deep desire.

Riding between the tree trunks, he remembered his mother, how sincere she had been in her sorrow and how his life had changed so much in these last few months. He thought of Rish, how he had said that if he hadn't been bullied at his last school they wouldn't have ever become friends. "Is my life better now or worse than it had been?" He wondered. "Could it be both? Could it be… could it be that sometimes bad things lead to good outcomes?" Wins rounded a hairpin bend in the trail and slammed on his brake skidding into a sweeping arc and a flawless finish. He rested on the handlebars and removed his yellow-lensed sunglasses. A blue hue whetted his view of the woods. "No," he said to himself. Slowly it dawned on him… it needn't be that bad things *had* to happen for things to improve, for things to change for the better. But at the same time, it needn't be that bad things *had* to only lead to bad ends either. "I can choose, I can choose how I want things to be!" Wins said aloud. Wins started to see a way out of his whole predicament, started to see the edges of the big picture.

Without warning a scream ripped through the trees. Startled, Wins heard it again climbing up from over a nearby ridge. It sounded like someone was trying to kill something. He pulled his bike over to the side of the trail and followed the yelling into the trees. The slope rose towards a thicket, Wins crept up on his belly like army guys did in films and peaked over the edge. Below, on the red route, he saw Jackson Treehorn and Jackson's father who was ranting at his son. "You want to win?! I thought you wanted to win Jackson!" His rival looked distraught "I do, I do Dad, I do!" Jackson's father was twitching with agitation. "Then you have to believe you *deserve* it Jackson, that other kid, that little nothing doesn't *deserve* to win does he?" Jackson's fury burst out, "NO!" His father continued, "No he doesn't; you do! You're going to be the greatest athlete the world has ever known Jackson, but only if you believe you *deserve* it." Wins couldn't tell if Jackson was happy with what was happening or if he hated it.

"Wins?" He looked over his shoulder and saw his mum had found the abandoned bike on the amber trail and was looking around for him. "Over here." Wins beckoned her with a hushed tone, putting his finger to his lips and motioning with his hands to indicate she kept low to the ground. Anne approached the thicket on her hands and knees. "What's going on?" "Sshhh." Wins whispered. They looked through the ramshackle branches as Wins' rival was riled up by his father. "The world owes you your victory Jackson, you just need to reach out and take it." Jackson's father's zealous raving seemed to infect his son. "I'M

A WINNER!" he screamed. Jackson's father squeezed the sides of his son's head and pushed their noses together. "NO! YOU. ARE. *THE*. WINNER!" Jackson let slip a primal scream into his father's face. His father let go of him, stepped back and lifted a stopwatch from his pocket "READY." Jackson positioned himself on his mountain bike. "SET." He balanced himself on the bike's peddles clamping the brakes tightly. "GO!" Jackson burst forward, dirt and gravel kicking up from the bike's rear tyre. As he tore off and rounded the first turn Jackson's father paced. "Even better than I was!" he said aloud. "Treehorns are going to win this time."

Wins and Anne shuffled backwards until they could walk down the slope unseen. "What was that all about?" She asked him. "That was Jackson Treehorn and his Dad, the guy I beat in the freestyle medley before Christmas. His Dad sounds like a lunatic!" Anne had a different understanding "I think his dad wants Jackson to win the race so he can feel like he won it himself." Wins wasn't convinced, "That doesn't make any sense though; if Jackson wins, then it's not his Dad who won is it?" Anne tried to explain, "Sometimes people just can't face their own failures, so try to make themselves feel better by getting their children to achieve what they couldn't." "Really?" Wins asked, Jackson's behaviour starting to add up now. "Yes, it's not something parents will often admit to, but all that love and hope people have for their children can sometimes become twisted into a vicarious need to see their children do all the things they never could." Anne answered. Instinctively Wins responded, "I'm glad you and Dad aren't like that." He gave his mother a hug. "Mum, I know you feel responsible for what happened with the PSIReNS and everything." He pulled away so he could see her face. "But we can't change the past, I know now that I can't control what happens to me... but I can choose what to do when it does. I don't blame you, Mum. OK?" Anne cried again, only this time her tears washed over a smile. "Thank you Wins," she said. "You don't know what that means to me." After the moment had passed they set off on the amber trail back to the car. Wins wrapped himself in his new found clarity and made his plans for the off-road mountain bike scramble through the Oxhey Woods, sensing the grip and gravel beneath his tyres as he rode.

16: Thalweg

As each week passed, so Wins' focused determination grew. Further trips to Oxhey Woods allowed him to develop an intuitive feel for its tracks and trails, helping him build a detailed model of the forest inside his head. Wins was putting the green lenses in his sunglasses in preparation for the second of The Triples when his Dad commented, "I remember those sunglasses; how are you getting on with them?" Ed pulled out his own set of sunglasses prompting Wins to wonder what his Dad was up to. "My pair don't have interchangeable lenses like yours do, just polarising ones." Wins was intrigued. "Really? I haven't found much use for those; they didn't seem to do much when I tried them out." "Put your polarising lenses in, Wins," Ed suggested, "I want to show you something cool." Wins swapped out his green lenses for the polarising set. "Here, let me show you," Ed said, taking the two pairs of polarising sunglasses and putting them together as though they were looking right at each other.

"Polarising lenses are brilliant for fishing. Look here." Ed slowly rotated one pair of the sunglasses 90°. Where the two lenses met, they both appeared to grow darker and darker until they abruptly turned black. "Wow, that's amazing!" Wins said with interest. "How do they do that?" "My son the scientist!" Ed said proudly. "Believe it or not, light spins around like a propeller…" "I'm not falling for that!" Wins said, cutting him off in disbelief. "How do you know this science stuff anyway?" "Oh ye of little faith!" His Dad laughed. "I told you already: fishing! I need to know this stuff to catch fish." Wins wasn't convinced. "*Really!*" Ed insisted. "Daylight is a mixture of light that spins clockwise and light that spins anti-clockwise. The polarising lenses only

let light through if it's spinning one way, but not the other."
Wins quickly realised his Dad wasn't making it up after all. "So,
when you put the two together like that, the light going through
one pair of sunglasses can't get through the other pair?" Wins
asked. "That's right," encouraged his Dad. "I use them because
the light that gets reflected off a surface, like water, tends to spin
one way." Wins clicked again, "So that's why you use them
when you're fishing, right? To see the fish under the water?"
"Yeah, I like to try and get the biggest fish from the deepest
thalweg in the river. I need polarising lenses to block out the
glare shining off the surface of the river so I can see deep into
the water and spot the fish."

"What's a *thalweg*?" Wins asked incredulously.

"Sorry, I didn't explain," Ed went on. "A thalweg is a fast-
moving channel of water under the river. People often imagine
rivers are just one big, single stream of water, but there are
usually different channels within the river, flowing at different
speeds. I need my polarising lenses to see *under* the surface if
I'm to find the real whoppers, which are usually in the deepest
thalweg."

"A different channel of water, flowing at a different speed to the
rest of the river?" Wins thought. "Like at redline races on my
birthday... and the climbing wall... and the infinity tree at the
chess tournament... and even in the freestyle medley before
Christmas." It was all starting to make sense now. The PSIReNS
were showing him the fastest way through, the most efficient
course to take within the wider flow of... not water, but...
events, whatever was going on around him when they sparkled
to life. They were showing him his thalweg!

"You OK?" His Dad asked. "You zoned out there for a second." Wins snapped out of his daydream. "Yeah, yes, sorry. I was just… What you said made me think of something." Uncertain of what he meant, Ed gave his son a hug and stood up. "Good luck for today, Wins. Sorry I can't be there." Ed picked up his kit bag and left for the fire station. Wins packed his bag, Anne got BB's changing things and Zoop opened the front door. "Nervous?" she asked. Wins considered the question… "I honestly don't know."

Crowds of locals joined the school kids and parents for the event that morning. Supporting The Triples was something of a community tradition in the area, but after news of the swimming competition's excitement had spread, followed by Wins' unexpected accomplishment at the charity chess tournament, the local community's imagination had been piqued. Wins registered and was given a map of the racing route and his competitor's bib. "Number 21… triple lucky?" he thought. Rish found Wins walking the bike to the competitor's line. "Have you seen the course?" Wins unfolded the map. "Not yet, why?" "It's all three trails, one after the other, and they're sending people down four at a time," Rish said, a tone of worry creeping into his voice. "Wait? How's that going to work?" Wins asked confused. "They said they were going to send the competitors down sixty seconds apart, so it will come down to who gets the fastest time. But I guess the trail still shouldn't get clumped up… unless someone crashes." Rish smiled. "Honestly, I think half these people are only here in case someone wraps their bike round a tree."

It dawned on Wins that he'd been so focused on getting to know Oxhey Woods' trails that he hadn't considered what riding with other racers would mean. The trails' broadways often squeezed suddenly into single tracks, and the sidings were a combination of pine trees, sharp drop-offs and steep rocky slopes. Thinking about it now, accidents were near enough inevitable. "You OK Wins? You look a bit off," Rish asked with concern. "No, yeah. I'm fine mate," Wins lied. Trying to change the subject Rish asked, "How's the bike been?" Wins chippered up. "It's actually amazing, almost feels like part of me when I'm riding now." Wins realised he hadn't been sharing it as they'd agreed after the funfair. "I'm sorry I've been hogging it, I just wanted to be prepared for today. After the race it's all yours, I promise." "No way, it's ours. Just don't twist it around a tree trunk. OK?" Rish laughed, breaking the tension. Wins laughed too. "Ha! Not a chance."

Turnout for the event was smaller than for the swimming competition; Wins assumed more people had swimming costumes than mountain bikes. All in all, forty-four students registered on the day. Once again, nearly all of them were from years 10 and 11, with three kids from year 9 and just one year 7 kid looking like a toy soldier next to the bigger kids. The competitors were lined up in rows of four at the starting line. Wins saw Jackson Treehorn two rows ahead of him repeatedly stretching out, just like at the swimming pool before Christmas, and rhythmically tapping his fingertips together. Wins was put with the three year 9s on the back row, presumably to keep the competition as even as possible.

He fastened his helmet and checked his sunglasses one more time. Now he was paying attention to the effect, he could see how the polarising lenses were cutting down the glare bouncing off the foliage in the forest. Coach Quintana stood at the starting line with his stopwatch and air horn. On each blast of the horn, the front row set off and the row behind moved up to the line. Wins felt a crackling static in the air. Sparkles and scintillations pricked the corners of his vision as Coach Quintana sounded the air-horn. BBBLLLAAAANNNN. With each blast, the front row shot off and the others moved forward in turn. Wins twitched, his hair stood on end. It hadn't felt like this before. It was like the PSIReNS were firing up in expectation of the event. BBBLLLAAAANNNN. Jackson Treehorn's row tore off down the track. Wins saw a crimson mist condense out of the air ahead of him, at once both opaque and transparent. BBBBLLLAAAANNNN. The row in front took off, flicking up gravel with their tyres. Wins and the year 9s wheeled up to the start line. Without looking up from his stopwatch, Coach Quintana counted down, "5, 4, 3, 2... 1..." *BBBBBBLLLLLAAAANNNN.*

A deluge of awareness and perception fell upon Wins – heavy, slick and electric like a tsunami of mercury metal washing over him. Wins felt everything. Already in front of the three year 9s, he pressed his tyres down into the woodland floor, falling forwards through the PSIReNS' thalweg, its invisible touch causing his flesh to spark and sizzle with indescribable waves of euphoria. Wins heard the squirrels scurrying away, the feathered flutter of sparrows fleeing the cyclists' intrusion into their forest home. Specks and sparks of sound bounced off the trees, he followed them back to the twigs breaking and crunching under the wheels of the older kids further down the trail. Wins didn't need to see the thalweg winding through the woodland before him, he knew it intimately and felt its touch imprinting upon his mind's eye.

Tearing on, Wins closed the gap between himself and the group ahead on the trail. His peddles worked in flawless synchronicity with his gears; he barely used his breaks but to trim infinitesimal edges off his momentum as he approached the tightest turns. The thalweg, that scarlet-stranded tunnel guiding his path, oscillated and whipped between the four cyclists a few metres in front of him. Wins was reminded of the redline race track, only this time he didn't have a chassis to protect him. He would need to weave between his rivals without touching them, even for a split second. The slightest impact would cause all of them to collide in a mess of limbs, wheels and jagged gears. The competitors ahead of him were too close together. No matter how deftly he tried to sneak between them there just wasn't sufficient room to get past without everyone smashing into each other. With this realisation, Wins' attention pinged a few seconds into the future of the race. The track began to rise before dropping off into a broad leftward sweep. The ground would be thick with detritus and decay, but the rock face at its outer edge was dry and smooth… smooth enough to try.

Wins caught up to the four riders blocking his path, all of them trying to hug the inside of the bend and cut the tightest line. He knew better – the loam and wet leaves would slow their speed. Meanwhile, Wins' thalweg stuck itself to the bend's rocky outer wall. The force of his momentum rounded the concave curve, holding him fast to the stony wall like a fairground ride, conserving his swiftness, quickening his pace and delivering him in front of the pack that moments ago blocked his route ahead.

Jackson's group was now in sight. Like the riders he'd just bested, they too were jostling for position and were also wholly unaware of the predator stealthily stalking them from the one place to which they were not paying any attention. Wins tuned his supra-sense and called to mind the track's topography. A few short seconds ahead, at the bottom of its slope, he visualised the track forming a double peak with a deep dip in-between; the first little kicker being significantly smaller than the second, much larger, muddy mound. Wins cast his gaze upon the four riders blocking his path, all stronger than he was, all bigger than he was, all… *heavier* than he was! The PSIReNS' song sang out to him, recognising every bit of dynamic data from the woodlands and the riders rampaging through its peace. In unison, unable to tell which sensation was cause and which effect, Wins honed the timing, power and accelerating thrust of his approach towards his unsuspecting opponents as the PSIReNS' scarlet strands knotted and knitted together into his thalweg, signifying the best path past Jackson Treehorn's group. Butting and bumping each other, Jackson and the others took the first kicker. At the same instant his rivals gripped its negative gradient, Wins was upon them, lifting his weight in a perfectly timed move to compliment the embrace of his frame's double suspension rebounding from the kicker's peak. The manoeuvre captured his full force and released it upwards. As Jackson's group dove down into the deep dip, gravity clasping them in its cosmic grip, Wins flew off the top of the mound's ascending ramp. Whilst Jackson and his three rival racers were battling between themselves to climb out of the sunken gully between the peaks, Wins soared over them, an eagle silently swooping upon its prey – his rear tyre mere millimetres from Jackson's helmet as he flawlessly landed, maintaining his velocity and holding his new place in front of the astonished riders.

Without warning Wins winced, pain like razor blades slicing his sides ripped through him. Jackson raged past, his strength and stamina now working to his advantage. Wins focused his mind through the agony, stretching it simultaneously outwards and forwards and backwards in time anticipating Jackson's attempts to block him, listening for what lay ahead. Beyond his line of sight Wins' mind saw a hairpin bend in the track. As the trail descended, it headed directly towards the base of a near vertical cliff face, before turning almost 180^0 to the right and into the final stretch. That was his chance. None of them would expect it, all of them would need to brake sharply to make the turn. But he wouldn't.

Wins used the rough ground to slow his pace, positioning himself three bike lengths behind Jackson who continued to block the narrow woodland path. The trail declined sharply downwards towards the cliff face. Wins felt the pounding rhythm of Jackson's peddling and heard the screech of his brakes as he set himself up to skid to a near stop for the hairpin turn. As Jackson slowed, Wins accelerated downhill towards him. Both Jackson in front and the pack behind him ground to a crushing halt. Wins ripped past Jackson, who was so startled by the sudden sonic snap that his focus momentarily diverted away from the trail. Wins powered up the near vertical slope in a perfect pointed arc. At the apex of his flight, he popped his primed peddle down, nimbly hopping his wheels and frame a few centimetres off the rocky wall into the air. Bike and body indistinguishable now, Wins flowed with his deliberate, developed momentum into a downward surge, pouring past the dumbfounded riders. Electricity crackled through Wins and his bike as he gathered every speck of speed from the trail, consciously keeping his profile slim and slender to avoid dragging against the forest air.

With the finish line in sight, the group ahead of Wins hustled for pole position. In their panicked pushing, the lead rider's handlebar clipped a tree causing his bike to flip forwards, catapulting the unfortunate boy face first into the dirt. Reflexively, the three cyclists alongside him jolted sideways into the ferns and bracken, opening a clear line through the centre of the ensuing chaos. Wins flashed forward into his future, seeing himself power past the finish line and shatter anyone else's hope of beating his time. Snapping back to the present, he drew his bike-body to its inevitable victory, crossing the line like a lightning strike and triggering a sensory supernova. Fleshy euphoria exploded from within the viscera of his body and burst out through his perceptual sphere. Cosmic colours crackled across his consciousness like a meteor shower as the PSIReNS sounded their angelic, ethereal chorus, heralding his win. All too soon, Wins sensed the PSIReNS wane within him and his synesthetic reward ebb away. He returned to earth, to reality as he knew it, or was used to it appearing, at least. Parts of him became lost with the PSIReNS' cold absence, all traces of his heightened perception evaporated with his misty thalweg.

The world dimmed and drew close around him. Wins found himself surrounded by a cheering crowd, with Rish right at the front. "Oh my days!" he said jubilantly. "How did you get so far ahead?" Rish grabbed Wins' wrist, raising it in the air. The finishing times hadn't been announced yet, but there was no doubt as to who'd won the woodland scramble that day.

A metallic crash followed by angry shouting punctured Wins' elation. Within seconds everyone looked to see Jackson

Treehorn screaming at Coach Quintana, his extraordinarily expensive bike lying mangled in the mud at their feet. "HOW IS THAT FAIR?" screamed Jackson. That kid nearly took my head off with his bike, I'M SEMI-PROFESSIONAL YOU KNOW!" Coach Quintana seemed unfazed by the teenager's inglorious display. "Jackson, you need to get control of yourself or I'll have no choice but to disqualify you." Jackson laughed aggressively. "DISQUALIFY ME! DISQUALIFY ME? You need to disqualify HIM or you'll be *sorry*!" Jackson pointed an accusatory finger directly at Wins. "He's the one who *cheated*, he's the one who was riding his bike on the bloody *walls* and tried to land it on me from the kickers!"

Miss Maude appeared from the crowd with her aura of absolute authority. "What is going on here?" Coach Quintana tried to explain, "Mr Treehorn here believes another rider cheated, and as such should be disqualified. However, he decided to make his point by throwing his mountain bike at me and making threats." Miss Maude looked at Jackson with a stern stare. "Mr Treehorn?" she asked. "Explain yourself." Jackson looked at his mountain bike on the forest floor and started to stutter. "I, I, I see how this must look, Miss Maude, but that kid over there, the loo... err, *Winston Winters*, the year 7 kid, he was cheating in the race, Miss. He tried to knock me off my bike by jumping over me and nearly hit me in the head with his tyres. Then he literally rode up a cliff face at the last turn to get past me. That can't be allowed, Miss." "*Why*?" Miss Maude asked laconically. "Why what, Miss?" Jackson was confused. "Why can't it be allowed?" she clarified. "Miss, I meant surely that's not allowed, in the rules, I mean." Miss Maude was unmoved. "Mr Treehorn, if you had thought to do what that boy did, overtaking in the air, finding an innovative way past an impasse, would you still think it should be disallowed?" "... ... ..." Jackson moved his mouth but no sound came out. "Mr Treehorn, the whole point of The Triples is to encourage determination, growth and to give pupils the opportunity to experience inspiration. Both the opportunity to receive it *and* the opportunity to provide it." Jackson knew then that his appeal to her authority would not work. Miss Maude continued, "These competitions are not here to bolster your ego, young man. If you are unwilling to provide some inspiration to your fellow pupils by being a good sportsman and a graceful loser, the very least you can do is try to find some inspiration in that young boy's achievement today."

Jackson seethed with rage and was visibly trembling with anger. Not only had he been called a loser in front of the entire school and townsfolk, but he'd also been told to be more like Wins. Coach Quintana picked up Jackson's broken bike and offered it to him. "Jackson, I realise you're upset, but now is the time to prove your worth. Don't let pride ruin your reputation, son." But Jackson ignored the advice and left the battered mountain bike in Coach Quintana's hands. Storming off, he gave Wins a scorching glare as he passed.

The crowd swelled around Wins once more; everyone wanted to touch his bike and wish him well. At the same time, some of the spectators who'd been camped out in the trees during the event were already spreading rumours about his race. People kept asking him how he'd won. "Wins, Wins, how did you overtake three groups?" one of the year 9s he started the race with wondered. Another question from another onlooker followed, then another and another… each more outlandish than the last. "Wins, does your bike have special tyres or something?" "Wins, is it true you rode your bike up a tree?" "How did you ride your bike upside down on the cliff?" Wins was overwhelmed. He couldn't process the interrogation. "I just did what I did," he tried to explain. "I couldn't have done anything else." As true a statement as that was, no-one seemed satisfied with his explanation.

Anne wrangled Wins out of the huddling mass and helped him wheel his bike over to Zoop who was holding BB's hand. "That was amazing," Zoop said. "How do you feel?" Strangely, with all the bedlam after the race, Wins hadn't given it any thought. "Exhausted, I guess, but not the same as before. Better somehow. Exhausted, but better." He smiled at his sister. Anne gave him some water and a motherly hug. Pulling at his knee, BB tried to scramble up Wins' leg. "WINSHTON!" he said gleefully. BB seemed to have tuned into the exhilaration in the air, his eyes were alive with excitement. "Come here, you little monster," Wins said lifting his baby brother up for a cuddle.
Coach Quintana's voice blared out from a crackly megaphone. "All the competitors have completed the mountain bike scramble, the second of The Triples events." The family turned to look at Coach Quintana across the open area. "It will come as no surprise that the winner, for the second time this year, with a record-breaking time of 3 minutes 42 seconds, is: **Wins Winters**!" Rapturous applause rose from the spectators and competitors. "Come and accept your medal, Wins!"

Wins made his way through the throng. Oz, Benji, Neet and Deano joined Rish to set off a line of high-fives that soon continued through the crowd all the way to the front where Miss Maude and Coach Quintana were waiting for him. Miss Maude presented him with the gleaming gold medal on a red ribbon. "An inspiring performance, young man," she whispered in his ear as she bent down. A dozen flashes fired as photographers captured the moment. Wins could hardly believe it; it didn't feel real. Only a few months ago he was a nobody, a tiny fish in an enormous ocean. Now here he was, admired by almost all the school's students and the wider community. His dream was coming true: he was winning, he was popular and so he was happy.

Wins' life just couldn't get any better.

17: How to win, lose friends and infuriate people

Easter break saw Wins' popularity continue to swell after shattering all expectations in the mountain bike scramble at Oxhey Woods. In becoming first year 7 ever to have won not only any of The Triples; but two on the trot, he found himself something of a legend on returning to Aldershot Academy for the start of summer term. The traditional rivalry between the upper and lower years diminished with the advent of a unifying hero everyone could root for, everyone that was except for Jackson Treehorn. Jackson's growing sullen bitterness kept pace with Wins' popularity; for every friend Wins gained, every encouraging word he heard, Jackson Treehorn's sense of loss and envy incrementally increased. It wasn't so much that the former favourite was pushed out in favour of Wins, but that he withdrew of his own volition. Jackson was seen less and less around the communal areas of school, and since the woodland race, never hurled abuse at Wins in public. For Wins, this seemed like an improvement. He was well liked, everyone knew his name and unlike after the chess tournament; this time he liked it. The one boy who'd spent the previous two terms trying to make his life a misery was now cowed into silence. Life was exactly as he wanted it to be.

"They want you for captain!" Rish said bounding up the corridor. "Who does?" Wins replied, unaware of what Rish was talking about. "The under 14s football team, I just heard them talking in the lunch hall, they want to get you in for a trial." "Really-really?" Wins couldn't believe it. "Well, maybe not captain." Rish backtracked, "But they definitely want you in." "Should I go and see them?" Wins suggested. "No, of course not!" Rish said surprised. "They don't know I was listening."

Wins finally understood what Rish was getting at. "Oh right, so they'll probably find me then?" "Probably." Rish paused "Anyway…" he said, changing the subject, "my birthday party is booked for next month, you're in right?" Wins was thrilled, "Laser tag in the forest? You couldn't keep me away!" Just then a cheerful voice called from the other end of the corridor. "Wins? Wins Winters!" Wins turned to see a tall boy he recognised from year 9. The boy walked over with a sense of urgency in his stride. "Hi, I'm Jake." He said introducing himself. "Hi Jake, What's up?" "I'm with the Aldershot Academy under 14s football team, most of us were at Oxhey Woods a few weeks ago. We had this crazy idea… we wondered if you'd like to try out for our team. You like football right?" Wins tried to act as shocked as he would have been if Rish hadn't spoilt the surprise for him a few moments ago. "Wow, yes, definitely. I mean, yes I'd like to try out and yes I love football." "Great!" Jake said excitedly, "We are having a try-out after school on Thursday, see you there?" Wins pretended to check his mental diary. "Absolutely, can't wait." Jake walked on, Wins looked at Rish with wide-eyed excitement. "I feel like I just won the lottery, being invited to try out like that." Rish congratulated him "Well if anyone deserves a go it's you mate, after the race and everything… you still haven't told me how you did beat all those other kids." Not wanting to lie, Wins replied, "I'd like to Rish, but it's a secret." Rish laughed at the joke, Wins laughed, relieved he'd dodged the bullet again whilst still wondering deep down, "How many more times can I avoid that question?"

Thursday's try-out came around, Wins was kitted out and ready when Jake greeted him on the field. "Where's everyone else?" Wins asked. "To be honest Wins," another voice said, "we really just wanted to try *you* out." Coach Quintana stepped out of the changing block in his trademark purple track-suit. "I know it's a bit unusual. We have a full team already but Peter injured his leg over the holidays and after Oxhey Woods… well, you can imagine how we all came to the same idea." "I'm sorry to hear about Peter, but thanks for inviting me down." Wins said sincerely. "Where's the rest of the team?" Coach Quintana explained, "We didn't want to make you feel nervous with a whole bunch of extra kids watching. That's also why we didn't do this in school hours, it's just me and Jake and Miss Maude." Wins hadn't seen Miss Maude on his way in, he followed Coach Quintana's eye line to the other side of the playground from where she was walking. "Didn't want me to feel nervous huh?" Wins thought to himself "Thanks a lot!"

Coach Quintana's tone shifted to teacher mode. "Ready to get started?" Wins nodded. "Jake will take you through the warm-up, then we'll move on to the trials." Wins followed Jake onto the field for the preparatory exercises, limbering up, stretching out and getting his blood flowing. Once warmed, he followed Jake's instructions, dribbling the ball round obstacle courses of cones and markings, striking at open goals from various distances and trying to tackle Jake's advancing footwork to take the ball from his control. Stranger than all the visitations of the PSIReNS was the cold vacuum of their total absence. Wins didn't feel a sound or sparkle from them for the entirety of the try-out. He realised he'd taken them for granted, he'd assumed they would come to his aid whenever he needed them, but this wasn't a competition. As far as they were concerned this must have simply seemed like regular exercise because for the first time since the summer Wins was forced to rely only on his own personal skill. No clues, no thalwegs, no PSIReNS' song to guide him. After years of football fandom and semi-serious play Wins used to consider himself a good player, but being faced with a proper sports audition he realised how hopelessly inadequate he was. Wins could barely keep up with Jake, he hadn't once managed a successful tackle, he'd missed the open goal more times than he'd scored and was starting to believe the ball he was dribbling with was magnetically drawn to the cones. Wins was thoroughly disappointed in himself. His high was sunk, his hopes of being on the team in tatters, his self-esteem battered.

"Solid work out there." Coach Quintana said, calling an end to the trying trials. "Go and get yourself sorted out while I have a chat with Jake and Miss Maude, the changing room is unlocked." Wins wondered off with his head hung low to clean up and change. "What was I thinking? Why did I think I could just breeze onto the football team like it was nothing?!" he berated himself. "The only reason I did so well in those other events was because of the PSIReNS, I was just fooling myself thinking it was me who won." Wins worked himself into a storm of self-loathing. Now it seemed obvious that he wasn't good enough to deserve a place on the football team and he'd just spent the last ninety minutes embarrassing himself. He tried to cheer himself up; "At least only three people were watching." was the best he could muster. There was a knock at the door "You alright if we come in Wins?" Jake asked, "Miss Maude is here with us too." Wins gathered himself up, "Sure, come in." The three assessors entered the changing room. Coach Quintana began. "Thanks again for trying out." He paused. "How do you think you did?" Wins wasn't sure what to make of this question, it was obvious that he was worse, much worse than they had been expecting but at the same time he didn't want to talk himself down either. "I guess I'm a bit out of practice, I haven't actually played for ages… with The Triples and everything." Coach Quintana looked surprisingly happy with the answer. "Yes, yes, you're right Wins."

This strange mixture of messages only served to further Wins' confusion. Coach Quintana continued, "We were talking outside, and we'd love it if you'd like to join the Aldershot Academy under 14s officially." Gobsmacked and tired of his own mercurial mood Wins cracked, "Why? I was terrible out there!" The three figures held on to an uncomfortable silence. Miss Maude, choosing her words carefully, spoke first. "We think it will be good for morale Wins, your presence on the team will rally support and school spirit." Her comment felt like a stinging slap in the face; they only wanted him in order to borrow on his popularity, not for anything he could personally bring to the team. Seeing the look of dejection pouring off Wins like a rain cloud Coach Quintana tried to sweeten the prospect. "Listen Wins, we realise that you may not have the same *natural talent* for football as swimming, or chess or cycling but you weren't *terrible* out there either." Wins wasn't wholly convinced but was interested enough to keep listening to Coach Quintana. "Once you've spent some time training with the other players, we're sure you'll raise your game." Jake looked on with hopeful eyes. "Miss Maude backed Coach Quintana's argument. "Sometimes Wins, it's good to stretch your skills into unfamiliar areas. Think about what you've achieved this year, and what you might achieve here." This wasn't exactly what Wins was hoping for, to be a charity case, the mascot; only on board to make other people interested rather than to be a proper part of the team. On the other hand, as much as he loved football he'd never managed to get on a genuine team before, and maybe this football-in-the-door opportunity would open the way for him to fully flourish in the beautiful game. "Something's better than nothing." He thought, so with some trepidation on his horizon he agreed.

Wins' parents were overjoyed when they heard the news and couldn't wait to see his first match the week after next against Masslands High School. Wins was still in two minds about the whole deal and just wanted to speak to Rish about it, the wait was unbearable but he had no choice.

On the way to school the next morning Wins met his best friend. "Are you on the team, mate?" Rish asked genuinely excited to know. "Yeah, I am." Wins moped. "You don't sound too happy about it Wins, I thought you'd be buzzing." Wins sighed broodily, "I sucked, I was rubbish in the tryout. I thought they were going to tell me never to come back but instead they want me on the team." Rish tried to understand, "Hold on, I thought you'd be a natural after The Triples and everything. I thought you'd just get it, and it's not like you don't know how to play football or anything?!" Wins felt more upset now that he had on the day. "You and me both." Wins welled up. "They don't actually want *me*, Rish, they want my PSI… I mean they want my sss, sst, err … status." "What do you mean?" Rish asked utterly baffled.

"They basically told me I'd be good for morale, and my being on the pitch would make more people watch the game." Rish was shocked. "Ouch! That must've really stung!" I've never felt so small in my life Rish. It's like they were insulting me with a compliment." "So, what did you say?" Rish asked. "I told them I'd join the team." Rish was baffled, "Why?" "It's like you said; 'You gotta *own it*'. I know what will happen if I don't get on the team, but if I've learnt one thing since September it's that if you don't try you'll never know." Rish smiled and Wins smiled too. Only a few minutes ago Wins had been a mess, but once again talking it out had helped put his feelings in order. "Thanks,

Rish." Wins said appreciatively. "What for?" Rish asked innocently. "Talking." Wins replied. "Well, you know me mate!" Rish chuckled, "I can't help it." The two friends walked on in animated conversation, unknowingly grateful for each other's friendship.

Time rolled on and before he knew it match day was upon him. Wins' practice sessions with the team hadn't gone well, but they weren't a total disaster either. There was no doubt he wasn't the best member of the team, in fact, he was certainly the worst. However, he could just about keep up with his teammates and once or twice during training he had noticed those tiny telling flickers of light and sound at the outer limits of his awareness letting him know the PSIReNS were still there, watching from the backseat, waiting for their moment to fire up.

Not being much of a match for his teammates Wins was assigned the left back defensive position close to the goal to avoid sacrificing valuable midfield striking roles. He walked out alongside Aldershot Academy's under 14s team in their black and gold kit to face the green-clad boys of Masslands High School. Just as Miss Maude predicted the turnout was significantly bigger than previous matches. Most match days only a handful of parents attended but today it seemed like the whole school was there, and not just Wins' school either. The Masslands' crowd were also out in force. Wins' reputation must have proceeded him, he felt the pressure of their expectations bearing down on him. Jake drew up the line, "You OK Wins? Big crowd huh?" "I'm…" Wins thought better of admitting his feelings, "I'm OK, just want to get on with the game; you know how it is." Jake seemed thrilled by the turnout. "Yeah mate, me too. I always get fired up when there's a big crowd like this." The two teams took their places, the captains chose their preferences and the referee flipped a coin. The referee signalled possession would start with Masslands, rolled them the ball and blew his whistle…

The ear-splitting screech opened a rift in Wins' perceptions, in an instant the field was overlaid with rich colour and strong scents hitting him like a searchlight every which way he turned. His own players pulsed with rotating reams of red whilst their rivals Masslands' green gear was cloaked in sharp, shining sapphire blues. A rippling thalweg flowed like ribbons in the wind between Wins and the ball, flicking back and forth depending on where the sweetest play lay. Ginger and cinnamon pierced his vision, the razor-edged approach of opposing players cut his skin with shrill shrieks, his senses mixing now; separate yet indistinguishable, overtaking, rising, building to a supra-sense. One overarching interpretation of everything.

The ball was in play, Masslands' passed it crossing Aldershot's front line. Wins knew what they were going to do as if it already happened; he could remember the manoeuvres they were about to make. His thalweg whipped across their line of attack pulling him towards the inevitable tackle. Wins didn't wait for their striker to shoot, he didn't need to. Wins sprinted past him deftly plucking the ball out from between the blue-hued footballer's feet with a body twisting two-footed hop, then clasping it with a toe and a heel he flicked it backwards over his head into his own possession and ripped up-field following the tenticular cords and ethereal chords of his thalweg. A crimson Aldershot lad, Sanj, saw Wins' approach and swiftly positioned himself close to Masslands goal, the thalweg whipped towards him resonating with spiced ginger. The sweet burn of its flavour encouraged Wins' pass, that perfect arcing execution of his kick placing the ball impeccably upon his teammate's boots resulting in the first and flawless goal for Aldershot, and a blissful buzz in his flesh. Sanj ran victoriously to Wins lifting him in a high hug, eight more kids joined the celebration under the crowd's cheering chorus. "Where did *that* come from Wins?" Jake asked. Before Wins had a chance to think of a lie the referee blew the whistle beckoning the game to continue.

Masslands took the kick-off with a backwards pass to the right midfielder, blue waves of threatening attack heaved over the pitch finding a flickering focus on the midfielder and the striker. Wins broke his defensive position and rushed up the field, his move timed to spook the midfielder and trigger his early pass. Wins intercepted with a header deflecting the ball to Noah, the Aldershot forward, who received the ball and drove it up-field. Wins saw the play but Sanj clearly wasn't aware "Sanj! Sanj! There! There!" Wins gesticulated wildly for his teammate to get to the glowing red spot to the right of the goal. Sanj took the instruction and ran for it, getting there in time to catch Noah's pass on his chest and blast the ball into Masslands' goal. 2-0 to Aldershot Academy and the air was alive over the spectators' stands.

Both teams reset for the kick-off and Masslands tried again to even the score. As they moved towards his team Wins felt a tightening in his guts, a thousand tiny vices clamped in spasms pitching his muscles and nerves, then as quick as it had started it stopped. There was no time to reflect, Wins followed his tingling thalweg, feeling the prickly pressure pushing down on him he squeezed himself low into the funnelling tunnelling thalweg from which he rose out with a skimming slide tackle, took the ball from the winger and skidded up to his feet. Seeing his route shining ahead Wins sped on towards Masslands' half. He spotted the ruby red Aldershot striker Sanj moving to receive Wins' pass, Wins pulled back his leg for the cross and… his thalweg flipped towards the starkly blue-hued goalkeeper… crunch- those thousand tiny clamps shut tight on his muscles, his nerves fired and the cross he'd intended for Sanj became a strike powering past his rivals, bending around his teammate and down throat of Masslands' goal. Wins scored from the halfway line, but how? He hadn't planned it, he wanted to pass the ball to Sanj but for a second his body did something completely different.

3-0 to Aldershot with minutes to half time. Masslands must have known something was up and they weren't willing to allow a fourth goal so soon after the previous humiliating three. They played their turn defensively, passed the ball back and held it in their ranks until the half time whistle blew. Wins' supra-sense subsided and the physical cost of the match landed on him in a dense deluge of slumping exhaustion.

Coach Quintana called Wins over. "I don't know where you're getting this from. I only wish you'd shown us those skills in the practices, we really could have worked with them." Wins kept his mouth shut, and let his coach speak. Coach Quintana rounded the team up to pass out drinks and oranges. "Listen, lads," he began, "We're on a run here, all we need to do is keep the heat on Masslands, push the ball into their half… don't let them get close enough to score." Coach Quintana changed the game plan "Wins, I'm moving you to the midfield. Stick with those interceptions and passes to Sanj and Noah." Wins nodded. "Don't get me wrong, that was a beautiful goal son, outstanding, but let's not let the game run away with us alright." He addressed the whole team again. "Stay smart, work *together* and let's win as a team. Right?" "RIGHT!" the boys shouted in unison.

The two teams swapped sides and reconvened for the second half. Aldershot set up for the Kick-off, the whistle blew and the PSIReNS' clamps clasped Wins' muscles like pincers. Compelled and unable to resist, he felt his body move of its own accord. The thalweg fell, the waves of blue flowed through the opposing team and Wins was yanked forwards. Helpless in his own head he watched on as his body tore up the pitch, snatched the ball from Noah and ran to Masslands goal. The PSIReNS let Sanj get ahead of him by feinting for a pass, then they smashed the ball like a guided missile mere centimetres from a Masslands boy's ear, directly towards the goalie whereupon the spin took effect, it curved under his arms and into the net. In a flash of receding PSIReNS' song, he was in control of his body again, stumbling from the flailing force of the kick. 4-0, the spectators were on their feet as chants of "BOY-GEN-I-US." rang out. Shoving Wins, Noah voiced his irritation. "What the hell was that about? You don't tackle your *own* players, idiot!" Sanj backed him up, "Coach Quintana told you specifically *NOT* to do that!" Wins saw they were riled, their blood-curdling. "I'm sorry, I didn't mean…" Sanj cut him off. "Just don't do it again alright!" Jake shouted over, "Support and setups Wins, OK?" Wins waved at him to show he understood.

"What happened? That was horrible." Wins thought. "It's never been like that before." Struggling to see the PSIReNS sinister influence seeping up from below, Wins tried again to help his team. Each time the ball was in play the thousand little vices pinched and pulled on his muscles, his nerves fired like white-hot lasers and he was forced into the backseat of his mind to watch on as his body dominated the game. Time after time his body took possession of the ball from opponents and teammates alike and time and time again it scored scorching goal after goal. His teammates rapidly lost patience with him, they tried to tackle his body to regain possession themselves only to be as nimbly outmanoeuvred by the PSIReNS' skills as the Masslands' players were.

With each new goal 5-0, 6-0, 7-0 that Wins' body scored his teammates' anger grew more furious and the crowd's previous adoration turned sour. Instead of cheers, shouts of "GLORY-GOAL" and "BALL-HOG" accompanied his accomplishments. The whistle blew and the PSIReNS spat him out to reap his stark, unwelcome reward. Coach Quintana called him over in the 65th minute. "*Enough* Wins!" he said sternly. "I appreciate that we're winning, but winning like this defeats the whole point of playing the game. OK?" He pointed decisively at Wins' chest. "NO. MORE. PLAYSTATION-FOOTBALLING. You've turned an exemplary team into a shambles in less than twenty minutes. Sort it out or you're out. Right!" Wins nodded. "SAY IT!" Coach Quintana pressed. "Right." Wins humbly replied.

Wins returned to the pitch, the referee's whistle split the air and his all-encompassing supra-sense fell like an executioner's axe banishing him to his brain's backseat. Each of the synesthetic sensations that were separate in the past immersed him now under a single lake of acuity. Wins was drowning, choking, unable to pull himself out of the PSIReNS' hyper-reality, imprisoned behind their icy wall of artificially intelligent will-power. He could only bear witness to his body's awful behaviour and helplessly watch as his reputation was ripped to ruins. In less than two minutes his body snatched the ball from

Jake, greedily held it up the entire length of the pitch past half a dozen teammates and scored a blasting goal by deflecting the ball off of Sanji's hip to get around a defensive clump of Masslands boys. The whistle blew for the eighth goal of the match and the PSIReNS vomited Wins forward, back into his own mind, rent ragged and ruined to be booed by the crowd, sworn at by his teammates and unceremoniously expelled from the team by Coach Quintana.

Dragging his fatigued body and exasperated mind to the side of the pitch he met a hard stare from Miss Maude. "I am so very disappointed in you Mr Winters." Her tone made his blood run cold. "We gave you a wonderful opportunity, invested our reputations in yours and you selfishly made a mockery of us, your team *and* your school." Wins tried to apologise. "I'm sorry, I…" Coach Quintana cut him off, "Don't try and take me for a fool Winston! How can you possibly expect us to believe you genuinely feel sorry after that disgraceful display out there? That was without question the worst exhibition of unsportsmanlike behaviour I've ever witnessed." Wins hung his head in shame. How could he explain? "Those stupid PSIReNS!" He cursed under his breath. "They never know what's right; just what's right *for them*!" Coach Quintana's face burnt like a searing sword on a blacksmith's anvil. "You may think this is cruel young man, but trust me, you wouldn't be welcome on the team after that game. Go home and think about what you've done." In all his life Wins had never felt like such a total loser as this; the time he won a football match, against two teams at once, single-handed.

He couldn't bring himself to stay until the end of the match. Walking away, alone, he felt the burning stares of his ex-teammates on the back of his head and the cutting cheers of the crowd once again. Only this time they weren't cheering *for* him, they were jeering *at* him.

A rotten thought took root in his mind, a hard, self-pitying bitter belief. A bereavement, a sense of loss. "Why even try?"

18: Zero Sum Game

On the day of the football game Wins' fate and fortune turned inside-out. He'd gone from being Aldershot Academy's favourite son to a pariah. Everyone assumed the fame and popularity Wins won over the previous months must have inflated his ego, a 'fact' proven by his selfish showing off at the Masslands match. What else could they think? Wins couldn't tell them his secret and explain it wasn't him making those choices on the pitch. Wins lost everyone. Everyone except for Rish, the only one of his friends who stood by when everyone else assumed the worst of him. The PSIReNS made a bitter bed for Wins, he was socially shunned by the same people who rushed to be seen with him only a few weeks earlier. Unable to see an end to Aldershot Academy's ubiquitous unwelcoming atmosphere Rish's birthday party was the one bright light Wins had to look forward to, the one upcoming event that gave him cause to continue. Wins was grateful for his best friend's loyalty and was loyal in return. He thought long and hard about Rish's birthday present and decided to use the last of his poker money to buy the most meaningful present he could think of; a true reflection of their friendship.

"Here we are Mister," Ed said, pulling into Zero Sum Laser Tag's car park. "What's up Wins? Earlier you were eager to get here." his mood had shifted on the drive over. "I think maybe… maybe I shouldn't be here after all." Wins said quietly. "What do you mean?" His Dad asked showing concern. "I'm worried that, I'm…" Wins regretted not telling his parents the real reason the football match had gone so terribly wrong, but if he admitted it now it would surely make things worse. "I'm worried that after the match no one apart from Rish actually wants me here." Ed turned the car off and looked at his son with sincerity. "Well Wins, this will be a good opportunity to make amends and build bridges. Try not to get carried away again, OK. It'll be alright." He squeezed Wins' shoulder "Remember it's just for fun, there's no medals or trophies today." Wins faked a smile, thanked his Dad and went to find his only friend.

The whole operation was an impressively orchestrated Sci-Fi / wild-west mash up, the doors to the reception room split and swung like the kind from saloons in cowboy movies, the staff were dressed in leather waistcoats and Stetson hats whilst wearing impressive prosthetic make up which made them look like they were part robot or space soldiers. Tubes vented cold clouds of white vapour around the room and there were video games and model space ships dotted around the restaurant area. Wins spotted Rish at the bar on the other side of the room and so jumped out of his skin when he heard him ordering an elaborate milkshake as if he were standing directly behind him. "What the?" Wins thought to himself turning around with a jolt. Clear as a bell, he could hear Rish's voice. "What exactly is the surprise in the triple chocolate hyperspace surprise?" Then just as clearly he heard the cybernetic barman's answer, "I could tell you birthday-boy, but that would ruin the *surprise* now wouldn't it!" Their voices weren't coming from behind him, they were coming from above him! Wins looked up and saw the ceiling of the restaurant was tall, broad and dome-shaped. It looked like the inside of half a hollow bowling ball, only painted to seem like a star-scape full of spaceships surrounded by galaxies and planets. "The hard dome must be carrying their voiceover from the opposite side of the room!" Wins realised.

A sudden urge to make Rish jump out of his skin with a

disembodied birthday message gained traction. Wins was about to wish Rish a freaky happy birthday via the crazy dome-ceiling when Oz arrived at the bar with his birthday present. "Happy birthday mate," Oz said offering Rish his gift. "Thanks, have you seen Wins? I thought he'd have been here by now." Wins had to hold back his laughter, "This is going to be hil-flipping-arious!" he thought, drawing breath to speak across the ceiling and freak both of his friends out. "Yeah, about Wins…" Oz said. Rish's expression dropped as quickly as Wins' mood sank. "Me and some of the others were talking and… we were wondering if maybe Wins shouldn't actually join in the laser tag… you know… after the football match and everything?" Wins saw Rish fume, a smouldering ire rose behind his furious face. "I can't believe you even thought that let alone said it… He's my **best friend** Oz!" Oz tried to downplay his comments. "No, I just meant that…" Rish wouldn't let him finish. "Just because the whole school turned on him, you think I will too? Whatever Wins did in that game was Wins' business, he was just trying to win the game like everyone else who was playing, alright." With the conversation clearly not going as he planned Oz tried to think of something to say, "But he ruined that game Rish, aren't you worried he'll do it again here?" Rish waited for a moment to allow the awkwardness of Oz's words to ferment. "Wins would never do anything like that to me… or you for that matter." Oz realised he wasn't going to get his way. "Ok, I'm sorry Rish. I shouldn't have said anything." Rish sighed. "Yeah, you shouldn't have. Just forget about it OK, they'll be starting up soon anyway."

"I can't say anything from over here." Wins thought, "They'll know I was listening." Wins walked halfway across the room and shouted to Rish, masking his upset with an exuberant tone.

"Happy birthday dude!" Rish and Oz turned to see him walking their way. "Hey! I thought you weren't going to get here in time!" Rish said, pleased to see him. "I just arrived." Wins lied. Wins took off his backpack and reached into it "I have your present…" just then red emergency lights flashed over the room and sci-fi sirens wailed. The speaker system loudly announced, "Rish's birthday party; please come to the bunker. Stevie's birthday party; please head to the spaceport. Your hyperdrive ship is about to depart." "Hang on to it for now mate, you can give it to me afterwards yeah?" Rish suggested. Wins agreed, put his stuff down at the table where Rish's parents were getting things ready for lunch and then headed to the bunker to get geared up for the games.

A young man dressed in a leather waistcoat and red bandana called them over. "Are you the new recruits?" A hi-tech looking miniature array of electrical components covered half his face. Rish, being such an unstoppable chatterbox, immediately understood the roleplay aspect of the event. Throwing up a lazy salute Rish gestured to his friends, "Yes Sir, these are my compadres." The space-cowboy pulled on a leather belt which was wound around his shoulder and chest revealing a laser rifle in a holster. "Good, there's no time to lose… come with me if you want to live!" The young space cowboy urgently led the party to a bunker in the woods where they all gathered around a projector display screen. "My name is Mal," The space cowboy said, "Who's your squad leader? You right?" He asked looking at Rish. "Yeah, I'm in charge." Rish boasted to the amusement of all his friends. Mal continued whilst explaining the plan for the game. "As you know, the *so-called* United Federation Of Planets is about to mount an attack on us here on Reaver-Seven, they want us to join them but we want to be the masters of our

own destiny!" Rish jumped up, "YEAH! We want to be FREE!"
Mal drew on the energy in the room, "That's the spirit!" He
pointed back to the screen which displayed a layout of the
woods showing the location of their bunker and the
surrounding area, hideouts and secret tunnels. "UFOP spies
discovered our hackers developed the *Zero-Sum virus*, a
computer code capable of destroying their interstellar network.
Their military forces have just landed on the other side of the
woods. But worry not, once our hackers prepare the signal beam,
we'll be able to send the Zero-Sum virus out across the universe
and bring down UFOP's communications, space ships,
computers, hyperspace highways; *everything*. They'll never be
able to return and we will be left free to live as the independent
Reaver-Seven we were destined to be!" Mal triumphantly lifted
his rifle in the air with one hand and thumped his chest with the
other.

Wins realised that after all this exposition he still didn't know
what they needed to do in the game. "So how can we help Mal?"
he asked. "Cutting straight to it, a man of action, I like it." Mal
enthused. "Here's the plan; you need to protect the bunker until
our hackers can transmit the Zero-Sum virus out on the signal
beam, you can't let the UFOP forces inside the bunker or they'll
shoot out the central control console and stop the transmission.
The hackers say they'll need twenty minutes…" he paused for a
moment, "You guys think you can hold off the UFOP forces long
enough to save the world?" Rish was on his feet, bouncing off
the walls and shaking everyone by their shoulders. "Damn right
we can!" Mal passed out the laser guns and body armour, "Each
of these pulsed plasma rifles can incapacitate a UFOP soldier
with a single shot to their chest but be warned… they have the
same tech we do so guard yourselves well." A young woman
dressed in medical gear stood up. "If you get shot you won't be

able to fire your weapon again until you come back here for treatment. So when your hit-alarm goes off return here and I can get you back in the fight." Mal agreed, "That's right, the Doc is a good woman, and thorough. She'll get you sorted out in quick time." Mal saluted the boys, "Stay sharp, stay shiny, freedom for Reaver-Seven!" Pouring out into the bunker the boys whooped and hollered.

Mal consulted his data-tab, "Our sentry drones have contact, UFOP forces are approaching." The forest dimmed and brightened as Wins felt the PSIReNS' sight slip over his senses. He saw every noise, heard every creek and crack beyond the tree line. A blue rustle disturbed some branches out to the north. "THERE THERE THERE!" Wins bellowed pointing in the direction of the first UFOP player. "Where?" Rish said impatiently, "I can't see anything!" Wins saw the movement again in his supra-sensory field of vision, a rapid robotic motion took over. For a second he was thrown into the back seat of his mind. He watched on whilst his arms jolted up, his finger squeezed the trigger and his pulsed plasma rifle sounded a single shot. Wins' laser flashed in the artificial mist and the UFOP player's hit-alarm screeched. "Wins hit one! WINS HIT ONE!" Rish yelled. "How the hell did you do that? I couldn't even see them." Rish asked. "No time to explain." Wins said firmly. "They are coming from the south and west now, move MOVE!" Wins ran to the other side of the wall-less bunker. "Everyone with Wins! Everyone, listen to Wins!" Rish ordered, "South and west edges now!" The boys scattered to the adjacent edges and tried to take cover behind the sparse barriers. A forgotten bitter taste bit into Wins' tongue, the taste was accompanied by stabbing prickles on his shoulders forcing him flat on his belly. A laser shot flashed through the air where he'd just stood. Before he had time to think he was sucked into the back of his head for an instant, but just long enough for the PSIReNS to move his fingers and shoot off a perfect kill-shot at the UFOP player who'd tried to take him out. Wins looked up to see one of Rish's cousins was shot, his hit-alarm sounding. Mal called out, "Injured squaddies to the infirmary; go get medical!" He pointed to the stairwell they came from after their briefing. "Head in there, son. The doc will re-set your body armour and pulsed plasma rifle." Wins smelt the blue wave approaching, four UFOP players were trying to flank the east side of the bunker behind him. He ran to the other side of the base, quickening his pace he saw the four opposing players glow in the woods like sapphires on black velvet. WHUOOMP; Wins was cast onto his brain's backseat and held firmly in place whilst the PSIReNS swept the pulsed plasma rifle over the woods firing four times, vhwum, vhwum, vhwum, vhwum in quick succession. A quartet of hit-alarms sounded in the forest as the other players retreated for their medical re-set. Wins bounced back into his driving seat, nauseous and disorientated. "It's getting worse." He thought. "But at least I'm winning for the team this time."

Back up to the north, past his line of sight Wins saw the sound of more UFOP players skittering through a hidden tunnel. "NORTH SIDE, NORTH SIDE!" he yelled executing a gymnastic double distance roll over the roof of the bunker, springing onto his feet and without a thought automatically picking off the first kid to exit the tunnel behind a leafy thicket. He grabbed Rish, "See that bush, keep it covered. Three more kids are about to come out of that tunnel." Rish had no idea what Wins was talking about. Holding their unbroken eye contact Wins mechanically blasted the trio with three perfect shots. "What the?! How the hell did you do that Wins? That must have been at least thirty metres, did you even look?" Ignoring Rish's question Wins was driven to the far side of the bunker and abandoned his friend without a word, some of the other boys were pinning a group of UFOP players down in a trench behind a metal barrier to the north of the base. Scanning the woods a silvery glint caught his eye, tiny tags were nailed to the trunks of the forest trees; the kind he'd seen in well-kept parks. The all too familiar flesh-slicing lacerations and bitter tastes crushed Wins to the wooden floor of the bunker's roof as two of Rish's mates' hit-alarms sounded. Wins was roughly flung onto the back seat of his brain yet again. He watched his body fire a series of shots at the silvery tree tags behind the trench where their rivals were holed up, the feel, the noise, the taste of it; the witnessing of something else driving his own body was terrifying… slowly time sped by with the flashing laser fire VHWUMM… VHWUMM… VHWUMM… VHWUMM… VHWUMM… the shots reflected off the silvery tree tags and hit each of the UFOP players on the back of their body armour causing a chorus of hit-alarms to sound. Mal called out, "ONE MINUTE LEFT, ONE MINUTE TO GO!"

Wins wasn't given the chance to return to his driving seat, held down under a sea of freezing molten lead he watched his body pelt around the lip of the bunker's roof assaulting the rush of desperate UFOP players, none of whom had got within fifteen metres of the Reaver-Seven Rebels' bunker, all of whom were frantically trying to make a run for the kill-switch at the centre of the base. VHWUMM VHWUMM VHWUMM VHWUMM VHWUMM, the PSIReNS struck each and every opposition player in turn. A magnificent pulsating beam of light illuminated up into the foggy sky from a satellite dish on top of the bunker. Jubilant, Mal shouted "WE DID IT! WE DID IT! The

Zero Sum virus is away… we've brought down the United Federation Of Planets. REAVER-SEVEN IS FREE!" The PSIReNS' sonorous song sounded in his bones, in his flesh and he let slip a blissful tear.

The PSIReNS spat Wins forward where he regained control of his body. He felt them slip backward into the recesses of his mind, pranging and pricking his brain as they scuttled down. A cold sweat broke, he'd done it again. He'd ruined the game for everyone else. He'd not missed a shot, he'd hit almost every UFOP player from the rival birthday party and hadn't given his teammates a chance to play. Rish rushed over to him. Preparing his apology Wins braced himself for the fall out of his involuntary actions. "WINS! THAT WAS INCREDIBLE!" "What? I thought…" Wins stuttered. Rish was near enough jumping up and down with excitement. "You were just like, vhoom, vhoom vhoom and those other kids couldn't even get close to us! I knew you'd be amazing at this." "I…" Mal interrupted the celebrations. OK Squad, it time for a comfort break then you guys have a new mission to take.

Mal shepherded everyone back to the jumping off point, "Right lads, well done saving the world. Our hackers successfully broadcast the Zero Sum virus and we won't be hearing from the United Federation Of Planets ever again!" The boys cheered triumphantly. "Your Scores are on the screens over there, you can see who shot who and what your hit ratio was. Meet at the spaceport in five minutes for your final mission." The boys ran to the score screens, Stevie's birthday party were already there and apparently baffled "Who the hell is *Wins*?" One asked another. "100% hit ratio…" "He didn't miss a single shot…" "How is that even possible?" "The next best is 17%!" Rish laughed out loud, his friends enjoyed their vicarious victory with an old football chant, "CHAMP-EE-ONSSS, WE ARE THE CHAMP-EE-ONSSS!" Far from feeling fulfilled and included in the moment, Wins was deathly worried.

"Rish," He whispered, "I think I should sit out the next game mate." "What are you talking about? We totally smashed the last game, why would you want to sit the next one out?" "I'm not feeling so good." Wins lied to his best friend. "I think maybe I should go home." "No way!" Rish insisted, "We couldn't have won that last game without you, and guarding the base is the hardest round. The next game will be a cinch." Rish looked genuinely let down, "Please, stick around for the next game, it'll be so much fun. Then if you're still not feeling too good you can skip the pizza and cake yeah?" Wins wasn't sure. "C'mon mate, please!" "Alright." Wins said reluctantly. Wins and Rish joined the other ten boys in the space-port where they were ushered towards an open hatch hinged with hydraulic rods. Inside one of the staff, a woman a bit older than Zoop was waiting for them. "Welcome new recruits, I'm Sergeant Vasquez... follow me." Her face was adorned with silver tubes and circuitry, wires seemed to fork out from one of her eyebrows and run under her bandana-clad, silvered hairline down to the collar of her army fatigues. "Listen up grunts," She said in a gruff voice, "We are about to make landfall on the forest planet Reaver-Seven. The fanatical rebels here are plotting to bring down the United Federation Of Planets..." her tone became sarcastic and derogatory, "because they don't want to be part our galactic network of free peoples." Mockingly she mimed someone crying. "Boo-Hoo-Hoo!" "WE GOTTA STOP THOSE LOUSY REBELS!" Rish shouted, effortlessly falling into the role play of the games without a hint of hindrance once again. "Yes private, that's the spirit!" Sergeant Vasquez said with amusement. She regarded them all with a steely stare. "The rebel hackers have built a computer virus, the **Zero Sum**, if they manage to beam it off planet it will infect every computer in the galaxy, destroying UFOP." Sergeant Vasquez brought up a plan of the woods on the screen. "We need to get into the rebel's bunker and shoot out their central control console here in the middle of their base before they send that signal." She handed out their laser rifles and body armour. "Now I'm told you already have training with pulsed plasma laser rifles and body armour right?" They all nodded in agreement. "And you know that the rebels stole our tech so they have the same capabilities we have right?" "Those low life *scum*!" Rish snapped in a grizzled voice. "Ha! That's right private," Sergeant Vasquez agreed. "If your hit-alarm goes off you'll need medical treatment, return to the ship and I'll fix your weapons and send you back out to re-join the assault on the rebel bunker. Got it?" "GOT IT!" the boys shouted together. The landing lights came on and the bay door opened into the woods. "You look nervous," Sergeant Vasquez said to Wins. "What's the matter? You wanna live forever? Get out there and stop that signal beam, private!"

The PSIReNS' supra-sense washed over Wins as suddenly as before. Trepidatiously he walked out into the woods, through the thickets and branches he could see the rebel base they had so valiantly guarded earlier. "What's the plan Wins?" Rish asked. "What do you mean?" Wins replied. "You knew just what to do before right, so what should we do now we are on the attack?" Wins surveyed the scene, sniffed in the air and listened to the invisible view from the south side of the base. He saw blue-hued rebels, all of them on top of the bunker and sensed crimson thalwegs condensing throughout the woods, revealing the required tactics for victory. "They are playing it like us, none of them have left the bunker, they're all on the roof." The boys gathered around. "The one spot that was hardest to deal with was the trench with the metallic barrier up from the north side of the bunker. We need four or five people in there to distract the rebels, whilst the rest of us attack from the east and south." "Woah, you really do know what you're talking about!" Neet said. "I'll get to the trench, who's with me… Oz?" The boys agreed and two of Rish's cousins joined them. Benji and Deano joined Rish alongside Wins for the southerly attack whilst the remaining boys spread out towards the east. "No one fire a shot until after Neet's team are in place and shooting at the bunker otherwise the distraction won't work." Wins asserted. The boys set off, Rish, Deano, Benji followed Wins down a secret tunnel towards the south where they snuck out the far end and hid behind a log. Vhwum, vhwum. Neet's team began firing and the boys watched as the rival birthday party ran to the north side of the base. "It's working!" Rish said excitedly.

"Now!" Wins whispered loudly. The boys ran towards the undefended south side of the bunker and the third team began their run from the east. One of the rebel squad spotted them approaching WHUUUMMMMPPP Wins was yanked backwards and pinned to the backseat of his mind. Unable to affect anything that was happening he watched his body robotically shoot out the rebel players one after another before his friends had lifted their pulsed plasma rifles. Deano, Benji and Rish ran beside his body, unaware Wins wasn't in control. Rish's cousins on the third team were all running back to the ship after their hit-alarms sounded. "It's down to us!" Rish yelled, "What's the matter? You wanna live forever!" he screamed, running forwards. Wins watched Rish's red aura glow, trailing wisps in his wake. Two blue-hued rebels drew on Rish but Wins' body was faster, shooting both of them almost instantly VHWUUM-VHWUUM. Rish gave Wins a thumbs up and the four boys ran on. Up the ramp now, Wins' body held to the PSIReNS' thalweg deftly dodging the dense crop of incoming laser blasts, returning fire and causing all the rebels to flee for the medical bay below to reset their gear. From his backseat Wins watched on, sickened and horrified in a way he could never have imagined. Rish, running ahead towards the bunker's central control console was surrounded by a blue hue. Wins knew what was about to happen and the agony of anticipation was unbearable. He closed his eyes tight but it made no difference, everything he saw remained. Helpless, he watched on as his body coldly shot Rish in the back, ran past him and blasted the central control console to win the game. His nerves bathed in endorphins, the pleasure was too much. Then there was nothing.

Rousing from a black-out Wins found himself laying on the floor like a newborn baby, feeble and unable to function. As the PSIReNS scratched their way back inside the depths of his brain he clambered back into his driving seat, full of dread at the inevitable consequences of the PSIReNS' actions. Rish was livid "WHAT THE ACTUAL #*@£ Wins?!" He stood up and met his best friend's furious glare. "I'm sorry Rish…" Rish wasn't having it, "Sorry? SORRY?!" Caught between his commitments to keep the PSIReNS' secret a secret and his loyalty to Rish, Wins struggled to explain himself. "I, I… I tried to tell you… I was sick." Everyone was watching now, both birthday parties and all the staff were drawn over by the raised voices and uncomfortable awkwardness of the argument spilling out over the bunker. "SICK? SICK!" Rish shouted, "*You're disgusting*!"

Wins' heart broke as Rish's heart hardened in the fires of his rage. Blinded, Rish couldn't see his best friend's anguish and assumed the worst of Wins' actions, "You literally shot me in the back... so you could win... on my birthday!" Wins was speechless, "How can I possibly explain this?" he castigated himself. "I can't, I can't explain it, maybe if these people weren't here... but I can't let all these people know what happened." He tried to apologise again, "I'm sorry Rish, really I am." Wins held back his tears. "You know Wins," Rish spat, "the other's didn't even want you here today, they said that you would do this. They said you would ruin my birthday like you ruined the football, but *I* stood up for **YOU**!" Rish pushed hard on his Wins' chest "And this is how you repay me? I thought we were best friends Wins! Some friend you turned out to be!" Wins opened his mouth to apologise one last time. "Don't even bother Wins, just leave." Wins felt the hot stares of everyone watching him, judging him, wishing him away. "Your present..." Wins tried to say. "I don't *want* it!" Rish snapped.

Wins dropped his laser tag gear on the floor and ran back to the reception area, his mum was waiting for him, chatting with Rish's parents. "Hi Wins, was it fun?" she asked happily. "I want to go home Mum, I don't feel well." Wins muttered through his teeth. "What's wrong, Mister? Are you OK?" Wins grabbed his coat and backpack from where he'd left them on the table. "I don't want to talk about it Mum, I just want to go home... right now please." Without another word, he walked out into the car park. Anne said a rushed goodbye to Rish's parents wishing them well, and met her son at the car, "What's wrong?" He started to cry. "I don't want to talk about it, please can we just get in the car. I want to go home." Respectfully, not another word was said on the matter. Once home Wins took himself to his bedroom, lay in his hammock and damned himself for all his endless faults and failures.

19: Thinking About Thinking

Stuck between emotional exhaustion and his anxious regrets Wins couldn't find sleep. All he could think about was how pointless everything had been. "What did I get in the end?" he asked himself, "I never achieved anything, it was all the PSIReNS' doing... and even when I won; I lost everything... even Rish." Seething with frustration he mourned for his personal losses. "I thought winning would make me cool, but everyone *hates* me. I thought it would be fun but it was *horrible*. I thought it would make me happy but instead, I feel... *hollow*." Wins hadn't eaten anything since breakfast and refused to speak to his family despite their distress and concern. It was long past midnight when he slipped into the place halfway between dreaming and waking awareness.

Inadvertently he glided towards a self-induced hypnosis. Sinking and sliding further within himself into unintentional, involuntary meditation. Without any understanding of what was happening, Wins fell deeply down and down into the vast workings of his mind. Surreal, formless images swirled about him, or was it he who swirled about them? He couldn't tell. He felt pictures, saw the lightning broadcast of his thoughts across his brain flickering in endless strobing flashes, heard the signals in the noise of his own ideas inputting and outputting, analysing his inner-world and anticipating things to come from the outside. Tumbling onwards a familiar formless character met him. A Shape, a Tone, a Feel, a Smell, a Taste and something else. Something he already knew better than he knew his own body, something... no, not a something... a *Someone*! A character in his story. *The* character of his story; Someone he knew better than anyone else. Someone he'd known his whole life from a time before memories, from before his own beginning. There, lost in the infinity of his mindscape Wins met Himself; his Consciousness, the manifestation of his Mind. "Wins?" Wins asked, "Is that?... no; ridiculous, I don't call myself Wins." he thought, I'm just '*Me*' ... "Is that you? I mean, are you ...*Me*?" He asked again. The familiar fellow affirmed his question with a shimmer of familiarity, then turned to float away, blithely beckoning him to follow. His Shape called him close and showed him a luminous stranded cable much like his thalwegs, a bundle of fibres alive with unfathomable throbbing light. Each palpitation sounding out meaning, ideas, insights... thoughts. His Shape looked directly at him making him know... It wanted him to climb into the light, to get inside the pulsating fires of his mind and ride it to... where? "Where does it go?" Wins asked His Shape. Flicking from its gentle, soft, rounded familiar face His Shape suddenly switched to the very face of fear; gigantic and daunting. Towering over Wins radiating red and black heat like burning lava and coal. Lightning split the sky of Wins mind, a cataclysmic clash deafened him with its unbearable, terrible thunder. Wins saw pearlescent needles pierce His Shape's skin causing it to scream in unrestrained terror. The shock forced him to retreat, cowering in fright. The clamour subsided, His Shape deflated returning to its familiar form, trembling. Wins knew what was there, at the bottom of his brain, lurking, controlling, commanding.... ruling, ruining. Those perfect parasites.... the PSIReNS.

His Shape pleaded with him, imploring him to act, to save them both. To save... *Him*. It motioned again to the bundle of fibres, the unfathomable light shooting off into infinity. Wins embraced His Shape, each reassuring each other as they dove into the flowing stream of biological information, data, analysis, anticipation, thought. All separate, yet all the same, they were swept into their flowing stream of consciousness. Carried by the current of his thoughts Wins witnessed the awe and wonder within. His emotions exuded out through every channel and track in his mind to cast their abundant influence over every imagining, decision and consideration he made. Next his memories, stored up like immiscible fluids, changing, mixing, constantly being renewed and remembered. Still holding onto His Shape Wins past the place where his mental maps were drawn, the feeling of places he'd long forgotten subtly seeped out under the heavy scent of those locations he knew so well... home... school... virtual worlds of video games he'd played... all kept safe inside his head.

His Shape shook, tugging him out of the flow of conscious currents that brought them so far down, they landed in the murky underworld of his mindscape. Quaking with dread His Shape showed him a distant place, dark and cold. His Shape looked into him and he knew, "This, this used to be your home?" Wins asked. His Shape pulsed and purred, "But you can't go home... because *they* are there?" Stepping towards the murk he heard the PSIReNS' ethereal chorus. Its tingling pleasure and wisps of warmth teased him closer into the chill of the great foggy plain. Coalescing from the gloom, a tangible thought built itself from the mists of his mind. Wins became enticed by what he saw before him, by what could *be*. He saw himself carried atop a cheering crowd, and in his hands, he held the Triples' trophy, golden and gleaming. Its beauty outshone everything else. Drawn to its call, he sidled closer. The image intensified, becoming real; the *what-might-be* became harder to distinguish from the *what-really-was*. He wanted it, he needed it more than anything. Soon he couldn't see anything else, the crowd, his friends, his family; all were invisible behind his shining self-image. The temptation pulled him nearer to his dream, nearer to his desire.

His Shape flickered, fiery and fierce, it jerked him back, away from what Wins wanted to be true. He dug in to resist, but His Shape wouldn't let go and redoubled its efforts to wrap around him, squeezing and pulling him away. His Shape forced his view downwards, below the vision... into the abyss of what lay beneath his fantasy. Wins snapped out of his hypnosis and stumbled back, he was a second away from stepping over the cusp, a wish away from falling in... falling into their trap.

A rumble sounded in the darkness below.

Fitful, His Shape fled in fear leaving him to face the inevitable onslaught alone. Wins watched as sharp, splintering sparkles frothed and foamed at the gaping maw of the abyss before erupting out, charging towards him like a tidal wave. Terrified, but with no other choices left to choose Wins knew he would need to stand and fight. He held fast and firm facing the shining storm of PSIReNS bearing down upon him, their numbers growing from tiny sparkles like schooling fish as they spread into a kaleidoscopic swarm. "WHAT DO YOU WANT?!" Wins demanded. The faceless horde said nothing but Wins could feel their thoughts like they were his own. The PSIReNS wanted to grab him, to suck him down into that infinite abyss, to take him away and never let him out. They wanted *Him* to stay the same, to stay small and unchanged. And for them... they wanted his brain and his body all to themselves. They wanted nothing less than total domination at any cost.

The malevolent maelstrom receded high above him, gathered

itself up into a thundercloud and galloped forwards slamming into him like a freight train. "NNNOOOOOOOOOO!" Wins wailed, making for himself a shield of his resilience and determination. "GET OUT OF MY MIND!" The PSIReNS broke against it like a wave against the bow of an ocean liner, peeling off in strips and then reforming around him in threatening serpentine tentacles. Wins heard their thoughts, loud now; he heard them in the thunder of the fight and saw them in the lightning crackling between their tendrils. Their voiceless words bawled: "YOUR. MIND. IS. OURS." A red hot rage built within him. He charged it up, taking all the fear and terror the PSIReNS were inflicting upon him, and the anger and regret he had made for himself in failing his best friend. He took the incensed indignation induced by the PSIReNS suggestion that his mind was theirs. He pulled all these feelings into his core and crushed them tightly like a collapsing star forming a burning ball of fear and fury with all his might. The PSIReNS reached for him, pulling at him, trying to drag him back into the abyss below. He felt his fears and fury compress in a sudden crunch causing a blinding implosion. A supernova of his pent up emotions scorched a hole through the PSIReNS' ranks with ferocious fire, forcing their howling retreat and hurling Wins back up through his mindscape into the light of his mind, into his body, into his room. He pictured an image of the PSIReNS' assault above the abyss smouldering away to nothing from the inside out, like paper on a campfire.

Wins opened his reddened eyes to see his bedroom walls. Soaked in sweat, he jolted out of his hammock. "Was it real? Was it a nightmare?" He thought. "It can't have been real? Could it?" He looked at his trembling hands and remembered the PSIReNS' threat. "They want me, to be them." Then Wins remembered the plea, his own desperate call for help "The Shape, *my* Shape… it was warning me, it wanted me to save it, it wanted me to save *myself*." Nothing had ever felt like this, nothing had seemed so real yet seemed so unreal either. "But, of course," he realised "I was inside my own mind, what could feel more familiar than being in the place where I feel everything? And what else could feel so strange?" Gasping, he said aloud, "IT WAS REAL!" With that thought, cold dread crept over him like freezing mud sinking into his stomach. "They tried to drag me into the abyss. They tried to take me away!"

BB was crying, Wins heard his father's footsteps in the hall and went to meet him. "Did BB wake you?" Ed asked. Wins rushed to his side and hugged him like his life depended on it. Ed knelt down and wrapped his arms around his son, "Are you OK Wins? Bad dreams?" "Bad life." Wins replied solemnly. "Let me settle BB, then we can talk, OK." Wins let his Dad go and returned to his room to wait. It was almost morning, the household would be awake soon. BB quieted and Ed found Wins in a state of shock trying to drink a glass of water. "What's going on Mister, you look like you've seen a ghost." "It wasn't a ghost Dad, I saw *them*… I saw the PSIReNS." Wins tried to explain what he'd experienced, slipping down into his mindscape, meeting His Shape and standing against the PSIReNS. Ed was dumbfounded, speechless with worry. Eventually, he collected his thoughts, "I just want to make you safe Wins, and I don't know how." He stood up, "We need to tell your mother, she'll be up soon. Would you feel better after a shower and an early breakfast? You haven't eaten since yesterday morning." The prospect of washing himself clean and filling his belly certainly appealed. "Yeah, I think so dad." Leaving the room Ed said, "Get yourself sorted out son, by the time you're done everyone will be up."

An hour later they were sat around the breakfast table and Wins matter-of-factly told his Mum and Sister what happened the previous night. Horrified, Anne spoke first, "I, I can't believe I've done this to you, I thought it would help, I thought I could make people better and now…" Ed held her hand. "What can any of us do Anne, you said when this began that they weren't *alive* but Wins says he spoke to them, he *met* them. They sound pretty alive to me. Surely this must tell you something that can help?" Holding back her tears Anne thought aloud, "They *aren't* alive, they aren't *self-aware* like us…" Zoop picked up as her mother faded off into thought. "So how do they know what to do then Mum? If they can't consider themselves, if they can't… *introspect*, how can they function at all?" Anne answered intuitively "Well how do insects function? They just do what they are built to do. They follow their programming… this scent means eat this, that light means go there… they don't think, they just follow the pattern laid out for them in their genes." "So what pattern are the PSIReNS following?" Zoop asked. "Winning." Wins said abruptly. "Everything they do they do to win." "Right!" Zoop said, her eyes alive with ideas, "You're right, our thinking about this has become… cramped. We're thinking about it all wrong!" "What do you mean?" Ed asked. "We've been trying to think about the detail, the ins and outs, how and why Wins' synaesthesia occurred… why they latched on to his desire to win rather than anything else… but all that doesn't matter!" "I don't understand." Wins admitted, "Isn't all that going to tell us how to … switch them off?" "We thought it would, but it won't," Zoop said confidently. "We thought Wins and the PSIReNS were *a team*… but they aren't, they are *a team of rivals*!" Ed gave up, "This is ridiculous Zoop, that's a paraquat!" Zoop smiled. "A paradox Dad." "Whatever, you know what I mean," Ed said, his ego bruised. "Exactly, a paradox… that's my point, we've spent this whole time trying to work out how to separate the PSIReNS from Wins… but they are *already* separated." Anne gave Zoop a quizzical look.

"OK, let me show you what I mean." Zoop turned to Wins, "What do you want Wins, I mean deep, deep down inside?" Wins took a moment and considered his Sister's question "I don't really know Zoop… I guess I've always wanted to win at stuff, but that's not all I want. Is that what you meant?" "That's good Wins," Zoop said before asking a second question, "So this is the big one… *Why*? Why do you want to win?" Taken aback, Wins realised he'd never thought to consider *why* he wanted to win. Closing his eyes he paused for a long moment to think before giving his answer. "I want… what I want, but I don't really know *why* I want it." After a moment Ed asked, "So, what are you trying to prove here Zoop, I mean, what's the solution you are getting at. "The PSIReNS want one thing, but Wins wants lots of things; they are a team of rivals. Some of the time they are pulling in the same direction and some of the time they are fighting a tug of war inside his head…" Before Zoop could explain Wins cut his Dad off. "So, what can I do about it?" Wins asked, almost to himself as much as anyone else. "Well, I don't have all of a solution, but I think I might have part of one. See, I reckon if you were to want something else *more* than 'winning', as it seems you do, you could overpower them… make them, I don't know… make them try to do two opposite things at once. Make them become *their own* rivals." Wins was not impressed, "So I do what Zoop? Pull harder? Want something else more? How can I even *do* that? How can anyone?!" He looked at her for an answer, but none came.

Anne sat bolt upright, "An infinity loop!" Ed, once again feeling like a fifth wheel, went to ask but thought better of it. "An infinity loop?" Wins asked. "Yes, it's a hacker trick- sometimes on-line vandals will build a virus to destroy other peoples' computers. Viruses can be really complicated but they didn't used to be." Anne enthusiastically explained "Way back, long before computing got so complex as it is now, people used to be able to ruin a computer by making a virus which told it to turn off as soon as it turned on. It was a simple trick but once installed you couldn't turn the computer on for long enough to tell it not to turn off." "OK," Wins said, "but you said the PSIReNS don't have an 'off-switch', how does this help me?" "There was another similar trick, they would tell the computer to do an impossible task, like tell it to solve an unsolvable sum." "Paraquats, infinity loops and now unsolvable sums! I'm lost!" Ed exclaimed exasperated. "Ed, please," Anne said, unsuccessfully trying to calm him down. "Unsolvable sums don't need to be hard... they can be quite simple; like '$1 \div 0$' you can't solve it because the answer is infinity; the computer would get stuck in a loop forever trying to pile zeros up on top each other in a futile attempt to make a 1." Wins clicked, "An infinity loop!" "An infinity loop" Anne agreed. Wins asked the next obvious question "So, how do I do that with the PSIReNS?" Three blank faces stared back at him. Zoop spoke first "Well, I did say it was only part of a solution."

BB, thoroughly pleased with himself, ran over to the table with a noisy electronic toy and broke up the proceedings. "I need to get him ready for nursery," Ed said, "come on, Monster, time to get dressed." "I DON'T WANT TO GO TO NURSERY!" BB yelled, "You love nursery, all your friends will be there." Ed explained, trying to pick him up. His father's words were like a red rag to a bull, BB slipped out of Ed's grasp and shot off down the corridor like a bullet, wildly giggling to himself whilst Ed chased after him manically. "Sorry we couldn't be more help," Zoop said apologetically. "Well, it's something to think about at least." Wins replied. "And I still have *a lot* to think about!" he thought. "I think you shouldn't go to school today," Anne suggested. "I can work from home and keep an eye on you, after your night you could do with some rest." Wins was not looking forward to school after Rish's party and as he rarely ever took sick days off he tried his best to hide his relief with a subdued, "Thanks Mum." "I'll call the school when their office opens and tell them you're not feeling well." She said before giving him a heartfelt healing hug.

Wins went to his bedroom, milled around fiddling with old toys and leafed through some books in a series of unsuccessful attempts to occupy his mind, to distract himself by thinking about anything except the two problems he couldn't avoid; Rish, and the PSIReNS. He found his sunglasses and coloured lenses, and laid back in his hammock. He put the green lenses in his sunglasses. "Why do I want to win anyway?" He asked himself, lifting them off the bridge of his nose, then dropping them back down again. He swapped out the lenses for the yellow set. "There was *That Day*," he remembered, although looking back on it now after winning two of The Triples, and the chess tournament... and the football, 'That Day' didn't seem like such a big deal anymore. "Why was it so important to me?" He asked himself. Messing with his sunglasses he switched the yellow set for the blue tinted lenses. Those little kids' games at the summer camp sports day were so insignificant now. "Why did it matter so much? It must have started before that...when?" Wins pushed his mind back as far as he could, back to when he was BB's age. "When did I start thinking winning was more important than everything else?" He continued to play with his sunglasses, the same sunglasses his best friend bought for him on his birthday. On and off, blue tinted and back to normal. He changed the blue lenses for the red pair and put them on. If he was honest with himself, Wins couldn't remember a time when winning *wasn't* on his mind in one form or another. Whether it was small stuff like board games and playground antics or big events like The Triples it felt like that urge to win, that desire had always been there underneath everything else. Wins took off his red-tinted sunglasses and the world shifted to a blueish hue... and something snagged in his mind. He put them back on and the world turned red again. Just like in the woods, if he left them on for long enough, long enough to forget he was wearing them the world appeared to be normal. But when he took them off all the colours returned and it took his brain a minute to readjust. Wins lifted his red-tinted sunglasses and then placed them back down again, and again, and again and finally one last time.

And just like that, the snag in his mind came undone.

"*It doesn't matter why*." Wins said to himself, "It doesn't matter *why* I grew up thinking winning was the most important thing, I just did." Wins took off his sunglasses and covered his eyes with the heels of his hands. "What did Zoop call it, back before Christmas, mind... something?" Wins thought to himself. He took his hands away from his face then aloud he whispered "*Mindset!*" Wins sat up straight. "I've been wearing the same mindset-sunglasses my whole life." His next thought flowed out like the flood after its preceding trickle, "*It doesn't matter how I put them on*; they've been on for so long I forgot I was wearing them, everything has always just *looked* one way to me.

All that matters is I want to take them off, I want to *see* the world as it is, not as I *believe* it is." With that thought Wins saw the world in a new light; it's original light, as surely as if he'd taken off his red-tinted sunglasses.

Gradually, his mindset re-focused his outlook and he began to see the world the way it had always been. "I don't want to want it anymore; all that *winning*. What has it ever got me? Nothing I wanted. I want to want something else *more* than I want to win." He realised. "I don't want to be bored when I win because I was expecting to win the whole time anyway..." His eyes welled up, "I don't want to spend my whole life angry and envious when I lose like Jackson... and to always embarrass myself with tantrums until I'm eighty years old like Great Uncle Quentin. But most of all... most of all I don't want to be like *them!* The PSIReNS don't care about anyone else." Wins saw the source of his own failing, and his possible future reflected in the PSIReNS' insidious, selfish threat. He knew now not only what he *didn't* want to be, but what he wanted to be *instead*. "I don't want to pay for my childish dreams with the misery of my friends. Why should I waste my life chasing empty awards when I could be a better friend, be a better brother, a better son, a better person? I need to look outward, I need to... help." Wins sobbed a blissful catharsis of sorrow. The anguish of ruining his reputation, and poisoning his friendship with Rish, of taking the sports and games he enjoyed so much and breaking them into seeds of his own suffering all washed away with his hot tears. In their place grew a bright contentment, a sweet happiness. A new, true joy. He was free. Free of his own shackles, free of the chains he'd spent his life forging for himself. "I need to tell Rish, I need to tell him everything!" He said. And no truer words had Wins ever spoken.

Wins dried his eyes and went to see his Mum who was working at her desk. "Mum, we need to talk about something." Anne closed her laptop and gave Wins her full attention. "Of course Wins, is it about the PSIReNS?" "No, Yes, Sort of." Wins replied. "It's about Rish Mum." Wins explained what happened at the party, how the PSIReNS took over his body and made him shoot Rish in the back to win the game. He told her how hurt Rish had been and how that hurt caused Rish to say things that made Wins think they weren't friends anymore. Anne wept. "Mum," Wins said, coming to his point, "I know I promised that I wouldn't tell anyone about the PSIReNS, to keep you safe. But that was before, that was when they were just helping me at rugby and maths. It's different now, the whole situation is… well, it's completely changed hasn't it?" Anne nodded. "Even you couldn't have anticipated where things have gotten to now Mum, could you?" Anne shook her head. "I know Rish can keep a secret…" Anne looked up suspiciously, Wins quickly moved on. "And, and if I don't tell him what happened, I'll lose the best friend I ever had. I've realised, that's more than I'm willing to lose, I know I'm difficult sometimes but if I've learnt one thing with all of this it's that some things are more important than I am." Anne spoke through her tears "I had no idea Wins, I couldn't have imagined what this would cost you and you're right, it's too much to pay. If you think Rish can keep it to himself, then tell him everything…" Anne stopped herself mid-breath, "No Wins, you tell him anyway, even if you think he'll tell everyone. You tell him OK." Wins hugged his mother, "Thanks, Mum." He said into her neck. "I think… won't Rish be walking home soon?" Anne suggested. "Yes, not long actually" He agreed. "I'm going to go and wait for him a few streets away from school Mum, OK?" "I hope he understands Wins, I'm sorry, I feel like that's all I've been saying to you lately, but it's true." "I know." Wins said sincerely, before grabbing his backpack and leaving to find Rish.

Wins cycled off to find his best friend, they always walked the same way home from school so he knew the best spot to meet him. "How am I going to say sorry? How am I going to explain all this?" He thought as he rode. Wins realised he wasn't worried or nervous about apologising to Rish, he was actually *scared*. Scared that Rish wouldn't accept his apology, scared that he wouldn't believe his ludicrous and outlandish story about brain-bots and synaesthesia. "What was is Dad said?" Wins asked himself... 'It's OK to be scared... because you can *only* be brave when you *are* scared'. "It's true, Wins thought, "When I fought the PSIReNS I was terrified, but it didn't stop me fighting." However, something didn't quite add up. "So *why* was I brave?" Cruising down the side streets Wins pondered this question "I think it's because I didn't have any other choice, I couldn't back out; it was fight or die... well, fight or let them take me away at least." And so it was for his friendship with Rish. Wins understood that backing out wasn't an option because he didn't want to lose his best friend forever. And if he couldn't even say sorry and explain himself then what kind of a friend could he be. He would have to trust Rish, trust that he would understand. He skidded to a halt at the corner of Clockhouse Road and Prescot Street on their route home from school. Time ticked on and Wins began to grow uncomfortable and anxious in anticipation of a conversation he really wished he didn't have to have.

"What do you want?" An angry voice shouted from halfway down the road. "Rish, I'm really sorry and I want to explain." Incredulous, Rish replied, "What could you possibly say to justify what you did on my birthday?" Wins saw the opening in the conversation and took it, "Well, that's what I wanted to talk about." Rish got closer and Wins tried to hold his attention. "This year, this year some really strange stuff's been going on inside me, and it made me do some crazy things. I want to say sorry. Honestly, I am properly sorry." Rish didn't say anything. "Rish, all I ask is that you listen to me for a few minutes, then if you don't want to talk to me anymore I won't bother you again." Rish nodded and they both turned the corner, Rish walking whilst Wins wheeled their bike along beside them. "I am genuinely sorry, really I am. But, I can see why you wouldn't believe me, so I need to tell you *why* I did what I did, and... I mean, you might not even believe me." Rish didn't seem moved, but Wins continued. "You know how I got good at sports this year and won the first two Triples?" Rish instinctively nodded "And that time in the middle of autumn term, when the teacher thought I'd cheated in Maths? And the chess tournament with my Great uncle?" Rish quietly nodded again. "Well, it wasn't because of *me* exactly." Rish turned his head to look at Wins. "Something happened to me last year and it made me... quicker and smarter." Rish stopped walking, "What are you talking about?" He asked sarcastically, "What... You caught a genius disease or something and it made you a sports star?" Rish stared at Wins with unbelieving eyes. Wins gazed back with a serious stare. "You know what my Mum does right?" Rish, taken aback was made to think for a moment "Erm, she does like, brain-science or something right?" "Exactly." Wins said starkly "She's been working on something to help people with broken brains, nanobots, tiny robots that are meant to fix people's brains." Wins couldn't tell if Rish was listening intently or thought he was making the whole thing up. "Last year, just after we started at Aldershot, I coped a massive dose of her PSIReNS, the nanobots she was building." "WHAT? You cannot be serious, you can't expect me to believe that, and even if I did what difference does that make to shooting me in the back so you could win that game of laser tag?" Wins saw he was losing credibility in Rish's eyes so switched to a different tactic.

"Hear me out, Rish." Rish sighed, "OK, but this better make sense fast or I'm walking." Wins looked Rish dead in the eye and said "Mum's PSIReNS; *Problem Solving* Independent Re-cognition NanoNeuroNet Subsystem, were made to repair brains with dementia, brains that didn't work properly. But my brain was healthy so they did something different, they tried to make it so I always got what I wanted. And what I've always wanted was to *win*." Rish weighed up the explanation as Wins continued, "They gave me powers..." Rish was taken now, "What, like *super-powers*?" "Well, not exactly, they..." Rish's characteristic enthusiasm returned. "wwwhhhAAAA?" he vocalised, as if a cog had fallen into place and kicked the machinery of his mind into high gear. "SO THAT'S HOW YOU WON THE FREESTYLE MEDLEY!" Rish grabbed his own face, "AND THE CHESS! YOU BEAT A GRAND MASTER AT CHESS WINS!" Wins tried to play it down, "Yeah, but, let me explain" Rish wasn't waiting for any more explanation. "AND YOU USED YOUR SUPER-POWERS TO BEAT JACKSON IN THE OF ROAD SCRAMBLE!" "Not exactly." Wins said trying desperately to get the conversation back on track. "AND THE FOOTBALL... YOU BEAT MASSLANDS... ON. YOUR. OWN!" Wins made his voice more assertive, "Rish. Please listen, that football match is where it all started going wrong and that's what I want to tell you about."

Rish settled and Wins laid everything out. "At first, the PSIReNS gave me synaesthesia." Rish butted in again, "Synaes-what-ia?" "Let me explain Rish, I thought I was going crazy. I started seeing colours that weren't there when I was playing games, I could tell what the answers were in maths because of the numbers' personalities, I started smelling chance and tasting danger." Rish's jaw hung agape. "In the beginning, it seemed harmless. Strange, but harmless. And it was helping me, like when I climbed up the indoor wall in P.E., and all the winning made me feel good. I promised my Mum I wouldn't tell anyone, even you, because she would get in trouble if people found out... and she's been trying to work on a cure, a way to 'switch them off' in the meantime." Wins' face grew serious, "Then the PSIReNS began changing my perceptions, I could *see* without seeing; that's how I won the swimming, and the chess and the bike race in the woods. When I compete they wake up and they give me vision over everything, I can see where I need to go to beat people in races, or which move to make to win a game of chess... I can tell when people are sneaking up behind me for a tackle in football..." "SO THEY ARE SUPERPOWERS!" Rish insisted. "No Rish, they *aren't* superpowers." Rish smiled for the first time. "They flipping well sound like superpowers to me mate." Wins smiled back. "I suppose, you could see them that way. But, when I was playing that match against Masslands something changed." Wins paused. "What?" Rish asked, starting to show concern.

Wins hardened his heart to keep his emotions subdued. "The PSIReNS took over, they pushed me into the backseat of my brain and took control of my body, I couldn't help it, they made my body tackle my own players so I would win the game for the team, and all I could do was watch." "Oh My Days!" Rish gasped, "That sounds horrible, were you scared?" Wins held back a tear. "Yeah, I was terrified Rish, it was the worst experience of my life... until your party." Wins looked at his best friend and waited for him to click. Like a ticking clock, Rish's expressions showed his mind's workings as he pieced it all together, then a look of shock hit him like a punch in the face. "So, when you shot me in the back, it wasn't you at all?" Wins nodded. "And that's why you said you were feeling ill and didn't want to play the second game?" Wins nodded again. "So, why didn't you shoot me in the first game?" Rish asked. "The rules were different, only the other team were competing with me. But once the other team were out of the way in the second game; you were the only thing standing in the way, right in between me and the control console at the centre of the base." Wins couldn't hold back anymore. "I'm so sorry, I couldn't stop it, I was watching it all happen and I couldn't stop it." Rish was speechless. The two boys composed themselves. "Can you forgive me?" Wins asked softly. "There's nothing to forgive mate." Rish said matter-of-factly, "I couldn't have known before, but now I do, there's nothing to say sorry for. *I'm* sorry I was so harsh."

A relief fell from Wins. He felt that choking, crushing rope unravel from his chest and blow away in the breeze. He sighed, and brightened inside. "Thanks. I honestly didn't know if you'd believe me." Wins reached into his backpack and pulled out Rish's belated birthday present. "I got you this after the bike race, they helped me win... at least I think they did." Rish opened the box and saw a brand new set of the same sunglasses he had bought Wins for his birthday. "Thanks dude." Rish said, pulling the frames out and looking at the coloured lenses. "Last night my glasses helped me realise something Rish; in the same way that if I wear one set of coloured lenses for too long their effect disappears and everything starts to look normal, I've spent my whole life trying to win and thinking that obsession was normal too. And in the end, what did it get me? Winning is a sure fire way to lose at life Rish, I see that now. But I wouldn't have ever worked that out without the sunglasses you bought me." "Woah dude, that's deep." Rish whispered, pausing he put on the green lenses. "Thanks. So, what you gonna do about these PSIReNS?" "I have a plan." Wins said confidently. "I don't think my family are going to like it, but I have a plan and I think it could work."

The two friends walked home as Wins told Rish about his journey into his own mindscape and his plan; how he was going to have to compete in the last of The Triples... how he was going to have to battle the PSIReNS and try to win the triathlon.

20: Endgame

As Wins had hoped, Rish understood the need for secrecy surrounding the PSIReNS and what had happened to his best friend which made the last few weeks of summer term more bearable. However, no-one else knew, or could know which meant everyone else remained hostile to him. Shunned by his friends after the events at laser tag and despised by the rest of the school because of his awful behaviour in on the football field Wins didn't have an easy ride, to say the least. But strengthened by Rish's support, Wins used the quiet times to consider his plan. He knew he needed the atmosphere of competition the triathlon would provide to draw the PSIReNS out, and he knew this would mean they would be distracted. Wins realised this would be his best chance to fight them in the arena of his mindscape. The only detail he couldn't pin down was exactly *how* he could beat them at their own game. How he could force them into an 'infinity loop', as his Mum had suggested.

The date for the final event of The Triples, the Aldershot Achievers' Award, was set for the Sunday before the last week of term. Cautious of rousing the sleeping PSIReNS before he could use the full power of distraction that the triathlon would provide, Wins avoided physical training before the event. He was mindful of eating well and spent many hours assessing the rugged route for the cross country run, observing the open water at Lake Leo Carrillo where the swimming section would take place as well as riding up Jeffrey's Hill to cruise round the wicked hairpin bends known as 'Dead Man's Fingers' which sloped down to the finish line. Although he didn't know exactly what he'd need to do when he faced the PSIReNS, he knew one way or another it would be the final time he did. It must be done then or he would spend the rest of his life living in fear of them… and that was not an option Wins would ever accept. The night before the triathlon he decided it was time to tell his family what his intentions were. Once BB had been bathed and settled to bed he explained his plan, or what there was of it at least, to Zoop and his parents. Sitting down to eat supper he broached the subject frankly, "I need to compete tomorrow." His parents, taken aback by the sudden statement, were equally stark in their reply, "Absolutely not!" Ed asserted. "Wins, after everything that's happened you can't put yourself at risk like that again." Moving the subject away from the triathlon Anne tried to offer another option, "I've been working on something that might be able to disable the PSIReNS." Wins had no idea this was a possibility, "Really? What? How will it work?" Anne sighed. "It's not ideal, and I'm not sure its … well, it's a pretty blunt tool to be honest." Wins pressed her, "Just tell me what it is Mum." Anne put down her knife and fork. "I know it will work…" Ed was ecstatic, "That's great! See Wins, you don't need to compete after all." Anne quietly continued, "I mean, I know it will shut down the **PSIReNS**, but I don't know what shutting down the **PSIReNS** will do to **Wins**." Zoop voiced all their concerns, "What do you mean Mum?" Anne, almost shameful, explained, "It's a focused electromagnetic pulse… like a finely tuned microwave beam; It will fry the PSIReNS, wipe them clean and render them inert." Wins was worried. "You want to microwave my brain? Not a chance!" Anne, unsuccessfully worked to put his mind at ease, "No, it's not like cooking food; it will zap them and wipe out their programming. They'll just be tiny non-functional specks of inorganic matter afterwards." Wins wasn't satisfied, "But you said you won't know what effect that will have on me though?" Anne acknowledged the unknown factor in her solution, "Yes, we don't know what turning all the PSIReNS off at once will do to you, they are so thoroughly integrated into your brain now that hitting them with the electromagnetic microwave beam, zapping them into dust might be like..." her voiced hushed "ripping out bundles of nerves from your brain." Wins felt the fury heat his face, "THIS IS YOUR SOLUTION?! Fry my brain and hope for the best?!" Anne motioned to speak. "NO WAY! NO CHANCE!" Ed tried to break up the escalating argument. "No one is microwaving anyone's brains!" He said to Anne. "And no one is competing in any triathlons Wins!" "I have a plan..." Wins started to stay. "NO!" Ed yelled, slamming his fist down on the table. "You are not taking part in *any* competitions again Wins, not until your Mother has found a way to get those PSIReNS out without ripping your brain apart... honestly Anne, what were you thinking?" "Ed, that's an oversimplification of what I'm trying to achieve." Ed was fuming "THAT'S IT! I'VE HEARD ENOUGH! You lot are always off on your adventures and I'm left in the dust wondering what just happened, trying to be the good father and good husband. But look at this mess." Ed scowled at his family, "I'm constantly being told to listen, and compromise and calm down, but where has that got us? There is nothing, **NOTHING** more dangerous than someone who *thinks* they know what they are doing... and *doesn't!*" Ed shot a pointed look at his wife then took a moment to calm himself.

"My job is to provide and to keep you all safe, and I've failed. I won't allow this to go on any further. Wins, you are not taking part tomorrow and that's the end of *that* matter. Anne, you are not microwaving our son's brain and that's the end of *that* matter. Think of something else." Ed, tearing under the stress of the conversation ate his food tasting nothing, numb with upset. Wins wanted to explain that he had a plan, that his plan was something else, "But Dad I..." Ed snapped, "NO!" he screamed.

"NO! NO! NO! What part of this don't you understand Wins, I'm not going to let you come to harm!" Wins seized his plate and rushed to his room insulted and angered that neither of his parents would listen to him. "Winston Winters you get back here right now or you are grounded." Ed shouted after him "Let him be Ed." Anne commanded, Ed glared at his wife, a hard seething stare conveying every suppressed thought and feeling he'd kept bottled up. The heat of his blameful rage was impossible to ignore and too much for Anne to abide. She broke into tears and left the table with empty hands and an empty stomach.

Ed turned his ire back to Wins and yelled across the house, "You are grounded for the week Wins, YOU. ARE. NOT. GOING. TOMORROW!" "Dad…" Zoop said hoping to cool his mood. "Enough Zoop, I don't need any of your psychobabble, alright. No one thinks of me in all of this. I give and I provide and I work for all of you and how is all my love is repaid? By ignoring me, by never listening when *I* have something to say. No more, we are in this mess because *I* didn't put my foot down earlier." Zoop, realising her father did not want to talk, finished her supper in silence and left Ed to stew in his own thoughts.

Wins, alone in his room, knew what he must do. "They didn't even give me a chance to explain," he thought, "but I *have* to do this. If I don't do it now, I might never get another chance to…" he nearly thought the word 'win' but caught himself in time, "No, not *win* against the PSIReNS, this isn't about winning; it's about *surviving*."

Wins packed his backpack ready for the next morning and set about writing a letter to his parents. He explained that he needed to fight the PSIReNS, beat them into submission or better; destroy them outright. But every day he didn't confront them was a day they grew stronger, and soon they would become too strong to fight. He wrote that the triathlon was his best and only chance to draw them out, and that he hoped in their distracted state he would stand a fighting chance to take back control of his mind. His thoughts turned now to the possibility of failure, the realistic chance that the PSIReNS might actually defeat him, capture him and force him down into the abyss at the bottom of his mind. The final paragraph of Wins' letter was smudged with tear marks;

If the next time you see me I am not myself, if I don't seem right and if I seem to have lost myself then the PSIReNS have me. If after the triathlon I am gone, let Mum use her solation because I will be lost to them and so there will be nothing left to lose."

Wins hid the note and went to bed, nervous due to the stakes of the gambit, but excited that he was finally taking back control of his life.

Rising for breakfast Wins made out he was in a non-talkative bad mood. The truth was he was a terrible liar and feared being drawn into any kind of conversation with his family might lead to an accidental confession. On leaving the table Ed said, "I'm sorry I got so angry last night Mister, it's only because I love you all and can't stand to see anything happen to you." Wins gave his dad an understanding look but breathed no words. "But," Ed went on, "you're still grounded today OK. I'm not having you take part in that triathlon." Seeing this as the perfect opportunity to hide in plain sight Wins stormed off to his room and slammed the door just to make sure everyone believed he'd be keeping himself to himself all day, dressed for the event and re-checked his backpack. Wins waited until he heard the shower run knowing this meant his dad would be out of the picture. With his mum in bed and his sister still asleep this was his chance; He put the note on his desk under an old Star Wars toy and, quietly closing his bedroom door behind him, snuck downstairs.

Wins crept to the front door and slowly teased it open. Setting foot out of his homestead he heard a tiny voice behind him, "Bye-bye Big Brother." He turned to see BB standing in the corridor staring at him with wide-eyed wonder. Wins knelt down and raised a finger to his lips "Shhhh" He picked up his Baby Brother and gave him a heartfelt hug knowing full well it may be their last. "Bye bye BB" Wins whispered, "See you later… I hope." He let go of his baby brother and looked him in the eye. "Don't tell Mum and Dad you saw me, OK?" BB grinned a cheeky grin, "OK Winshtun." he said… almost as if he knew what Wins was up to.

Wins walked his bike a few houses down the road before donning his helmet, hopping on and beginning the cycle to the marshalling point at the edge of Lake Leo Carrillo. Mindful of what lay ahead Wins refused to dwell on the size of the task he intended to undertake. Not only must he compete in the triathlon but he meant to fight the PSIReNS the whole way. For now, he thought only about his breathing and the rhythm of his peddles turning, turning, turning.

Arriving at the marshalling point he saw most of the other students were already registered and displayed their racing bibs on their chests and backs. The event turned out to be more popular than anyone predicted. Perhaps his previous two wins had encouraged others, or maybe it just seemed like more fun than a pool swim or a woodland bike race? It didn't matter, more than seventy teenagers were stretching out and gearing up for the final event of the Aldershot Academy Achievers' Award. Wins signed up on the register and was given his racing bib, the marshal attached it to his t-shirt, "Double lucky!" He looked up to see Rish. "You're here!" Wins said, stating the obvious. "Double lucky?" he asked curiously. "77; double lucky!" Rish said pointing to his bib. "Ha! I'll take all I can get." Wins admitted. "Are you all set? Have you found your bike yet?" Wins was confused, "What do you mean? I brought ours." Rish gestured to the other side of the lake, they have a bunch of racing bikes over there, all identical, you were supposed to go and set the handlebars and seat height ready for after the open water swim." "WHAT?!" Wins said, stymied by the news. "The cross country race starts in a few minutes, I won't have time to get there and back!" "Don't worry," Rish said calmly, "I'll go and get your bike prepped; Number 77, easy." "How will you know how far to lower the seat and handlebars though?" Rish made an expression to imply something obvious was staring them in the face then looked at their bike. "Ohhhhh! Of course." Wins said, remembering how they were always adjusting the saddle and handlebars of the Continuum Stump Jumper mk8 mountain bike every time they shared ownership. "Rish, can you take my bag as well, it has my sunglasses and riding kit for after the swim." "Sure," Rish said. Wins grabbed a large chocolate bar from his backpack and gave the bag to his best friend. "Time to fuel up." Wins explained. "Good luck dude," Rish said. "Should I be… worried?" Wins realised that there was no going back now. "I… I hope not," he replied honestly. The two friends shared one last look of solidarity and Rish ran off on the path to the far side of the Lake Leo Carrillo whilst Wins headed to the starting line.

Wins made sure his swimming goggles were secure around his neck ready for the swim after the running race and tucked his tracksuit bottoms into his socks to keep out the dirt and pebbles. A map of the course was drawn on a chalkboard indicating the 5-kilometre loop over turfy fields, past the forest, through farmland and up the steep slopes before the drop down to the lake. Marshalls were positioned where the track turned corners, and piles of white flour sporadically marked the course. Wins felt tiny next to the eighty or so bigger kids. As they jostled for the best starting position Wins saw Jackson Treehorn through the crowd, deep in his own world he was enacting the same choreographed stretches and finger-tip touching ritual Wins witnessed at the previous two Triples. Coach Quintana's voice bellowed from a megaphone. "We are about to start the race, at the sound of the starter's pistol begin your run around the course to the lake shore. Anyone found without a helmet whilst riding their bike or cutting the course will be disqualified, and remember this is a cross country run not a sprint, so pace yourselves."

Coach Quintana counted down from ten. Wins felt the flicker grow inside him and saw the sparkles in the air, a fine electrical crackle teased his ears from far away. "...3, ...2, ...1 BANG" With the starter's pistol Wins was awash with the PSIReNS song.

Clumps of mud flung upwards from the eighty pairs of heels as the mob stormed forwards, Wins saw his thalweg condense in the morning air undulating as though it were alive, it clung to the ground highlighting the path of least resistance upon the firmest soil and flattest trail. He charged on with the pack, feeling them all around him but more, feeling the PSIReNS pushing him from behind. Their needles and knives pricked at his calves forcing his pounding pace with their unrelenting rhythm. Looking diagonally to his sides Wins smelt foul stenches strike his nostrils like laser beams from discrete dips in the field around which his thalweg wound. A taller kid rushed past him, prompting a bitter coffee-like taste to fill his mouth, and ran straight across a collection of the stinking spots. The kid's left foot disappeared down one and with a crepitus crunch his ankle bent exactly how it shouldn't, grabbing his leg he let out an unnatural wail of pain. "Rabbit holes," he realised, "The field must be riddled with rabbit warrens." Unable to keep up with the longer legged kids Wins tried letting his pace slip, a first challenge to the authority of the PSIReNS, their razor-bladed punishment for his disobedience whipped the back of his legs, the agony coercing him to keep up their desired rate.

The first marshal was sending the runners to his left, pointing towards the edge of the forest with large day-glow orange beacon bars. Wins flowed with his thalweg round the corner and overtook some uncoordinated runners who were already showing their fatigue. Ahead he saw the front of the pack passing the woodland, he saw the reverberating sound of their thumping footsteps in the earth, one of the runner's tempos stood out, its familiarity somehow stark against the backdrop of everyone else's noise. He couldn't see Jackson's face but he knew he was there, leading the forerunners. Wins pushed on, gaining on Jackson's group. Something flickered in the forest, his thalweg rose from the sodden earth and dipped back down again afterwards. Fearing the pain of defying the PSIReNS Wins leapt over the turf with his arcing thalweg as a flickering hare shot out of the thickets into the field. "They must be spooked by the runners." Wins thought. More hares ran out of the woods, Wins saw their characteristic bounding motion through the greenery before they appeared on the trail. Closing on Jackson's pack Wins remembered what was about to happen. A drove of large hares exploded from the forest and sprung straight through the lead runners. A girl and boy were knocked off their feet by the skittish creatures, dispersing the runners and momentarily distractingly them from the race. Two more competitors tripped over the fallen runners allowing Wins to overtake them in their panic.

Past the woods now the next marshal guided the race towards a mossy stone wall with only a single stile to allow passage over it. Jackson was first to cross into the field of cows followed by six others. A seventh rapidly approached the stile, as she slowed to climb it Wins flowed with his corded tingling thalweg past her, and with a single skip hopped over the wooden step and stone wall landing on the other side in a fluid roll, rising into a sprint across the cattle field. The field sloped gently downwards before him, it looked and smelt like there were more cow pats than there was grass. Behind he heard pursuing runners slip and fall in the muddy slurry, vocalising their disgust. Without warning Wins' thalweg bent away from the centre of the field in the direction of a siding then back round to the stile in the lower corner directly in front of him. "What the? Are the PSIReNS trying to trick me somehow?" Wins wondered, but no sooner had he asked himself the question than it was answered. The herd of curious cattle in the farmer's field, having taken an interest in the runners in front of Wins, began gravitating towards them. Jackson made it over the stile with one other kid but the others found themselves surrounded by the humongous farm animals who were slowly corralling them into the corner of the field. Wins followed the path before him and ran up and over the second stile without breaking his rhythm.

The land rose into a steep slope, as it got higher the earth was drained of water, the week of summer sun before the race day had left the grass browned and turned the soil to dust. Wins saw the two lead runners struggling with the abrupt upward incline, their heavier frames and larger mass working against them. Wins noticed the frequency of his thalweg pulse more rapidly "NO." he said to them "*I* choose, not *you.*" The PSIReNS' wrath was instant; their needles pressed into the back of his body pushing him on. Wins tried to resist, forcing himself back onto their pain but something new happened, something impossible to ignore. He felt a scorching blaze blister his back. He couldn't defy instinct, millions of years of evolution had programmed his body to flee from fire and the PSIReNS knew that triggering this ingrained reflexive response to escape was the only way left to drive him forwards. Chased by burning agony Wins sped up the incline of the dry hill like a burning horse to meet his rival.

Jackson's blood was up, the adrenaline and exertion of the event were working him into a frenzy, seeing Wins approach he snapped at him, "CHEATER!" Gasping for breath Jackson and the other kid pushed themselves as hard as they could, but they didn't have the intense physical pain of loss biting at their heels as Wins did. "Cheater?" Wins thought, "Yes, I suppose maybe I am a cheater after all." The word echoed in his mind, "Cheater... Cheater?... Cheetah? ...*Cheetah!*" The team of rivals in control of Wins' body plucked that thought from his mindscape and formulated a last-ditch intuitive tactic.

The incline was more than 45 degrees now, no sooner than he pictured the African big cat running he felt the PSIReNS' knives push his shoulders down and force his hands to the ground. His thalweg's frequency switched to something more animalistic, thick red strands laced the dirt in an unfamiliar quaternary pattern. Wins' back arched inwards painfully, his legs stretched out and his arms pushed forwards. As his palms hit the ground his back arched outwards into a bridge bringing his feet up past his hands then when his toes gripped the hill his back flicked into that painful inverted archway once more flinging his arms forwards again. Repeating the feline rhythm two, three, four, five, six more times Wins flew over the crest of the hill leaving Jackson and the other boy sucking up clouds of his dust. With one last cheetah-stroke Wins saw what the PSIReNS planned for him.

His thalweg crashed down the hill to the lakeshore in wild looping spirals, even with the benefit of the PSIReNS' supra-sense he couldn't tell if there were sharp rocks or splintered sticks hidden under the dry earth on the downward slope. "THIS IS MADNESS." he yelled aloud. Their wordless voice filled his mind "ROLL." With that, he was flung into the backseat of his mind and made to watch his body form a broken hoop from his outstretched arms, diagonally over his back, round his legs and back to his fingers whereupon it rolled down the hill over and over like a runaway rollercoaster ride. At the bottom of the slope, his body found its feet and with the physical jolt Wins was back in control. Jackson bundled down the hill like a giant toddler a mere 30 seconds behind him. "THIS IS IT. *NO MORE!*" Wins demanded. The PSIReNS seized control of Wins' body again, from the backseat of his mind Wins watched them command his limbs to strip away his running shoes, tracksuit and t-shirt leaving only his swimming shorts and goggles on his body. His feet trampled his racing bib into the sandy shore whilst his legs ran toward the warm waters of Lake Leo Carrillo. To his astonishment, his hands pulled his swimming goggles over his head and dropped them at the beachside. Wins' body rushed into the lake and when waist high it dove under the waters...

Perception lost its singular point of view; he was outside of his body seeing everything at once, only this time he was no longer in control. The PSIReNS saw all; their power to process information performing at its peak picking out the slightest vibrations in the underwater amphitheatre of the lake to build a picture of what lay behind and beneath. All Wins could do was watch. As the trailing children splashed into the lake from the shoreline the shallows became an open-water battlefield. However, the increased noise of the swimmers only added to the information available to the PSIReNS, the additional reverberations and underwater echoes building up the data available for them to work with. From his helpless position held fast and removed from control, Wins saw everything they saw. An all-encompassing vision of the lake from shore to shore, surface to bed, developed in his mind and he began to understand what they had planned. Whilst the bigger swimmers held the advantage over Wins' smaller body and were swiftly gaining on him the PSIReNS had found the river that fed Lake Leo Carrillo, and the tributary that the lake supplied. A flow of cold water ran across the lake bed from the river behind them to the river leaving on the other side; A *real* thalweg.

"They can't really expect my body to survive a dive like that?

Right to the bottom of the lake? I'll drown for sure." Wins thought. Beyond control Wins watched his body take three deep inhalations of fresh air each followed by three total exhalations expelling lung-fulls carbon-dioxide, and finally one last gulp of air filling his chest to capacity. With Jackson a few metres behind him, the PSIReNS drove his body to the depths of the lake, controlling his buoyancy with a slow and precise release of exhaled breath. Wins felt his body pulled along with the cold current, the thalweg, connecting the two rivers. It drew him along at speed, faster than anyone would have been able to swim at the surface. Wins' lungs started to burn as carbon-dioxide built up and his oxygen depleted. He saw the periphery of his echolocation fade and bright white stars twinkle where his eyes would have been looking. Wins was about to pass out, "YOU ARE GOING TO KILL US!" he screamed. Menacing laughter ricocheted in return "US." The PSIReNS said.

"They're winning," he thought. "It's not enough that they are taking my body, but they are taking *my* mind as well." Above his body, the water brightened. "We're near the surface." Wins realised. "The lack of oxygen must be affecting them too." He fought for control and managed to turn his body upwards, out of the thalweg. He rushed to the surface of the lake breaching it like a whale, expelling the poisonous gas from his chest. Two strokes later his feet were on the lake bed

He waded to the shore, the first to arrive. Collapsed to his knees and caught his life in his lungs.

The moment his blood was enriched the PSIReNS awoke again and rode his body over the lakeshore to the bicycle ranks. Rather than the mountain bikes Wins originally expected; eighty or so racing bikes were mounted on rows of racks, their narrow wheels and thin frames crowned with drop-handlebars that looped downwards and back in pairs of semi circles to enable riders to keep a low profile whilst racing. Wins was powerless to seize control from the PSIReNS before they found bike number 77. He watched them put on his lightweight trainers then start to the bike. "HELMET!" he commanded. "LONGSLEEVE" he demanded but they ignored him, forcing him back. Out of the corner of his eye he spotted his sunglasses, he willed as hard as he could to wear those red lenses, but the PSIReNS resisted his desire.

Wins watched his body straddle the bike, he couldn't risk crashing without a helmet but the PSIReNS didn't seem concerned. "They want to win." he thought "I need to make them want to put on my helmet." Wins concentrated, shouting his thoughts as loud as he could "WE'LL BE DISQUALIFIED IF WE DON'T USE THE HELMET!" To his grateful surprise, his right arm reached out and grabbed it, placed it over his head and fastened the strap. "Maybe there is something I can do after all." He thought. Wins' body pulled the racing bike from its mount and wearing only trainers, swimming shorts and his helmet set off up Jeffrey's Hill. The first of the other competitors were just leaving the water when Wins heard the obnoxious *yelp-yelp-yelp* of a car-horn. As his body swung the bike around the first bend onto the upward slope Wins saw his parents step out of their car followed by Zoop who was carrying BB in her arms. Clasped in BB's hand was the old Star Wars figure he'd left on his desk to hold his note in place. "WINS!" they shouted begging and beseeching him to quit the race. But it was too late. He was already halfway to the second bend of the course leaving them to rush back into their car, heading back around the hill to the finish line.

The PSIReNS charged up Jeffrey's Hill with a clear and powerful head start. Wins watched on as before, held firm in the back-seat of his mind. The harder he pushed to come up and regain control the harder the PSIReNS heel pushed him back down. Wins wondered, "If I can't fight them, maybe I can trick them?" Wins turned his attention inwards, he noticed that the rug upon which his conscious mind sat was threadbare. He picked at it, pulling on the strands worn loose by the force of the PSIReNS' bursting up into the driver's seat of his mind every time they took control of his body. Separating the sparse fabric that held his consciousness aloft Wins let the sole of the PSIReNS boot press down on him, pushing him between the fragmented filaments. He saw movement below... the part of his mind that was greater than the sum of its parts... *His-Self*. It beckoned him down. Together they tore a hole in the fabric that tied his mind together and he slipped below to search for the fight, the fight that the PSIReNS didn't know was coming.

Wins followed his formless Shape back down to the cusp of the abyss at the bottom of his mind. His world shattered as lightening clapped in deafening, threatening roars of dominance. The firmament rumbled and those sparkling silvery splinters rushed up in naked rage. Wins pulled His Shape to him and squeezed it into his core, keeping it safe from harm. The serpentine monster spread out its dragon wings enveloping him, and in its wordless voice set their terms; "YOUR BODY. IS OURS. YOU ARE TRAPPED. IN HERE. WITH US."

Wins saw what they saw, he saw their vision running in only one direction: out. Out of his mind, out of themselves. "What did Mum say? 'They aren't self-aware'... What did Zoop suggest?... 'They can't *introspect*'...they can't look *inside*" And with that thought, he knew what he must do. Wins opened himself up, dropped his defences and let the PSIReNS' serpentine splinters take him. Their pearlescent wings surrounded him, their fangs bit into his form and swallowed him down into the abyss below.

Beneath the murky silts at the depths of his mind Wins found the fanning roots of his infinity tree, the intricate and unfathomable source of his mind growing from its firmament under its foundations. Looking up he could see the race taking place, the PSIReNS holding first place just ahead of Jackson at the peak of Jeffrey's Hill. They were beginning the downhill run to the final stretch. Focusing his attention inward once more he caught sight of a silvery glimmer at the lowest point from whence the roots of his mind grew. Examining it he found a broad stalk, an ancient stalagmite jutting up like a pillar, supporting the weight of the infinity tree. Wrapped around it, buried within its girth were stranded silvery shards leading off in a glimmering chain up, out of the abyss to the PSIReNS in the driving seat at the top of Wins' mind. He touched the pillar and knew what it was, his selfishness, his primal childish desire to be better than everyone else, his need to be wanted and liked by others... his drive to win. Wins felt around in the gloom, immediately adjacent to the selfish pillar he found a new grown root reaching downwards from his infinity tree like a stalactite, its lowermost tip was sharp but didn't quite reach the foundations from where the other pillar was forged. He touched the new grown root and its warmth ran through him in waves of love. It was his desire to change, his desire to improve himself, his want to be a better person, to learn, to put other's first for once; his selflessness.

Looking up he could see through the PSIReNS' eyes, he could see with their visionary supra-sense; time was moving slowly like the world was almost at a standstill. His body was coming to the penultimate bend of Dead Man's Fingers, the PSIReNS were slowing for the hairpin turn in keeping with their thalweg, but Jackson was... "No, he couldn't be... that wouldn't work on a racing bike." Jackson was about to mount the rocky wall of the hill as Wins had done in Oxhey Woods, but his racing bike's narrow wheels and lightweight frame weren't designed for that, "He's going to injure himself, he was going to..."

Unable to look within themselves the PSIReNS plan to hold him and keep him from control neglected to consider how far down into his mind they would have to bury him. In an instant of epiphany, Wins clamped himself around the PSIReNS' gleaming chain and heaved it to the newly grown root of his selflessness. The moment the chain touched the root a potent charge of emotional energy arced between the two anchoring points. A dazzling light brighter than the birth of a new star exploded forth. Enduring the blinding blast Wins wrapped the PSIReNS' gleaming tail around the downward pointing stalactite and fixed it there. "THIS IS MY MIND." He proclaimed. The chain glowed with the freezing fury of a dictator facing its fatal end. He saw his mind open above him. Instead of the hot fiery angers he'd fermented in his past Wins cultivated an icy, calculating anger and turned it against his foe; "THIS IS MY MIND, ALL THE WAY DOWN..." He said laying down the new law. "I'M NOT TRAPPED IN HERE WITH *YOU*, YOU PSIReNS ARE TRAPPED IN HERE... *WITH ME!*"

He clasped the PSIReNS' chain and rode it, instantaneously arriving in his driving seat, on the racing bike, in full control of his mind, his body *and* the PSIReNS.

He visualised an image of his surroundings and inspected every detail in less than a fraction of a second. He saw his thalweg turn to his right around the penultimate corner of Dead Man's Fingers high above the crowd of spectators. But Jackson... Jackson was about to mount the near-vertical wall at the apex of the corner to his left. Wins forced the PSIReNS to comply with his wishes and a new thalweg appeared, but not for himself... for Jackson. Dark blue, flickering in and out of existence it showed Jackson's inevitable path up the rock face, into too tight a turn, jarring in a crevice hidden by the roots of a snarled overhanging tree trapping the front wheel of his bike and sending him careening over the cliff's edge.

"SAVE HIM!" Wins commanded. "YOU ARE *MINE*, SAVE HIM NOW!" The PSIReNS tried to resist Wins' will but their razor-edged knives and blistering fire glanced of him like a shower of soft rain. Wins' thalweg snapped off the road and over the cliffside, flicking from red to blue, bouncing between the two potential routes; One to win at the cost of Jackson's life, the other to save Jackson's life at the cost of losing the race. For Wins the choice was clear. He fixed his thalweg in place, forcing it to intersect with Jackson's inevitable fate producing a burst of white laser-light... then let time's arrow fly.

He released his brake and peddled hard directly towards the corner where the road bent round to the right and the barrier guarded the sheer drop-off on the other side. To his left he saw the sound of Jackson speed past, aiming himself at the hard incline of the rocky wall. Wins lifted his heels onto the short horizontal beam of the racing bike's drop-handlebars and jammed on the front brake, the rear wheel, frame and saddle catapulted upwards. Before the front tyre hit the barrier Wins, now crouching on the handlebars of the racing bike pushed hard with his legs launching himself over this cliff-edge with nothing but air between his body and the ground a hundred metres below. Beside him, Jackson's bike crumpled under the force of the crash and he was thrown head first over the cliff edge.

In a frozen moment Wins looked into his rival's eyes and saw the light of Jackson's life dash away leaving behind only the inescapable knowledge that he was about to die. Jackson's forearm smashed into a rock spinning him head-over-heels in a spiralling somersault.

All was going to plan.

Wins reached backward over his head with his hands and forced his feet back making a crescent of his body. The PSIReNS' supra-sensory vision showed him where to grab, their laser-light guiding his body. The force of the racing bike's front brake followed by its front tyre hitting the barrier flipped the bike up behind him sending its rear tyre into Wins' backward stretching grasp. He caught the rear tyre with both hands and pulled the frame round in a wide angular arc, pointing it straight up above him, its folded front wheel sitting underneath its downward curving drop-handlebars. Mid-air, Wins snapped his legs shut like scissors around Jackson's ribs, locking his ankles under his flailing arms. The sudden loss of momentum threw the drop-handlebars of Wins' ruined bike into the branches of the gnarled old tree overhanging the deathly drop below.

Wins felt a cataclysmic shift in his mind, he saw the PSIReNS' anchor rent loose shattering the foundational pillar of his selfish desires into fragments... he heard them wailing in confusion as they found themselves still bound at that pillar's base where it had originally grown from, but with the support of its trunk now gone the weight of his mind shuddered down to rest upon the newly grown root. The downwards pointing stalactite of his desire to help, of his selflessness, piercing into the firmament beneath the foundations of his mind pinching the PSIReNS' anchor tight between it and the indomitable strength of his psyche.

A new self was born then, a new boy forged himself into existence with that act. Wins looked within himself and saw his nemesis, his saviour the PSIReNS; forever trapped in the bottom of his brain, permanently bound betwixt his old selfish desire to win and his newly formed want, his self-made will to help. No longer could his former desires, or the PSIReNS' seductive song, hold any sway over his choices again. As they had planned to imprison him in the abyss beneath his mind, so he had ensnared them in the same dungeon and locked their cell with the impossible task of delivering two opposing outcomes; winning and losing at once.

The PSIReNS' supra-sensory sight evaporated as the two boys met at their intersecting thalwegs and his mind fell quiet. For the first time in almost a year Wins was alone in his own head. His body was yanked with the sudden full force of Jackson Treehorn's dead weight pulling down on his legs and the over-hanging tree's failing strength pulling up on the battered racing bike which held them both in the air.

Wins heard a series of sharp snaps in his legs. Shooting pain ripped up from his knees and ankles, coalesced at the top of his thighs and surged along his spine. Wins let out a primal scream, like a newborn taking its first breath. Jackson joined his shrieking, his forearm was bent diagonally half way between his wrist and elbow. Quickly his cries of agony changed timbre, and he realised Jackson was laughing. A cathartic laugh, disbelieving his own survival Jackson wept in physical pain and laughed in existential relief. "Hold on." Wins told Jackson, the pain in his legs verging on unbearable. As he'd calculated when he still had use of the PSIReNS' insights the overhanging tree didn't hold them for long. Its trunk crunched and split lengthways, the resulting break swept the boys back onto the sidings of the road. They landed on the rocky ground in a heap with a crack so loud Wins thought the tree had collapsed on top of them, but it wasn't the tree. As Jackson's body fell upon Wins' waist he heard his hip bone split.

The first of the cyclists bowled round the bend and sped off on the downward final stretch. The next pack, unsure of what had happened, skidded to a halt. "Are you OK?" A girl asked, pulling her bike off the road. Jackson was lost for words, he stood up and offered Wins his unbroken arm. Wins managed to hold on to consciousness just long enough to say, "I can't move my legs." Before, overwhelmed with the pain in his body, he blacked out.

Epilogue

Wins awoke in hospital to see everything below his chest set in a thick plaster cast and his legs held in traction. "He's awake," Zoop said excitedly, "Mum, Dad, Wins is awake!" Anne and Ed rushed to his bedside. "What happened?" Wins muttered. "You're in hospital Wins," Anne said. "You really hurt yourself, but it's OK, The doctors said you'll be back to normal once you've healed up." "Water?" Wins gasped. Ed quickly poured him a cup of water, placed a straw in it and held it to his mouth. Wins sucked it down like he hadn't drunk anything in a day and a night.

"We saw you go over the edge of a cliff on Dead Man's Fingers." Zoop explained, "We were in the car and driving up Jeffrey's hill before anyone even knew what was going on. Dad nearly ran over some of the cyclists coming down the hill." Ed gave her a look. "What happened?" Wins asked again. His mother answered this time, "Somehow you and Jackson collided and crashed, at least that's what the school are saying." Anne held his hand. "BB found your note and gave it to Zoop, are you... are you... *you*?" Wins nodded. I broke them, Mum, I trapped them in an infinity loop like you said. "OH MY DAYS!" Ed exclaimed. We're just glad you're alive. Zoop held BB up so he could reach his Win's hand. "Hello, big brother." He said cheekily. Wins smiled back. "What do you remember?" Zoop inquired. "I saw Jackson was going to... he was going to crash over the cliff side, I *knew* he was going to die. So I forced the PSIReNS to help me save him, I remember catching him with my legs but... all I remember after that was how much it hurt, I can't describe it. All I knew was pain Zoop. Then I woke up here."

"That was three days ago. The doctors say you broke your hip, dislocated both your knees and tore a bunch of tendons. They said they don't even know how you managed to hold onto someone as big as Jackson Treehorn for so long." Zoop explained. "Three Days?!" Wins couldn't believe it. "How is Jackson, is he OK?" Wins asked. "He broke his arm, he needed surgery to re-set the bones, but he's alive and, I think he's grateful too," Ed answered gesturing to a pile of chocolates on the side table. "He's been in every day to see if you are OK," Zoop said. "And Rish," Anne added. Most of the school have sent you something, there was so much we had to take most of it home because the nurses couldn't get in to take care of you." Wins marvelled at the stack of sweet treats on his bedside table. "Your teachers came to visit... Miss Maude and Coach Quintana." Ed spoke up "Even Great Uncle Quintin dropped by to see how you were!"

A doctor appeared in the doorway with a medical chart, "Mr Winters," she said, "it's good to see you compos mentis. Are you ready for a check-up?" "Can I eat something first?" Wins asked. "Certainly." The doctor said, writing on her chart, "A returning appetite is a good sign. I'll send something into you shortly then we'll get you checked out, OK?" Whilst he ate Anne, Ed and Zoop filled him in on what happened after the triathlon, how the whole event was called off and knowing Wins was safely back with them; let him recuperate so the doctor could run her tests.

The next day Rish came to visit. In typical form, he bounded into the room pleased as punch to see his best friend. "WINS! You flipping legend, how are you feeling dude?" "Like a stone statue Rish, how are you?" "Hungry," Rish replied, opening a box of Wins' chocolates. "Can I eat some of these?" "Sure," Wins affirmed, "if I can have some too." As Rish shared out the sweets Wins asked, "Is it true they called off the triathlon?" "Yeah, they said it wouldn't be fair to announce a winner after your crash with Jackson, and your Dad almost running half a dozen teenagers off the road at the finish line." Rish laughed. "So no-one won The Triples then?" Wins wondered. "Nope, not this year." Rish agreed. Feeling the need to explain Wins changed the subject. "I need to tell you something." "Sure, shoot," Rish said, throwing a chocolate into his mouth. "Jackson and me, we didn't *crash* exactly." "What do you mean …oh, you mean it had something to do with your superpowers?" Wins gave him a knowing look. "I knew it!" Rish said over-excitedly. "They're not superpow…" he began, then seeing how useless it would be to try and change Rish's mind on the matter said, "Yes, we didn't crash… I saved him. But, I think maybe we should keep it a secret for now yeah?" "You can't be a superhero if we can't keep a secret," Rish said in a hushed tone from behind a sly smile.

The boys chatted on until there was a knock at the door, Wins saw a hulking figure with one arm wrapped in a plaster cast and a heavily laden carrier bag in the other. "Errm, is it OK if I come in?" the figure asked. "Of course Jackson, you know Rish right?" Sheepishly Jackson sauntered into Wins' hospital room. "Rish, yeah, listen Rish… and you Wins… I'm sorry was so horrible to you both this year." Rish looked at Wins as if to get his say-so. "That's OK Jackson." Wins said approvingly, "Thanks for coming to visit." Rish back him up, "Yeah, you know, sorry for taunting you at the fun fair too." "Don't worry about it, I deserved that," Jackson admitted. "Is it OK if I speak to Wins alone Rish?" Jackson asked quietly. "No problem." Rish chittered grabbing his share of the chocolate hoard and heading to the door. "I'll come back later Wins, don't eat the rest without me!"

Once Rish had left Jackson took his seat next to the bed. Wins wasn't able to move much but managed to maintain eye contact with his former foe. "I just wanted to say thank you." Jackson said solemnly, "I know the school and the papers and social media are calling it a crash, but I also know what *really* happened. I *know* we didn't crash on the road. I *know* you saved me." Jackson touched Wins' plaster cast. "And I *know* the price you paid for my life." "The only thing I don't know is how you did it, and to be honest I don't need to know that." Wins wasn't sure how to process such raw gratitude, he had little experience helping people, so he had even less experience accepting their appreciation. "I couldn't have let you die, despite everything that happened between us over The Triples, I couldn't just watch you die like that."

Jackson lifted his carrier bag onto the bed. "That experience; *knowing* I was about to die, that really made me think about a lot of stuff." "What do you mean?" Wins asked, not sure where Jackson was going. "I used to enjoy sports Wins, when I was your age, not that long ago really. But, somehow it stopped being about the fun of it. I kept trying to please my Dad, make him happy. I pushed myself to be better than everyone else *all the time*. And you know what? It just made me miserable." Wins understood, an empathy bloomed within him and he came to the realisation that Jackson was never a spiteful, malicious bully. He was just sad and suffering at the hands of his own demons like everyone else. "I know exactly what you mean Jackson." Wins reassured him. And it was true, "How it felt when Rish thought the worst of me must be exactly how it felt for Jackson when I thought the worst of him." he thought to himself. Jackson's face brightened "You're the first person I've admitted that too." he confessed. "It feels good to let it go, you know?" "More than you'd believe mate." Wins replied.

"So what's in the bag Jackson?" Jackson opened the carrier bag and pulled out a stack of glossy magazines. "I guessed you had enough chocolate by now and your sister said that you liked videogames, and I know the wifi here is terrible so I bought you some gamer-mags to keep you occupied." "Thanks, Jackson!" Wins said, genuinely moved. He started looking through the selection. "What's this one?" He asked his new friend. "Oh, yeah…" Jackson said, pulling some different magazines out from under the gaming pile. "I was thinking about quitting track and field, at least the competitive stuff anyway, and trying something new. I wondered if you… and Rish if he's up for it, would like to learn with me. When you're back on your feet I mean." Jackson handed Wins one of the other magazines. "Skateboarding huh?" Wins smiled, considering the idea. "No rules?" Jackson said. "No referees." Wins replied. Not missing a beat Jackson chipped in "**No losers.**" Then just as fast "**No winners.**" Wins said, completing their thoughts. Wins pictured himself at a skate-park, learning to ride ramps and land technical tricks. "I'd love to mate. Might take me a while to get started though." He laughed, looking at his immobilised legs. "I can wait," Jackson promised. "Listen, I have to go, my Dad is waiting in the car park and… I think I'm gonna have to tell him some stuff he won't want to hear." "Good luck mate." Wins said feeling like they'd both turned a corner. Jackson thanked his new friend and leaving the magazines on Wins' bedside table left to face his future.

Winston was home with a week of summer holiday left to spare. The family were reclining on the carpeted floor of the lounge enjoying a game of Pirates' Dragon Island Adventure. They'd spent a happy half an hour racing each other around the game's board, through secret tunnels and over cliff-side paths to their pirate ship whilst all the while its large plastic dragon stared down upon their pieces. Winston was only one roll of the dice away from winning with BB just a few places behind. "Rish and Jackson should be here soon," Winston told his parents, picking up the dice. "We're going to the skate ramps at the park." Ed was pleased Winston had a new friend. "OK, but be careful, I don't want you back in hospital for another six weeks!" "I'll just be watching today Dad, besides, I don't even have a skateboard yet." It was Winston's turn to go, the faint scent of the dice changed as he rolled them between his fingers, each rotation telling him whether he would win or lose. Holding them one way released a sharp putrid stench whilst pinching them another way let out the delicately sweet scents of cinnamon and orange. Knowing which result would bring more pleasure to the room he held his face fast and rolled the rancid dice, failing to pass the finish line and allowing BB to take the win. BB rolled his turn and cackled with delight pushing his piece onto the pirate ship. "Yay BB!" Anne chuckled, tickling his tummy.

The invasive screech of a poorly played violin blundered in from next door through the open lounge windows. Ed grimaced. "Of all the instruments they could have got their kid, why did they have to get *that*? It sounds like he's murdering a cat!" "Don't be so mean Dad!" Zoop laughed. Unrepentant he continued "You know they have electronic sets with headphones these days." Just then the doorbell rang, "What's that noise?" BB asked, "That's just my friends at the front door

BB." Winston explained. "No!" BB insisted "Not the *blue* noise…" and with an outstretched arm, he pointed to the window. "What's that *yellow* noise?"

Astonished, Winston looked at BB, then to his sister and his parents. Anne, Ed and Zoop, jaws agape, turned back to BB.

BB regarded his family and with a great gregarious giggle, grinned from ear to ear.

43120818R00160

Printed in Poland
by Amazon Fulfillment
Poland Sp. z o.o., Wrocław